MW01611470

OLD WOUNDS

A NOVEL

BETTI LOUISE LEE

atmosphere press

© 2022 Betti Louise Lee

Published by Atmosphere Press

Cover design by Matthew Fielder

No part of this book may be reproduced without permission from the author except in brief quotations and in reviews. This is a work of fiction, and any resemblance to real places, persons, or events is entirely coincidental.

Atmospherepress.com

TABLE OF CONTENTS

I dedicate this book to two people – my father, Ruben, and my brother, Malcolm. My dad was the most influential person in my life. He gave me courage, a strong work ethic, and a desire for better things in life. Malcolm gave me joy, insight into his extraordinary intelligence, and a reminder to laugh.
Both of them gave the greatest gift – love.

For that, I will always be grateful. I love and miss you both.

CHAPTER 1

NIA CARTER

Hi there, and nice to meet you. Let's get to it. My name is Nia Carter, and I am an Insurance Investigator, a mom and a pretty scrappy lady, and until my personal demon raised its head, my life was normal, almost boring. The last weeks have been interesting, interesting in the vein of the wrongly attributed Chinese curse, "May you live in interesting times." It's not really a Chinese curse, but that's another story.

My troubles began that day, a regular day, one that was being spent concentrating on my cases. I had an outstanding arson case that I knew would require a trip to San Francisco in the near future, but for now, it was going to have to wait. I needed to get out of the office, so after discussing it with my boss, Jason, I decided to trail a small case I'd been working on, that of a construction worker named Roland Burkhardt, who had fallen from a ladder and claimed serious back injury.

Roland had seen a doctor who pronounced him bruised but not broken and gave him a reprieve from work for two weeks. Unsatisfied with the doctor's findings and wanting to find a way to collect money for his bogus claim, he had consulted a chiropractor, who swore he had more serious injuries. We'd had dealings with Dr. Bowen, knew him to do whatever was necessary to allow his patients to collect Workman's Compensation in return for a phony diagnosis of illness. He skimmed his fees from his patients' skimming. Roland suffered from a well-known addiction – gambling – and his favorite spots were located in the casinos in the mountains west of Denver. Jason and I decided to let Roland play his hand and catch him when he used his ill-gotten comp check.

Around 11:00 a.m., I got my phone and laptop and drove to Roland's place, a small frame house on Sante Fe. I hid around the corner and sat in my car until I saw him come bouncing out. He didn't look like a man who had an injury, much less a back injury, when he hopped into his elevated pickup truck. I clicked off a few shots. Gunning his engine, he sped away with me in close pursuit. He drove a mile or so down Sante Fe, got to 6th Avenue, made a left and tooled up the hill on the way to Blackhawk. I followed behind.

The trip from Denver to Blackhawk takes about half an hour and is an exceptionally beautiful drive on a warm, sunny day. The winding route is lined with rocky outcroppings supporting towering pine, elm and aspen trees. Occasionally, big horned sheep or deer make their way down the hills, providing photo opportunities for the tourists. There are at least twenty-five casinos operating 24/7 in Blackhawk and Central City, and when their cash is depleted, losers slink out the door and back down the mountain.

Roland hit Main, with me closely following, turned left, and followed a man dressed in a green vest and derby hat into the parking garage of the Saratoga. At the last minute, I passed the Saratoga and parked my car in the Gilpin Hotel's lot. I knew I could keep him in my sights in the casino, since it was so crowded, he wouldn't notice me, but if I was right behind him in the garage, he might recognize my face and determine I was there to watch him, not to gamble.

Crossing the street, I entered and quickly found Roland at the cashier's window cashing a check. He had pulled one folded check out of his wallet and I overheard him tell the cashier that he was playing it safe and had brought only one check and no credit cards.

"Only brought one so just in case I lose, I won't blow the house payment." he stated with a wink and grin. The cashier counted out five hundred dollars in twenties.

The constant "DING!, DING!, DING!, DING!," of the machines created a cacophonous symphony to winners and losers. Casinos are loud and not a place for the faint of heart. Veterans of the experience are a cross section of society; all races, economic standings and sizes, each trying to hit the jackpot. At a line of nickel machines, a geriatric Black woman with a knitted cap that looked like an afghan was pulled up to a "Wicked Winnings" machine alongside a biker dressed in dirty jeans and a leather vest adorned with chains and conchos, intent on winning dollars in a "Miss Kitty" slot. They paid not an ounce of attention to each other.

Roland went straight to the dollar machines. He was sliding a twenty into the dollar mouth as I watched him from a bank of slots in the same row, separated by six gamblers. He hadn't looked to either side of him, merely fished his wallet out of his back pocket and sat down to the machine. He waited until the money was swallowed, then set to work hitting the play button, each punch eating three dollars from his investment. I sat down at a machine about seven down from him, put in a ten and hit slowly, playing a single dollar for each push of the button, looking over my shoulder at my prey. Within a minute, Roland won what must have been at least fifty dollars from the jaunty tune coming from his machine. Smiling, he continued to punch the keys and insert twenties. Although I was donating a dollar each play and going about it slowly (he was playing an average of nine for each one I inserted), my ten was quickly depleted. Sighing, I put in another. This was definitely going on my expense report.

Suddenly, Roland jumped up and gave one loud whoop. His machine was ding dinging merrily, and the light on top flashing red. I leaned down the line with the rest of the patrons and saw that he had won a jackpot of $1,000.00. He was smiling, hugely accepting congratulations, twisting left and right, a movement that would have brought pain to a man with a bad back. He was so happy; he didn't notice me clicking pictures with my phone. After about five minutes, the floor walkers came and gave him ten, crisp new hundred-dollar bills, which he kissed, then folded and placed in his wallet.

The other players had returned to the slots and I was the only one watching his actions. He looked around, searching for a new machine. He actually looked me in the face but his elation from winning dimmed recognition. He spotted another machine behind him and moved to it. Swinging his leg over the stool, he got busy inserting twenties. But this machine was not as kind as the first one. It ate a hundred in less time than it takes to brush your teeth, without giving a return of even a dollar. He put one of the bills he had won into the machine, which then returned less than half of its value. He hit the cash button and a paper payout ticket slid out of the machine. Pulling it out, he proceeded to a cash machine and cashed the ticket. My camera and I watched his every move.

Roland and I went to two other casinos, Bullwhacker's and The Gilpin Hotel. At each, I shot pictures of his winning with elation and losing with depression. After two hours of play, the depression was on top. Roland had lost not only the $1,000.00 he'd won within the first thirty minutes, but also the $500.00 in funds he'd gotten from cashing the check. He was broke and rifling his pockets for loose change. Finally, when he couldn't dig up more cash, he slumped back to the front door of the Saratoga, turned in his ticket stub and redeemed his truck. He didn't have enough to tip the valet.

I felt dejected as I followed him down the mountain because I'd lost forty bucks. I could only imagine how he felt. By my count, he had lost at least fifteen hundred dollars; 1,000 of the casino's money and more importantly, 500 of his own. He was destined to feel worse, since I'd taken numerous shots of him dancing when he won, and fairly kicking himself when he lost. Back injury my foot. This guy was milking the system and doing a piss poor job of it.

When we arrived at his house, he pulled into his driveway and I pulled into my accustomed spot around the corner. Soon I heard the unmistakable sounds of a spat, no, it was a full-blown argument, complete with loud voices and expletives rolling out of his house. The higher pitched voice was his wife's, I was sure. Roland's was low, rumbling and contrite. At first.

"You lost *how* much?!" she yelled.

Mumble, mumble, mumble.

"Five hundred *fucking* dollars?!" she yelled.

Mumble, mumble, mumble.

"Are you *crazy*?!"

Mumble, mumble, mumble. And then he came alive.

"I worked for it, not you, you fucking bitch! Get the hell out of my face!"

The next sounds were of furniture breaking or maybe it was the walls. Either way, a battle comparable to Gettysburg was going on in the house. I debated for a bit, and then dialed 911.

"Yes, could you send an officer to 1575 South Miramont? There seems to be a domestic disturbance of monumental proportions going on in that house, and it might be a good idea for you to look into it," I said.

"Yes ma'am. We received another call from their neighbors. Officers are in route," the dispatcher told me.

"Ok, thanks." And I hung up.

Red lights flashing, two Littleton police cars came to a screeching halt in front of Roland's house, just as his wife ran out the front door, turned and pitched what looked like a Dutch oven. Roland was right behind her and managed to feint left as the pot flew past his head.

"Bitch!" he yelled.

"Bastard!" she yelled.

The police were out of their cars and on him like flies on a turd. He twisted and wiggled, but they cuffed him and brought him to his knees. Neighbors stood on their lawns watching the melee, while I happily clicked away, capturing each of his dainty moves. Suddenly, Roland looked directly at me and recognition clouded his face. He opened and shut his mouth, resembling a fish out of water, and then his face crumbled. He knew he was caught. I flipped him a wave, smiled, got into my car and drove back to my office, chuckling all the way.

When I walked into Jason's office, I couldn't stop giggling.

"I got him!" I told Jason.

"Burkhardt?"

"Yup. Caught him in the act." I proceeded to tell him about my trip to the mountains and Roland's escapades. By the time I finished, we were both cracking up.

"You will see a bonus on your next check," Jason told me, still grinning.

"Great! I'll write up my report, download the photos and have it on your desk tomorrow."

"Works for me," he said.

"Would you do the court thing when it comes up for me?" I asked.

"Why?" he asked. "You've done all the hard work, so you should get the credit."

"Naw. I don't need any more scumbags trying to track me

down. I still have a restraining order against the last Workman's Comp creep. You can do this one."

"Okay, sure, if you say so," he said with a nod. You take it easy and get some rest. You done good, girl!"

Little did I know that I wouldn't be getting any rest for a while. My ex-husband saw to that. In all fairness, it really wasn't his fault that he was murdered.

CHAPTER 2

It was time for another day at the office, but it was a bit more trying than my normal, everyday prep for work. I had a slight, rather painful handicap in the form of a brace on my left leg. Luckily, it was temporary, to correct tendons I'd badly damaged when I tripped off of the front step. Normally I am agile, athletic, and anything but clumsy, but running after Alex had taken a toll. Anyway, a brace is hard to make a fashion statement with, so I decided I needed to cover it with a sock, and since tailored suits lose impact with socks, I changed about four times, finally settling on a skort and short-sleeved blouse. So much for dress-for-success.

Grimacing at the final product, I left my bedroom and made my way to the kitchen. Alex, my son, was already there, stylishly attired in a pair of red BVD's and blue Chuck Taylor's. He sat in our small breakfast nook, arms loosely crossed on the table waiting for his breakfast, his smile warming the room as he greeted me with a flash of a wave.

"Hi, Mom!"

"Good morning, son. You'd better get your butt up and get something to cover those skivvies or when I'm done with it, it'll be as red as those drawers are."

"Aw, Mom. I figured since Valentine's Day is next week, I can show off my new underpants. I'll look good!" He grinned and did a little pirouette around the chair then climbed back up and leaned on the tent created by his hands.

"Alex, you are such a con! I know that *you* know that Valentine's Day was three months ago! Clothes monkey butt – now!"

He slid me another drunken grin, hopped down from the booth, and headed for his bedroom. Oh, how I love my son! He is six, smart as they come, and as happy as a well-fed puppy.

Alexander Michael Carter's birth was the highest point of joy in my life, even over-shadowing my wedding day. The morning he was born, I'd crawled from my snug cocoon of sleep at 4:25 a.m. and dragged myself to the bathroom for about the thirtieth time to pee, but this trip proved to be different. The signs that I had been told to look for by my doctor and the numerous baby books that my girlfriends and family had given me were all there. If I had been groggy when I'd sat down to pee, my attitude immediately became comparable to lighting the burner of a gas stove – all fired up.

The toilet paper was bloody.

I was staying at Mom and Dad's in anticipation of the impending birth, and after washing my hands and face, I scuttled to my parent's room. It took four shakes and a pinch to get Mom to wake up so we could go to the hospital. Dad woke up in a flurry, totally wired and ready to go, and after he dressed, he duck walked me through the house, out to the garage, opened the passenger door to his blue pickup and helped me slide onto the seat. Mom climbed in the back seat. Dad drove speedily but cautiously to the hospital, and when we got there, jumped out, ran to my side, opened my door, cupped my elbow, and both of my parents led me into the building. Since I was expected, a nurse whisked me to a birthing room, helped me mount the high bed and we prepared for the birth of my son. After getting me settled in, my parents were ostracized to a visiting room and I was left alone.

Why is it that part of your body signals that it's time to void the precious little bundle and part of it seems to balk and want to hold on until the next ice age? My bodily conflicts were making me angry, and since Frank was not there doing his husbandly duty, I was alone – me and my bundle with no one to yell at except the nurses who came in periodically to check progress. Obviously, the one in attendance had been through this before and seemed understanding when I yelled, "SHIT!"

I lay there in a pool of sweat for what seemed like eternity, waiting for Frank to show, but I knew he wouldn't. Pain came as a sensation of something sliding into my body like a burglar, prowling around at a steady, mounting rate, reaching a peak then stealing away. Each intrusion left me gasping.

After a while, Mom and Dad were allowed back in, both carrying packages and grinning like two hyenas.

"Hi guys." I fluttered a small wave in their direction.

"Where's Frank?" Dad asked after he had kissed my forehead and wiped the sweat away with a cloth the nurse had left.

"Oh, I didn't call him," I murmured.

"Humph. I'm goin' to the waiting room." Two things I knew: first, Dad couldn't stand to be in the room when a woman was giving birth, although Mom had done it seven times, and second, Dad was going to call Frank to tell him his child was on the way. Mostly, Dad wanted to have the pleasure of cussing Frank out when and if he did arrive.

Mom sat at the side of the bed and looked down at me, occasionally wiping my face. Suddenly, I felt a rush of warmth in my nether regions, and Mom squeaked, "Oh no!" She called the nurse in, whose face fell when she looked down at my thighs. Hustling Mom out of the room, she picked up the phone, quickly dialed, and barked, "Get Dr. Merritt in here stat!" After a beat or two, she rushed on. "Alright. Then get Dr. Yoon! He'll know what to do!"

I pulled myself up and looked down. A pool of blood was soaking my bottom half and the bed, slowly seeping its way to the edges of the sheets.

"Lie back." The nurse gently grasped my shoulders and pressed me back down on the bed. Suddenly, I was very cold and started to shudder. I became dizzy, light-headed, totally disoriented, and very sleepy. I really don't remember much of what happened then, except being rapidly wheeled out of the room and down a long hall, accompanied by both of my parents and the monosyllabic chanting of Mom and a nurse, holding hands and vigorously praying. From the corner of my eye, I remember Dad, his lips moving in prayer, looking very pale, and clutching his bible with what seemed to be very shaky hands.

I awoke later, still groggy in a clean gown and bed in the recovery room. A nurse was fiddling with my IVs, and I asked her, "When do I go in to have my baby?"

"Oh, you had him already," she remarked cautiously.

"Him? A boy? Where is he?"

"Hang on and I'll go get the doctor." She left the room.

I lay back and started to cry, sure that my child was dead and that the nurse just hadn't known how to tell me. She came back with an Asian doctor in tow, his smiling face giving me a smidgen of hope.

"Mrs. Carter," he said, taking my hand. "You have a beautiful, baby boy."

"Is he okay? Is he alive?" I was bubbling spit and tears and shaking all over.

"Yes, yes of course! He's fine. If you wait just a little longer, one of the nurses will bring him in so you can see him."

I lay back on my pillows relieved, and the cold dread I'd felt when I'd first opened my eyes in the recovery room, crept away, leaving a calm so intense that I began to go to sleep. The doctor was talking to me and at first I was groggy and unsure of what he was saying.

"I'm sorry. What was that you were saying Dr.?" I asked.

"I said that I am Dr. Kent Yoon, and that you two almost didn't make it."

He took both of my hands in his. Staring into my eyes he said, "You experienced what is known as *Abruptio Placentae*, a condition that occurs when the placenta inexplicably tears away from the uterine wall, causing hemorrhaging and causing the blood to totally surround the baby. Your son nearly drowned in blood, and you nearly died from the loss of it."

"Shut up!"

He blinked and took a step back, not understanding my outburst. I held on to his hands and pulled him back to the bed. "I'm sorry, Dr. Yoon. I didn't mean that as it sounded. Please go on."

"Um, well, um.... placental abruption is a very serious and rather rare occurrence, and in many cases, both patients die. Many doctors are unfamiliar with the condition, and unless a cesarean delivery is immediately performed, death occurs. I have seen this condition on a few occasions and luckily, I was still in the hospital."

"Is my son going to be alright?" I asked.

"But of course! He swallowed a great deal of blood, but we pumped it out of his little tummy, and he will be fine. He probably will have black stools for a bit, but he is very healthy, and his scores were excellent."

I looked around him and saw a nurse come in holding a blue, wrapped bundle.

"Here he is!" Dr. Yoon exclaimed.

The nurse came over and placed the bundle in my arms, and I gazed down on a pale, tan face that was scrunched in an expression which simply looked as though he was wondering where he was and how did he get there. His hair was a straight, slick mass of black fur, luxuriously downy, covering his head and the tops of his ears. I couldn't see his eyes, but when he suddenly opened them, I was amazed at the deep azure color.

"You sure this is my baby?" I asked. "He has blue eyes."

"They will probably turn darker as he gets older, but he may just be a blue-eyed African American," Dr. Yoon said.

I wrapped my arms tighter around my son and kissed his shiny hair. Love for this person that I had just met felt as though it was choking me. He unscrunched his face momentarily and looked up at me, an expression of wonder in his eyes. He seemed to realize that I was his mother and at that moment, both of us knew that our bond was stronger than any man could create; a love that could only be made by God.

Alex is all boy. He'd vastly prefer to run than walk, has a simultaneous love and fear of animals, and adores his mother beyond all others. The color of his eyes has darkened slightly but they are still a dense blue, deep and serene as the ocean. One of the things I love about my son is the fact that he rarely becomes angry about anything, never sulks or talks back. Comedian – yes. Belligerent – never. I watched his little red behind skip down the hall, fingers scraping the wall, curly head bouncing to music in his mind. When he returned, a pair of jeans and a gecko-embellished sweatshirt covered his frame.

"Do you have all of your new soccer stuff? I put it beside your dresser," I said.

"Oh! Oh, yeah!" He shouted and ran back to his room. His enthusiasm for sports was insatiable, but I had some concerns. His father had been a star athlete, but I knew there was always a chance he would inherit my genes. The poor child has a curse on one branch of his family tree.

My family is African American, and although most white folks think all Black people possess two things, rhythm and athletic prowess, most in our family could neither dance nor play sports. In homage to our African heritage, my parents had given all seven of us strong, African names, but they could not give us athletic ability. Our names are distinctive but not the sort that cause behind the back giggles. They would never have put the anchor of Shaniqua on either of us girls or saddled the boys with anything close to Deshontay. Mom and Dad knew to the general Caucasian public, right or wrong, these names conjured ghetto images and could prove to be a hindrance.

My sister is T'ene, which is Swahili for 'love' and my older brothers are named Adam, since he is number one son, and number two, Bruk, which is pronounced Brook. Bruk means 'one that is blessed' in Ethiopian. Neither went out for sports. My brother Fynn, a name admired as strong in Ghana, had played soccer as a goalie, and his team had lost for three consecutive seasons. Whether it was because he graduated or not, the year before he started to play and the year after, they had a winning team. Khari, 'a strong warrior', had tried to loop a lacrosse ball, and received a firm whack on the forehead by his own stick. The blow had left a nasty scar. I was next in line after Khari. My name is Swahili for radiance or brightness.

Now Taye, he was the exception. Taye, whose African name means 'he has been seen', had toyed with the idea of an NFL career in his youth. He was all-state champ in high school, and by his sophomore year, large and small colleges vigorously scouted him. During high school, he had also played hockey, baseball, and basketball, and was the savior of the wrestling team. The years that he was on the teams were all winners. Taye even appeared to have an aptitude for golf. My other brothers couldn't hit a T-ball. We told Taye he was a mutant. During his sophomore year at Colorado State

University, he'd thrown himself into his studies and backburnered the sports, disappointing all of his coaches. He was more of an academic than an athlete and he wanted to become a veterinarian, not play with a football as a career. Funny thing – Taye could dance, too.

Alex came back from his room, navy sports bag weighing heavily on his shoulder. Smiling broadly, he reverently laid the bag beside his chair then climbed back onto his perch to his breakfast of Cheerios, toast and juice. He ate, pronounced it delicious, chewed his animal-shaped vitamin, wiped his mouth on the back of his hand, trotted to the bathroom, brushed his teeth with a singular forward and a singular backward movement, then came back and helped me grab lunches, hats, umbrellas, jackets, and the precious bag. We hit the road.

It was one of those steel gray days that are almost unfamiliar in Colorado; a day devoid of sunshine or fluffy clouds, pewter the main color hovering above our heads. The dull sky hung above the Rocky Mountains on the fringe of the western horizon, iced by a layer of grimy blue. The sun was hiding behind the lackluster curtain, stubbornly refusing to show its face. I was hoping for just a glimpse, to burn off a little of the day's moisture. It is a known fact that Colorado weather can change from glum to glorious faster than a Vegas showgirl, and that the sun shines 360 days of the year. Maybe not shine but at least present a glow at some point in those 360. It seemed that today was going to be one of the five when we weren't going to be blessed with rays. There was a chill in the air and a swath of drizzle misted our windows, but heck, it was Friday so even if we had a full-fledged thunderstorm spit on us, we didn't care. We were exceptionally late, so I didn't tell my son the usual stop and smell the roses but instead, bundled he and his gear into the car, snapped on seat belts, and took off at breakneck speed down Jordan Road.

Jordan Road is just that – a dirt road; a straight shot to

Alex's school, and I needed to try to make up for lost time. Thunder grumbled in the distance and within five minutes of leaving the house, silvery streaks of rain peppered the car, urging me to flick the switch for the wipers. Down the road we flew, my son holding on for his life. He knew the drill; had too much practice since I have a tendency to drive a bit, well let's face it – *FAST* - although in this particular instance I was being foolish. A dirt road is no place for excessive speed. I was going just too fast and the inevitable was bound to happen. We hit a gravel mogul.

"Hold on, baby boy!" I yelled to Alex.

We spun to the left. I countered with the wheel. We spun to the right, the rear of the car bounced, and I was not quick enough with my reflexes. We slammed into a culvert that was about two feet deep, tracing a path parallel to the road. The car came to an abrupt halt, and I thanked God for seatbelts. Alex looked shaken.

"I am so sorry, honey. Are you okay?" I asked him, stroking his forehead, kissing his little hand.

"I t-t-think so. You okay?"

"I'll live."

Cussing under my breath, I climbed out and surveyed the damage. Things did not look good. The wheels were suffering, both canted at an angle unfit for driving. The twisted left wheel, sort of up and back let me know that travel was to be accomplished by a call to AAA.

Rain came down, pelting so hard it felt like hail, making me glad I'd brought not only my long raincoat but also the matching yellow hat with the large brim that prevented water from draining down my back. It looked sort of silly and made me look as though I was ready to go whaling out of Mystic Harbor. Alex had one just like it that he refused to wear, and in its place, he had put on his little baseball cap before we'd left the house.

Alex and I started chatting sporadically, mom to son. "So,

honey, do you think you're up to playing forward this week?" I asked over the noise of the pelting rain.

"Oh, yeah, Mom!" he said, his face lighting up. "Coach said I may get to be the GOALIE next week!"

Hoo, boy, I thought. Goalie would not be an advisable position for Al. He didn't block well and catching anything smaller than a medicine ball might be hard for him. Good ol' Coach. He believed that soccer was to be played simply for the love of the game and with that in mind, he made sure all the kids got a chance to play.

We talked on, Alex's chatter bubbling in excited anticipation of joyful soccer success, me with thoughts of his let down when he realized he wouldn't have a career in sports. I would need to find a substitute for his energies, since he would most likely not be in line for any athletic scholarships. Nearly an hour later, the AAA tow truck showed up.

"Goin' too fast, were ya?" the crusty driver said. He was a young man, but he had the world-weary attitude of someone much older.

I shrugged. "I thought I saw a deer," I said.

Alex and I climbed into the cab of his truck, while he hitched the car up. My son looked up with trepidation. His deep blue eyes were two sizes larger.

"Don't worry Tonto. I've got this," I told him. "We are probably going to need to buy a new car, but we will cross that bridge when we some to it. Have a little faith in Mom, ok?"

"Ok, Mommy." He was relieved. Once again Mom had blocked the door and saved the day. At least for now.

I had the driver take me to the auto repair shop of my friend Larry. Larry was a true entrepreneur. He'd bought his first gas station two weeks after graduating high school and now owned five very prosperous full-service operations, including the repair shop. He would have been hurt if I'd called someone else to take care of my machine.

When Alex and I walked into the waiting room, Larry saw

us and jumped up from his big desk behind the glass window.

"Hey babe!" he cooed, giving me a perfunctory buss on the cheek. "Give the guys time to check it out."

We took a seat in the waiting room beside a businessman. He was gorgeous – thick, dark hair curling back from his handsome face. His complexion was dark, the color of coffee with just a rumor of cream, and as smooth as Alex's. He had a well-formed nose, nostrils slightly flared. When he stood to go get some coffee, he was a good distance above me – 6'3" or so – and the obviously Armani suit looked wonderful on his noticeably muscular body. His full, exceptionally kissable lips shaded a deep cleft in his chin; high angular cheekbones and eyes the surprising dark gray color of an angry sea accented his face. But those eyes were far from angry. They were gentle, kind, and concerned, and cuddled in the longest, thickest eyelashes I had seen since I'd looked into the eyes of my son. I was staring. Yep – gorgeous.

Alex poked me. "Mom, why you staring at that guy?" he asked, aiming for sotto voce and not accomplishing it. The guy looked at me and smiled. I smiled weakly, and if my complexion would have allowed it, I would have blushed. He stuck out his hand.

"David Dillon," he said. Shaking his hand, I told him my name. "Car mishap?" he asked.

"Well, it has never been advisable to speed in rain, but I wasn't cautious enough. What are you in for?"

"Oh, nothing too dire. I just needed an oil change, and Larry's crew always get me in and out. Who's this fella?" he asked, looking at Alex.

Alex, ever the gentleman, stuck out his hand and said, "Alexander Michael Carter. Pleased to meet you." I always had gotten compliments on my son's manners, and he always made me proud.

"Pleased to meet you too."

David asked Alex about school and me about my job, and I

gave him the short version of my livelihood.

"I play soccer and I'm really good!" Alex blurted. "I have a game this afternoon. Do you want to come see me play? It'll be a really good game! I play goalie and I'm really good!"

"Alex, stop bragging! Mr. Dillon is busy!"

"No. No, I'd like to come see you play. Where will the game be?"

"Mom! Mom, where is my game?"

I sighed and gave him the warning eye. "It's at the Kennedy fields, off of Hampden at 5:30. Field 6."

"Great!" David said. "I'll be there!"

"Oh no," I interjected. "You don't have to come."

David was adamant. "No, no. I'd like to come. I haven't been to a soccer game in a long time, and I want to see this soccer star play."

Alex was grinning like a hyena. "See Mom. He wants to see me play."

"You may not have a car, so if you want, I can pick you up from your office. I'll pick both of you up."

"No, that's ok. I'm sure Larry has a loaner I can use. Thanks anyway."

"Well in that case, how about we go out to dinner after the game? I'm sure this guy likes pizza." He looked at Alex.

"I *love* pizza!" Alex exclaimed. I frowned and shook my head no.

David looked at me. "Nothing fancy and no strings, ok? It's just a meal, ok?"

I sighed again and gave Alex another stink eye. "You are welcomed to come to the game, Mr. Dillon, and we will have pizza with you."

"Call me David."

CHAPTER 3

FRANK CARTER

In some small section of his brain, he knew, from the moment of his birth, that he was afraid of death. He knew that his fear was greater than was normal – most people were afraid of dying, but his fear was a constant companion. Even as a child, he'd feared the dark of the grave and dying, the two synonymous with each other. Why, he was never certain, but he had always known that he would be faced with both fears at many stages of his life. He now realized that both had locked hands and were with him this night.

He lay flat on his back in the trunk of an antique Chevy – about a '48 he thought – remembering the humped back. His long legs were bent, knees up, and for some reason, he found a little humor in feeling that he was like an enormous paper clip, coiled and ready for office business. It was a mammoth trunk, large enough to accommodate his six feet plus frame, allowing him to lie s-shaped prone with his rounded knees stretching for the lid. It was so very dark. He swallowed his lump of fear as best he could and wished that he had never come back home.

During his childhood, his parents paid scant attention to his fears, telling him he needed to be tough...be a man...grow up, and at the age of five, to aid in this transformation, he'd been forced to attend his grandmother's funeral. His mother plainly stated that he was to kiss the dead lips of his beloved grandmother, but he'd wailed at the top of his lungs when she'd suspended him over the open casket, the breath of it cool from days in the freezer at Bennett's Mortuary. His mother grudgingly yielded to the gesture of placing his hand to the marble-cold cheek to say good-bye.

When his child eyes looked at the face of the person he loved more than any other, he became afraid. This didn't look like his Grans. This thing was dark and sunken, the skin the muddy tones of a puddle bottom after a hard rain. His Grans was a dark, rich, chocolate brown. This cold, unmoving object wore pale, pink lipstick, a color his Grans would kink her nose at, her choice having been the brilliant red of a ripe, Delicious apple. The hair was in twisting curls, rushing over each other on the top of the head and around the cheeks, not pulled into the big, round bun Grans always wore at the base of her neck, a convenient receptacle she stuck his pencils into. He had seen them open the lid of the box and knew that Grans was in darkness when it was closed, and the thought brought a shiver to his shoulders. No, this was not his Grans, but instead a wax dummy dressed in Gran's favorite white, church suit. From that point on, his mind held the image of the dead, wrinkled face captive throughout his life, grasping it as though precious instead of feared.

By the time he'd reached Gilbert High School, his fears were of a more manageable nature, although they never receded too far into his subconscious. The pursuits of a teenager occupied his mind and his time, and allowed him respite from them. He was tall, handsome, and skilled in sports, all matters of high regard in the female circle. A self-taught and extremely gifted artist, he painted caricatures of his buddies, and dreamy, romantic, Vargas-like images of his girlfriends. His landscapes adorned the walls of the high school's rotunda, as well as the echoing lobby of the Women's Bank on 17th and Champa. He had a rare talent – the ability to draw any subject to an almost photographic quality. His specialty was humans; so lifelike they appeared to breathe and could, at any moment, walk off of the canvas. Girls always wanted to date guys like him – the captain of the football team, the basketball team, even the golf team. To be with him was a badge of prestige and though quiet and considered shy, he mixed well with the opposite sex, achieved an alliance with them, and came to know the beauty of caring for a woman. He sought perfection in all phases of his life, and as a natural progression, the pursuit spilled over, creating a desire for honors academically. A's were all he accepted and if he didn't receive one in a class, he quietly confronted the teacher to rectify the situation. Only one teacher had ever needed to discuss the changing of a B to an A. If not for the war, he would have attended the University of Colorado on a dual football/academic scholarship.

The call came for all young Americans to participate in the Iraq War, and although he did not agree with the politics of the time, he was not exempted. When coerced by his ultra-patriotic father to do his "God given duty for his country," he dressed as nicely as possible to make a good impression. He had his hair cut to shorten the thick curls, shined his shoes, made certain the crease in his slacks was so sharp it could draw blood, and wore the whitest shirt in his closet. He was accepted into the Marines, trained well, and became a model soldier. He was a bit afraid of leaving home and never returning but the thought was quickly squelched though not completely overcome. Though he'd never held a pistol, much less a rifle prior to his Marine career, he found that he had a natural aptitude for marksmanship, becoming the best shot in his platoon. The rigors of tactics invigorated him, as well as the study of night maneuvers and flanking, and he spent numerous off-hours studying the history, culture and political differences of a country he'd never lent much thought to prior to enlistment. He came to the realization that he wanted to be certain he got them, before they got him. All in all, his life was full; he was content.

Within the first week of his tour in the strange, dry country of Iraq, one of his closest friends, Scott Liggins, was blown to bits while doing night reconnaissance on the outskirts of Kuwait. Scott's body was unrecognizable. The fearful and confused feelings he'd felt at the death of his grandmother had long been repressed, but they came swarming back at the loss of his friend. He couldn't bear to look at the remains of the shredded body. The second week, a native child – dark hair framing an oval face the color of pine, almond eyes as dark as pitch, shoeless, her clothing tattered and dirty – walked into the encampment, grinned and threw a grenade into Jay Brown's tent. Jay had been the leading receiver on Gilbert High's team, and this time, although he ran as he never had on the football field, a shard from the casing flew straight and true, severing his spine, piercing his heart, and emerging through his sternum. He had cradled his friend and watched as the life vacated his body. Bubbling blood flowed freely from Jay's mouth and chest, painting his clean fatigues. The slick, red river coursed down his thighs to his knees, and finally to the dusty, brown earth.

That night, he smoked his first of many joints, and began to invent new methods to control the mental aberrations, which were beginning to torment him. It was then that Iraq brought out instincts he did not know his mind was in possession of. Volunteers were regularly solicited for night reconnaissance, and this time, he was the first to step forward. His stealth became legendary. He'd slide undetected into enemy encampments, assess the atmosphere then silently slaughter any victim with the misfortune to wander into his path. Before the sun stole the sky from the grip of the moon, he would silently return to the American encampment, carefully place the heads of his victims in a straight line on the stilled tracks of the tanks, and then slide into his bunk. Morning found him lying on his back in his tent, staring up through the canvas at the filtered sun, smoke from his joint drifting above his head. No one ever saw him sleep.

He'd been in the field for seven months when a bullet plowed into the fleshy part of his thigh, severing the artery, the fountain of gushing blood presenting him with a pass home. Recuperating in Denver at Veterans Administration Hospital, he'd stare at the treeless southern landscape outside of his window for hours. In the first month, he had many visitors; old school friends and Marine buddies who had also left the battle, but in time, their numbers tapered until the only non-medical or enlisted personnel he saw were his mother and father. Upon release from the hospital, he loaded all his earthly possessions in his duffle, moved in with his parents and went in search of a job. But the available positions for former football, basketball and golf experts were hard to find, so he hired on with a construction company and built houses south of Denver near Cherry Creek Dam.

A bright light appeared in his life, but he had endured so much desolation, he didn't know how to handle sheer happiness. He met a girl, a girl he had known when his life was more manageable, and after he had been home for some time, she had come back into his field of awareness. They had known each other most of their lives, but she had moved in a different circle. But just like bubbles frothing on the surface of a lake, they had met, fell in love and married. She loved him without reserve, and he tried but could not reach the deep commitment in return.

He loved her, but...

Their life together gave him respite for a time. It pulled him away from his torment, but he slipped away from her and sanity, as one would slide out of a disguise. Happiness was a costume, one he could not bear the weight of, and he could not keep it on for very long.

Although he enrolled in art school, he had difficulty concentrating, and after a time, he dropped out. Smoking marijuana and drinking whiskey with his remaining high school chums who were not in the service or college were his only pastimes. He still painted on the weekends, stonily sitting in front of a canvas from sunup until the light was but a memory, but his subjects were no longer the images of a contented, well-adjusted individual. He now committed as much bleakness as his brush could depict to the canvas, and if unsatisfied, would cover the surface with thick coats of gesso and titanium white to erase every trace of what had become to him, disappointing art. He was in the elite club of men and women that the service had trained in the art of assassination, showed the darkest segment of life, but had neglected to teach how to resume a somewhat normal existence once they had returned from their vacation in hell. His life had gone full circle and the turns it had taken were not all for the best.

The dark was almost over-powering now. Shuddering, he tried to turn over, but the movement was too awkward. He bumped his knees, and the handcuffs threw his balance off. Golden slivers would momentarily slide by to show where the edge of the trunk was. He could hear traffic noises and felt a gentle lurch each time the car came to a stoplight. At one point, although shackled to his fear, he dozed then came awake when the car stopped abruptly. He felt the doors open and heard voices drifting closer. He could smell a rank, fishy odor and determined they were near water. The trunk lid opened, and he could see stars hanging in the night sky. Hands gently lifted his feet out then grasped his manacled wrists and pulled him upright. A palm against his back steadied him. He sensed that they were standing on the banks of a lake, the gentle waves lapping at the shore. Night creatures sang to each other, lamenting their own set of unique problems.

He knew then that his twin fears, joined so closely in his mind as to become one, were about to come to fruition.

"It's such a shame." The voice was whispering as though they might be overheard. The whisper came from behind, and just as he remembered the identity of the speaker, a bullet slammed into the soft spot behind his left ear.

"I'll never be afraid again."

Frank's mind pulsed as life winged its way out of his body and into the night sky.

CHAPTER 4

We made arrangements for David to meet us at Kennedy. He had truly wanted to pick us up, but I didn't know this guy, and no way was I going to get into a car with him, even in a vehicle as gorgeous as his Porsche.

When I finally got to work, I was already tired. Walking into the bathroom, I turned and looked in the mirror. Yikes! My hair had gone from glossy, springy, ebony curls to a black Bozo-do. The thing rain does to African American hair is pretty phenomenal, and sometimes a pain. I retrieved a pick from my purse and tamed my locks to a curly, poufy Afro. Not bad and no longer a fright wig. I then leaned into the mirror to check my makeup, which consisted of mascara and lip-gloss. The mascara looked a bit muddy, so I decided to wash my face and start again.

My eyes are my best feature, so I never use shadow. No matter what color it is, it looks unnatural on me. My lips are slim by Black folk's standards, and I use gloss to enhance them. As much as I'd been cursed with the Carter lack of athletic ability, I'd been blessed with their clear, unblemished skin. At thirty, I didn't look a day over eighteen. Most of the time, my youthful looks served me well. I could still get into a movie as a student, but when I had to testify as an expert witness in court, the opposing attorneys sometimes rudely asked if I was old enough to be there.

I made it a point to take good care of my complexion and kept it as scrupulously clean as possible to keep the pores small and ward off wrinkles. I used my lotion to remove the mascara, then rinsed well and made do with paper towels for drying. Once I'd applied mascara and a slick of gloss, I was ready to start the day. Again. It was about time I did some work.

The walk back to my office was punctuated by "What happened, Nia?" and "You ok?" and "Anything you need?" from my co-workers. Great group.

"Nothing, guys." By the time I limped back to my office and sat down behind my desk, they had mustered around me. I told the story only one time.

Since the rest of my group was not sure if I'd make it in that day, my meeting had been cancelled. I determined I would be rooted to the spot the rest of the day. Crossing my legs was akin to a flailing because of the throbbing in my injured ankle, and I contemplated getting up that very minute, going to the bathroom again and peeing even if I didn't have to, while the pain was still intense. That way, I'd get the necessities out of the way and could prop my legs up on a stack of binders and stay stretched in that position for the remainder of the afternoon. I wanted to feel the burn only once more that day – when I got up to go home. While I was vacillating between going or staying, I called Ellen to find out what I had missed that morning. I knew I would need to catch up on our current batch of would-be criminals. After chatting with her for a few minutes, I hung up. The phone had just hit the cradle when it rang.

"Yo, girlfriend! Whuzzup?"

Truly a voice from the past. Laurinda Hickman was the only African American woman I knew whose sole desire in life had been to climb Mt. Everest, ride as a privateer in a motorcycle race and win, snorkel the Great Barrier Reef, lead an archeological dig at Machu Pichu, and a poisonous snake hunt in Australia. So far, she'd done the last three, and made headlines each time. Everest still eluded her, and I knew the bikes couldn't be far behind. She worked as a photographer and had never married. Although her beauty was legendary and men from all walks of life had pursued her, she had never been seen in the company of someone with whom she appeared to be enamored. She always appeared to hold herself above regular mortals, but since she was also a kind, genuine friend to everyone she met, it would be hard to hold animosity against her. Jealousy was not as easy to squelch.

We'd grown up together in a farming community about twenty-five miles southeast of Denver. Laurinda had one brother, LaVelle, who was my age. She was the same age as Khari. Her family had moved into the vacant house over the hill and down in the valley when she was three and LaVelle was a year old. Childhood for her was happiest when she traversed the twenty or so acres that separated our houses. There would be an almost non-existent tap at the door (many times Mom thought one of the chickens was loose) and Laurinda would poke her head in, timidly calling, "May we come in?" Laurinda and LaVelle would sidle into our small kitchen, take their places at our miniscule dining table and join us in whatever meal Mom had prepared. In the beginning, unlike us, they never said prayers prior to the meal, so a religious education was served along with the peas and carrots. Mom and Dad began to load them into our old station wagon on Sunday mornings to travel into town to New Light for church, hoping to salvage their little, heathen souls.

In the summertime after meals, we'd roam the fields – me,

Laurinda, LaVelle, T'ene and my brothers, pulling wildflowers for Mom and catching lizards, snakes and frogs which we put into five-gallon glass jugs we'd decorated to look like deserts. Flat, thorny cactus and little white bellflowers sprouted over miniature sand dunes, cooled by lakes fashioned from broken pieces of mirrors. Winter found us flopped back in the snow; arms and legs flapping to produce gigantic snow angels that we were sure passengers in low flying aircraft could view with envy. Or we stomped out our names on the vast plains of frosted white surrounding our house. We never quarreled but competition was fierce to produce the best terrarium, angel, or foot-pounded name.

Although we weren't related, I resembled Laurinda more than I did my sister. We both had large, dark, liquid eyes that caused most of the teachers to refer to us as the Doe Twins. I was small, a smidge shorter than five feet tall, with a delicate build. Laurinda was at least 5' 8", with long, spindly legs. Both of us had hair the heavy, sultry, darkness of black velvet – Laurinda's was long – down to her butt and full; mine is short and curly. But, while Laurinda had a mysterious beauty even when we were kids, I have always had an impish look, never beautiful, always cute. During that time in my life, it was somewhat neat to be told I looked like a black Shirley Temple, but after I'd passed about seventeen, it became a curse. I'd always wanted to be elegant like T'ene and Laurinda, but I knew I would always be just cute. In time, I've learned to accept the hand I'd been dealt.

Laurinda's mother seemed to be the only one who was blind to her obvious beauty, always trying to downplay her attributes. She braided her hair in two thick ropes then wrapped them severely around her head, a la Heidi. But Laurinda was like me: dark-skinned and far from Scandinavian, so the woven crown of hair only served to make her look ridiculous. While my sister and I were two of the most stylish girls in the school, Laurinda was forced to wear saddle oxfords, thick socks, white, starched blouses, and mid-calf skirts. It was not until they'd moved away from our neighborhood my junior year of college that I found out why Laurinda's mother had been forced to dress her to look like a dowdy schoolteacher. Her father, Sonny, a small, mahogany-brown knob of a man, was a wife beater, pedophile, drunk and child abuser, the molester of Laurinda since she was about three. Doris, her mother, thought that if she were made ugly, maybe he wouldn't bother her. It hadn't helped.

Sometime in June, the year which she and T'ene would have entered Grandview High as sophomores, Laurinda disappeared from our neighborhood. When asked, Doris said she had gone to Mississippi to spend her sophomore year with her aunt and uncle. Knowing Laurinda was not fond of the aunt, we were sure Doris was lying, but didn't broadcast our disbelief. One day, LaVelle pulled me aside and said without preamble, "Laurinda's a whore and she gonna have a baby."

I looked at him, eyes blinking like stoplights and dumbly said, "Uh-uh. How can you say something so nasty about your sister?"

"Where you think she is then? She not in Mississippi with Aunt Clea and Uncle George. She down there at the St. Stephen's, gettin' ready to bust." He folded his arms across his chest, defying me to dispute him. I turned my back and walked away. When I got home that afternoon, I talked to Mom. Mom had shaken her head and said, "Never mind, Nia. We'll talk about it when you're older." When Laurinda finally returned her junior year, her stay was short lived. She moved in with Mrs. Livingston, an aging widow at the church, and finished the remainder of her schooling at Gilbert High.

I hadn't seen her for over a year, although we talked every month or so, and I kept up with her escapades via newspapers and TV. It had been too long since I'd last heard her voice. In the years that passed, Doris had left Sonny and moved into Denver to a small townhouse on Locust Street. Before the divorce was final, she'd gone back to her profession, accounting, and from what we'd heard, he'd moved to southern Colorado and gotten a job as a gardener. She didn't get to enjoy her freedom from him for long, though. One night, while returning back upstairs after getting herself a glass of orange juice, she'd fallen down the stairs and died from a broken neck. Days later, following the smell, the neighbors had found her in a dried pool of transparent orange.

"So, how's life treating you, girlfriend?"

"About as fine as it can. Where are you? What'cha doing nowadays? Climbed any tall peaks lately?"

"Whoa, girl! One at a time! I'm staying here at Mama's house for a few days. Want to go to lunch to catch up?"

I forgot about my ankle, and chirped, "Ready when you are."

"I can't get away until about one. That work for you?" she asked.

"Fine."

"Where's your office?" she said.

I gave her directions and she hung up, her trilly laughter ringing in my ears.

By the time I got downstairs to the guard's desk, he was ready to leave his wife and kids for the beautiful woman in front of him. Tall and willowy, Laurinda was dressed in a fluid drape of black, the only color she ever wore, the silk of her dress swathed around her slender frame. Her long hair was pulled back in a barrette. She mildly flirted with the guard, batting her lashes in a way that would have made any other woman look silly, but this man was doing everything but salivating. I shook my head in pity for him. I'd seen a picture of his wife and kids, and for him, looking at Laurinda's elbow was a vast improvement.

"Hey!" she shouted when she looked up and saw me. "Whew! Why didn't you tell me you were the walking wounded?"

"Tell you in the car. Just walk slowly. How ya doin', O'Reilly?" I said to the guard. He grunted.

"See ya later, hon." Laurinda winked then flicked a wave in his direction, which brought a toothless grin to his face.

Pushing the revolving door for me, she took my elbow as I hobbled down the stairs, opened the door and helped me into the car. She was driving her mother's ancient Olds, its once red paint now dull, fading, and cancerous with rust. Cars were never something she worried much about, just happy if they started when she turned the key.

"So, what's the story?" she asked when we were buckled in and under way.

"Chasing after Alex, and this morning, my doggone car jumped into a ditch." I blurted it out to avoid her questions.

"Car jumped into a ditch. Yeah, right. You were driving too fast, weren't you? Girl, you need to slow down!" she scolded.

"Yeah, I know. It's not as bad as it looks," I said.

"It's worse!" she smirked.

"Droll, very droll." Switching subjects, I asked. "So, what brought you to town to see us country bumpkins?" I asked.

"Humph," she said, momentarily taking her eyes from the road and looking at me. "Let's talk about that after we eat. Where do you want to go and tell me how to get there."

I directed her down Drake Avenue toward the mall, intent on a meal at Cajun Canton.

"O-o-oh, yeah girl! Cajun Canton! That's just what this tired ol' body needs!" Laurinda drooled.

I hadn't realized how hungry I was when the fleeting thought of Bourbon Chicken made my stomach growl.

"How's LaVelle?" I asked.

"Humph! I don't know. That Negro always seems to get arrested just when he thinks somebody might be looking for him. Last I heard, he was in Maricopa County jail for hanging paper around the metro area, but when I called out there, they said he'd been let out and his parole officer was, if you can believe it, looking for him harder than I was. He never learns."

LaVelle had left Denver on the run from the law. He'd been involved in a minor robbery of a Taco Bell in the company of two other idiots, all three armed with fake guns, so he'd decided he'd outlasted his luck in our fair city. Laurinda said he roamed from state to state, taking construction jobs with small outfits that didn't ask too many questions. I hadn't seen him in more than five years and Laurinda said it was close to a year since she'd seen or heard from him.

"He usually only calls when he can't get bail. Guess he's been hustlin' pretty good lately," she said.

Most of the lunch crowd had gone back to their offices by the time we rolled into the restaurant lot. The pungent odor of spicy food tickled my nose as we walked to the door. Cajun Canton was a ten-table eatery owned by the husband from Louisiana who was the chef, of a wife whose accent remained thick, and still tinkled like temple bells. Ling Tao Johnson was as Asian as Joe Johnson was African American. They loved each other too much to allow the hurt of the cruel words and stares they had endured for nearly fifty years to pull them apart. Combining their love of cuisine, they'd opened their restaurant in the heart of the Black community during the early 70's and had never closed their doors. Cajun Canton was known all over Denver for strange sounding but scrumptious combinations like crawdads and sesame; combination rice and black-eyed peas; wontons and fried chicken. Many had tried, including me, to duplicate the mouth-watering Bourbon Sesame Chicken, but nobody could do it like Joe.

"Hi, missy!" Ling Tao chirped when we walked in. She always called me Missy. "How you? Ah, you fall again." It was a statement of fact. She had seen me when I'd been on crutches the past winter after I'd fallen on the ice. "You here fo' chicken? Joe!" she bawled. "Missy here fo' chicken! Two plate! How that boy?"

"He's perfect, thank you Mrs. Johnson," I said.

She patted my hand and passed it to her granddaughter, Jenny, for her to lead us to a table.

"How you, lady? Have not seen in long time," she said, walking beside us and patting Laurinda's hand.

"I'm fine, Ma'am. How are you?" Laurinda had to shake her head at the depth of Mrs. Johnson's memory.

"Ah...getting old, but still come to restaurant every day. Jenny not old enough yet to run things."

"Grandma!" Jenny scolded.

"Good to see you, Mrs. Johnson," Laurinda said as she slid into her chair.

"The food will be out in just a minute. Granny always knows what you like," Jenny said after pouring two glasses of sweet, iced green tea from a pitcher. She walked away in the direction of the kitchen. Ling Tao had resumed her perch on a chair behind the cash register, vigorously wiped her hands on a damp towel then deftly resumed folding wontons.

Laurinda sighed as she looked around. "She never forgets a face. I know I'm home now."

"So, to what do we owe the privilege of your visit?" I asked. I was chewing a breadstick I'd liberally covered in Louisiana hot sauce.

"Oh, well, I might as well tell you. Sonny died and I was the only one to bury the old bastard."

I stopped chewing. "When'd he die?"

"'Bout a week ago. Unfortunately, he had my card in his wallet with 'Daughter' written on it, so the coroner knew where to find me." She was staring out the window, a look I couldn't read on her face.

"What happened?" I asked.

"Police said it looked like he was drunk, and he'd slipped and fallen on a pitchfork in the shed. He'd been dead a day at least before Mr. G. discovered him. Don't know how the tines found it, but they got him in his little, teeny, tiny heart." She sighed.

"Was he still a gardener?"

"Oh yeah, and Mr. G. is paying for everything. He always struck me as perceptive, and I think he guessed I didn't want to. Sonny had been with him a long time. Ever since I left high school..." she trailed off. Her thinned lips were turned down as though she tasted something disagreeable.

She then told me serious therapy had been called for in the years following high school, and although she had bad days, remembering her dad, she was a determined woman, hell bent on making her life have meaning. She traveled and said smilingly, that she made boatloads of money from her photography, which had been featured in countless magazines and from the book of photos of her adopted home, New York, New York. She lived in a pricey townhouse overlooking Central Park.

After that, Laurinda and I didn't talk for a while, just sat in silence looking out the window at Fielding High School across the street. Teens milled on the lawn, one group lounging on the wall smoking, another clutch of husky fellows passing a football to each other. I remembered seeing three of them being wooed by CU on Channel 7 news. Girls dressed in skin-flashing shorts and tops, flirted with the would-be millionaire athletes with the determination of divorce attorneys seeking massive settlements.

"So anyway, I'm having them, the Monarch Society, cremate him, and I'll put the urn out there at Ft. Logan, since he was a veteran. I kinda like the idea of him burning twice, don't you?" Her smile was faint and her voice wistful when she said this.

"Well, here's our lunch." she said briskly as Jenny walked up with a tray on which were two plates loaded with combination rice and black-eyed peas, thin slivers of candied sweet potatoes and scrumptious bronze chunks of chicken, shimmering in a caramelized glaze and dotted with white sesame seeds. Morsels of green scallions and slivers of red pepper decorated the peas and rice, and in two bowls was the clear broth Joe and Ling Tao knew I loved. They knew I liked to slurp it as I devoured the chicken, rice and potatoes, so it was always served with my meal. Nodding her head when I grinned and saluted with my fork, Ling Tao smiled and returned to her task.

Laurinda and I did not speak a word to each other until most of the soup had been slurped and the plate held less than half of the original serving. "Will you be staying long?" I asked when I finally looked up.

"Oh, I don't know. I'm supposed to go to Chichen Itza in a month to six weeks or so, and I don't plan on coming back for at least a year, so I may just stay here till I need to get packed. I keep my passport handy just in case I decide to hop a plane."

"Well, regardless of the occasion, it really is good to see you. I'll call T'ene and the boys and see what's up for this weekend. We should all get together."

We talked a little longer about my family, avoiding all discussion of hers, finished our food down to the fortune cookies then, looking at my watch, I announced, "Let's fly, kiddo. My boss isn't in to check my hours, but I did get in late this morning." After I paid the bill, peeked in the kitchen to say hi to Joe, hugged Ling Tao and Jenny, we scooted to the car. Laurinda didn't say much on the drive back and I didn't press her. It was obvious that she had things on her mind. At my office, she helped me to the door.

"I'll call you tonight, okay?" she said.

"No. Call me in the morning. Tonight, I have a date with a handsome man.

"S'cuse me? You tryin' to find my man a new daddy?" She did the Black woman head wag, hands on hips, a smile playing with her lips.

"Lord, no! But this one looks like a real fine – and I do mean fine – candidate."

"Well alright. I'll call you in the am. 'Round 10, ok?"

"Works for me. See ya, hon." I said, hugging her. "It really is good to see you."

"You, too!"

She skipped down the stairs two at a time, her long legs flashing. It really was good to see her. Pushing the revolving door, I hobbled back upstairs to Fraud.

CHAPTER 5

When I returned from lunch, I did what I had to every day in my job: I tried to track down the bad guys. Most days at Shield were exciting work: tracking the guys who torched their homes, wrecked their cars, claimed workman's comp then partied on reported broken legs, or those who pretended to flush the wife's diamond down the toilet for the thrill and profit of collecting on their insurance. And those were the tame crimes. Humans are creative primates, and I'd seen my share of murders for the money. In my favor though, when it came to finding those who were trying to get away with it, my record was better than 80-20.

By 3:45, tardy or not, I was ready to get out of Dodge. I called Larry, who said he was happy to give me a loaner while they fixed mine. Larry and I had known each other since grade school, so he wouldn't want to charge me for the loaner or repair of the car, but I'd pay him anyway. My motto: owe no one.

"How 'bout I pick up some pizza, bring the loaner, and get you from work tonight?" he asked.

"Ah...I'm going to be late getting home tonight."

"Wha'? We always have dinner on Friday," he whined.

"I got here so late that I need to stay a while, and after that, Alex has a game. We can go back to our routine next Friday." The lie rushed from my mouth.

"Routine, huh? You never usually stay late if you get in late. If you don't want to see me anymore, just say so." Now he was angry and whipping himself into a world-class pout.

I sighed. "Larry, I'm tired and my ankle hurts, so can we dance later? I'll be over in a bit to get the loaner, if you still have one and if not, I'll just get a rental."

"Come on over whenever," he replied sullenly. I hung up.

Ellen walked out to the lot with me. She said, "You'd better go home and soak your ankle instead of going out to dinner."

She's so practical.

"And miss going out on a date with a hunk! Not on your life!" I hooted. "You know as well as I do, my dating life doesn't get me anything but cooking for Larry the loving and clueless, so a free meal with someone who can spell gets the old juices goin'! Just wait till you see him!"

She had agreed to take me to get the loaner and pick up Alex, so we ambled off to her Camry, and headed out. By the time we got to the school, Alex was waiting outside in a queue of other kids, all laughing and nudging each other. He talked all the way to Larry's, barely stopping to take a breath. Alex was like so many other six-year-olds – talking was something they did from the moment they awoke till they closed their eyes for sleep. It didn't matter that I didn't know exactly what he was talking about. It mattered that I seemed to be listening.

When we arrived at Larry's garage, he was in the process of completing a sale, his smile genuine and all encompassing. Larry was the master of customer service, which helped him get and keep customers in the highly competitive business he'd chosen. He bid the young lady goodbye then turned his smiling mouth's attention to my cheek, bussing it perfunctorily.

"How ya doing Alex?" Alex merely bobbed his head. He wasn't too crazy about Larry; only tolerated him because he was my friend.

"You did a good job on it this time," he said, bobbing his head in the direction of my car. It forlornly sat on the south side of the building, front wheels flat, giving it the look of a dog hunkering down on its front paws. It looked pretty pitiful. "I think it's finally time for a new mode of transport."

"Oh, no, Larry!" I squealed. "Say it isn't so!"

"Sorry, babe. When Jake brought it in this morning, I knew we couldn't fix it. Axle's broke. Could get it welded, but it'd never be completely safe." He reached behind him and selected a set of car keys from the pegboard behind him. "C'mon out front. There's a nice little Beetle I just bought to loan out. I'll give you a good deal on it, if you decide you like it. Anyway, keep it as long as you need to."

We walked outside to see the car. "What happened to your ankle? Do that when you creamed the car?"

"Heh, heh. Nothing gets by you, does it?" The car was a sweet little Volkswagen Beetle, black with black leather interior. I looked inside and was thrilled to see that it had a cd player and was an automatic. I knew Larry had bought it at the auto auction, and knowing how cheap he was, he'd probably paid half of its true worth. This just could be my new car. I opened the door and sat down in it, and my son climbed into the passenger seat. Larry put his hand on my shoulder as he handed me the keys.

"I'll take your wreck in trade and give you a really good deal on the price if you want," he said. "Deal?"

"Deal," I said.

We arrived at Kennedy, and sure enough, there sat David. He looked even better than he had that morning, or maybe I'd been delirious with pain. Naw, he looked good! He had changed into a navy polo and gray twills, understated elegance.

"How're you? How's the ankle?"

"Throbbing nicely." I was sarcastic again. I knew because he looked down at me and frowned.

"Sorry," I said. "I think it's called Tourette's."

"S'ok," he said. "Survived the day?"

"Sat a little more than usual and didn't walk around visiting as much. I was actually fairly productive for a change."

I asked David if he would give me enough time after the game to shower. He had cheated and gone home to change before coming to get me.

"Of course. What, you think I want to take some funky woman to dinner?"

"Funky? Well! I'll have you know I took a sponge bath in the sink in the bathroom of the fifth floor ladies' room the minute I got to work this morning. Actually, it was a paper towel bath, but we make do with what we have."

"Hey, David!" Alex yelled as we walked to the field.

"Yo, Al! How's it hangin'?" David asked.

"'How's it hangin'?'" I squealed.

"That's a guy phrase, Mom. Chill." Alex was down with it.

"Yeah, Mom, chill. We be guy talkin'!" David filled in.

Holding my left hand up vertically, I topped it with the palm of my right hand in a time out sign. "You chill, my man. Enough cool talk. I need this fella to speak SAE, if you don't mind. We have a college career to think of."

"You're right. I was running out of cool phrases anyway," David whispered.

Early on in his life, it was quite obvious Alex was going to need a degree with bite from a noteworthy school. He'd be hard pressed to make a living off of sports. Maybe he would find his niche as a sports attorney or perhaps a sports doctor, but the poor little fellow had two left feet and a short supply of savvy. He had heart, though. First minute of the second quarter, he ran for the infield, determination causing his eyebrows to 'V' like a pointer to lead him to the object of his desire – the ball. He sped past the other small combatants, homed in, thrust his left leg backward, pistoned it forward, missed the ball and scissored the air. He landed with a tooth rattling "plop." His arms were flat on either side, fists melted to palms, knees skyward. Play had proceeded a short distance down the field as David bolted and I hobbled up from our spot beneath the cool of a shady elm and ran to my wounded soldier's side. David and the coach reached him first. David was immediately down on his knees, an arm on either side, his large frame shading Alex from the sun. Alex's hands had become fists once more and they were rubbing his streaming eyes. David gently picked him up in his arms, whispered something into his ear, carrying him to me.

"Is he hurt?" I gasped.

"Naw," he said gently. "Just had the wind knocked out of him."

He carried him while I held on to a little hand. The whole time he was whispering to the child.

"I almos' had it, Mama!" he quietly sobbed as we sat back down. "I tried so hard!"

"I know you did, baby. Don't cry." He only called me Mama when he was very sad or hurt and, in this case, he was a little of both. David still had him cradled in his arms. The child reached out and strung his arms about my neck, sobs shaking his shoulders. At that moment, he made me very proud.

He turned to David and said, "Thank you," in a small, sad voice.

We sat out the remainder of the quarter with Alex in my lap, arms tightly wrapped like pythons around my midsection, cheek resting on my chest. He watched the play with what I thought was little interest but at half time abruptly released me then jumped to his feet.

"I'm going to see if Coach'll let me play again!" he announced.

"Good idea, fella," David said.

"I'll do better this time!" he yelled on the run.

After conferring with the coach and seeing an okay nod from me, he was put in as a forward. His steam had returned, and his legs were soon churning the air. I held my breath and prayed as he once again homed in on the ball and kicked. He miraculously hit it! The ball feebly careened off of the green-jerseyed chest of one of the boys on the opposing team, bounced off of another's head, landed, then slowly caromed into the furthest corner of the goal. The goalie made a valiant effort to beat the ball's slow progress, but much to Alex's joy, he was too late. My little player had scored a goal!

"What did you tell him?" I asked after David stopped jumping around.

"I just told him if he got a goal, we'd go get pizza after the game, and if he didn't, we'd be nice and take you out to dinner at a wear-a-tie place, like Baroque."

"You know, he hates ties."

"You're catching on," he said and resumed jumping and clapping.

Alex was the hero of the day and not the goat, as I'd feared. His teammates clapped him on the back and high-fived with enthusiasm and many shouts of 'Way to go, man!' at the conclusion of the game. We walked to the car, and he accepted the accolades with aplomb. His little face was stretched so tight, I thought his teeth should hurt. Once in the car, Alex smiled the grin again then made it a point to remind us that Papa, his granddad, would be as proud as we were.

"Sure thing. We'll call him as soon as we get home," I promised.

At the corner of Hampden and Monaco, the light caught us.

"I'll be at your house in forty-five, ok?" David yelled out the window.

"We'll be ready!" Alex chirped. I looked at his happy face and shook my head.

"Forty-five minutes." I called, turned on Monaco and headed south. David had turned left to go back into Denver.

We were home within twenty minutes. Dashing in, I made Alex go to his bathroom and start running the water. His face lost a bit of its glow at the mention of bathing, but his elation buoyed him back up and he went as told without a word. I followed him to his bathroom.

Suddenly, he turned. "You promised that we could call Papa and tell him about my game. Remember, Mommy?"

"Oh, yeah, that's right. Go get the phone."

I sat on the closed toilet lid and waited for him to come back. He came running in and handed me the phone.

"Hey, Mom," I said when I heard her voice. "Is Dad home?"

She said she would go and get him, and I put the phone in Alex's grasping hands.

"Papa, Papa!" he shouted into the receiver.

"Nana went to get him. Wait a sec."

Moments later, he again shouted, "Papa, Papa! I made a goal!"

I heard Dad's booming voice say, "Good going, fella! I'm proud of you!"

He and Dad talked for a bit, then, after saying I love you, he hung up. Handing me the phone, he climbed into the now full tub, grabbed his floating fire engine and began to make 'vroom-vroom' noises.

"Babe, Mom can't sit beside the tub tonight," I said, scrunching my face when I got up.

"I know, Mom." He zipped the toy over the bubbles. Leaving the bathroom door open so I could look down the short hall and see him, I trotted into my room, took the brace off, then all of my clothes then turned the faucets in my shower. I sat on the toilet seat and took off my shoes. When I took the right one off, my foot felt like a loaf of rising bread dough, spread to fill the shoe. When I took off the sock, I could see how bad it was, dark purple and fat. I stepped into the shower, soaped my body and leaned against the wall. Getting out, I lurched to the toilet, pulled a towel off the rack and sat down with my legs stretched in front. My entire leg was hurting. Tears flowed.

Knowing that I had to bite back the pain, I splashed icy water on my face to reduce my puffy eyes then patted them with tissue and looked in the mirror. I looked frightful. Reaching into the cabinet, I found my Tylenol and some seldom used eyeliner, popped two pills and followed them up with a handful of water. I traced a thin line close to the edge of my lashes, stroked black mascara on and stood back to survey the results. Makeup can be as good a cure as a vaccine for measles, erasing all vestiges of what had looked like a lost cause.

Now the hair. I plugged the rollers in and went to my bedroom while they were heating. Standing in front of the closet, I sighed. If I couldn't go out with him, I'd try to look good in. I called Pizza Palace, ordered a medium cheese and a Kitchen Sink. After lotioning with a perfumed body smoother, I pulled on a long, pale aqua flowered rayon skirt that rippled around my ankles, a cream colored, clingy, silk tee shirt and sandals. Back in the bathroom, I haphazardly wrapped strands around hot rollers. The heat would straighten the frizz. I finished rolling and limped down the hall to Alex's bathroom. He was still merrily driving over the bubbles.

He looked up at me and smiled.

"Alright then. Let's get out of the tub," I said.

He thrust his arms up to me and I grabbed his wrists and hoisted him over the edge to the rug. Wrapping his Scooby Doo towel around him, I sat down on the toilet lid and held him in my lap, starting our daily hugging ritual. He silently curled his knees up and rested his damp head on my chest.

"I love you, Mommy." He tipped his head and looked up

into my eyes.

"I love you, too, my darling." Kissing his forehead, I pressed my face against his head. His hair is soft as a dream. I gave him a long hug then began to briskly rub his body to dry him. When we were done with dry off, he grabbed the white underwear I'd laid on the counter, sat on the floor and rushed his feet into them. Leaving him, I returned to my room, removed the curlers and shook my head. A quick flick of the pick here and there, and I was happy to see that I looked as though I didn't have a clue of what humidity was. The curls bounced to my shoulders. Alex had finished dressing about the time the doorbell rang.

"I'll get it!" Alex yelled as he flew to the door. David was handing Alex a large, wrapped box as I rounded the corner. He looked up and I could see he appreciated my outfit.

"Nice." he murmured.

"Glad you like," I said. "Hope you don't mind, but my ankle really hurts. Can we stay in? I already ordered pizza. Hope you like yours with everything. If not, I got Alex his favorite plain cheese."

"Sounds good to me." Moments later, the delivery boy drove up, Pizza Palace flag waving merrily from the antennae of his antique Honda. Taking the pizza from the pimply-faced kid, David peeled a twenty and a ten out of his money clip. He gave it to the kid and said, "Keep it," when he attempted to give back change. The kid grinned widely, touched the brim of his red cap, and happily bounded to his car.

"Take them into the dining room, please." I motioned to the right. Following my direction, he took the pizza in and placed it on the table. I walked behind him, heading for the kitchen for plates.

"Hey, look." he said. "Why don't you just sit down and tell me where everything is?"

"That'll work. The plates are in the top cabinet to the left of the stove, glasses are in the cabinet next to them." I perched on a chair. Alex came running in clutching a new soccer ball.

"Look, Mom! David gave me a new soccer ball! Can we practice tomorrow, huh?" His eyes sparkled as he quivered with excitement.

"Honey, I don't know. I can barely walk."

"Oh, yeah, Mom," he said. "I'm sorry."

"Don't worry about it, fella. If it's okay with your mom, I'll come over tomorrow and kick a few with you, okay?" David looked down at me. He had three plates, glasses and a liter of Pepsi balancing in his hands.

Alex's head bobbed like one of those bobbly head dogs you see in the back windows of cars, and he grinned like a madman. David issued the utensils and I told Alex to get napkins from the kitchen.

"Okay, Mom!" He ran in and I could hear the cabinet door slamming. When he returned to the room, he laid a napkin beside each plate. He then quickly slipped into his chair.

"Mr. Alex, your cheese pizza." David said as he ceremoniously placed a slice on Alex's plate. "Mommy? Cheese or everything?" he said turning to me.

"Everything sounds good."

After pouring soda into all of our glasses, he sat down and pulled a piece of pizza off for himself. Grace was said, then we ate in silence except for my occasional admonition for Alex to slow down on his eating. He gulped, burped and smiled at me.

"Tell me more about your family," David said after we all had slowed down eating.

"Well, there's a bunch of us. Lucky seven." I said, ticking them off on my fingers. "Fynn's a stockbroker; Khari, a pilot; Taye is a veterinarian; and Adam is a cop. My brother, Bruk, and my sister, T'ene, are both professors at DU."

"Whew! Bet your parents are proud. Interesting names, and, pray tell, how did your dad support all of you?" he asked.

"All African names. To support us, Dad was a general contractor – a homebuilder. Started out by building a home for his family and discovered that he had a knack for it. Built one for the neighbors a mile or so down the road, and from then he was off and running. He was the premier custom homebuilder in Colorado for a number of years. This house was the first one he built in this neighborhood." I was staring back at the past and thinking about my childhood.

I continued, "This house was one of three and the area used to be more rural than it is now. Used to be all dirt roads. Dad bought the land, forty acres, built this house, the ones on either side and the two behind it; sold them then had to wait a while since he didn't have any more money. After that, he went to straight custom homes on contract. Carter Construction built at least one house in most of the towns east of the mountains here in the metro area. The biggest one was built for John Livingstone, you know, the producer? It's down in Parker. Big, old house with a tennis court and indoor swimming pool," I told him proudly. "Then the corporation guys came in and started building what they called custom homes. They're actually humongous tract homes. They did and still do, use about four plans which they make a few cosmetic changes on, then sell for boatloads of money. They pushed most of the smaller operations out and started eating away at Dad's territory. Dad had enough contracts in the works to hold them off for quite some time. His customers were loyal and wouldn't leave him, so he just bided his time until they were chomping at the bit. Finally, he gave in and sold. None of the houses are as well-built as the ones he produced, which kinda makes him angry, but after he got out, he and Mom built their dream house, and now they live on a little ranch on the outskirts of Evergreen."

"He must have made a pretty nice profit," he said.

"Yep. Dad made them pay. He wasn't really ready to retire, but now he's kind of a gentleman farmer. Has a few chickens, geese, ducks, a cow or two, and a horse for each of the grandchildren. He and Mom travel, kick back, and enjoy themselves. It's a nice life for them. We think he did pretty good for a colored boy with a tenth-grade education." I paused. "So, tell me about yours."

"Ah, well," he began. "Let's finish our dinner and I'll tell you about them later."

"Ok. Sure." He seemed evasive, but I decided to wait him out. When two cheese and three Kitchen Sink slices lay in lonely, gooey grease puddles, David leaned his elbows on the table and smiled at Alex.

"Didya get enough there, champ?" he asked.

"Um-hm. I'm full!" Alex pushed wearily from the table. "Can I go watch *Nemo*, Mom?"

"Go wash your hands and face first. Want me to put it in for you?" I asked.

"Mom! I'm not a baby. I know how BluRays work!"

"Well, la-de-da! Go on, Mister Man!" I laughed.

"Wanna come watch *Nemo*, David? It's a really good movie!" He was looking at David with big eyes and eyebrows raised nearly to his hairline.

"Not quite yet, fella. You go get it running while I help your mom with the dishes, ok?"

"Ok!"

"He's watched that movie at least fifty times." I whispered to David. "The newer Disneys don't seem to have the same draw for him as *Nemo*."

David smiled. Wagging his little butt at me, Alex high-fived David and left the room. We carried the dishes and empty containers to the kitchen where he tossed the empty boxes, and I loaded the dishwasher.

"Got a big baggie?" he asked.

"Cabinet to the left of the sink," I said.

He piled the leftover pizza into the baggie then put it in the fridge as I wiped the counter. I felt so relaxed, so at-home with this man. We were moving about each other in my kitchen, not talking but comfortable in each other's company, as though we had been doing it for years. When the cleanup was complete, I folded the towel over the sink divider and turned to him.

"Why don't you go into the living room while I make coffee?" I asked.

"Alright, that sounds good. Maybe I'll go check out *Nemo*. I've never had a chance to see it."

He strolled into the family room and came back in less than a minute. "Come check this out," he said waving me into the family room.

I followed him. Dory was scooting from coral to coral in an attempt to escape Marlin, but her swimming acrobatics were lost on my son. Alex was curled in his old comforter, his head resting on his pillow, gently snoring.

"Little man had a busy day," David whispered.

"Yeah, he's tired," I said.

David reached down and hoisted him up into his arms. Alex sighed then rested his cheek against David's chest. I preceded him, held the door ajar and led the way to Alex's room. He gently deposited the child on his bed then set about removing his clothes. I stood beside them and watched.

"You're pretty good at that," I remarked.

"I've had practice. My sister has three kids. Where are his pajamas?" he asked when Alex was down to skivvies. Rummaging in the dresser, I passed him a clean nightshirt into which he had corralled Alex's head and upper torso within a matter of moments. I helped him place my comatose little fellow under the sheets, kissed the soft cheek and we left the room, pulling the door gently behind us.

"Go on into the living room and I'll be in with the coffee."

"This has to be by your ex," he said, when I walked in with a tray laden with two cups of coffee, sugar and cream. "You did say he was an artist, right?"

"Right. That's him."

He was standing back from a painting of a brilliant pink

rose on a thorny bush with a realistic turtle in the background and a blue, cloud-decked sky. The painting is large – three feet by four – and dominates one wall of my living room. If you look closely, you can see the branches of the rose bush form a man and woman, preparing to embrace. The overall effect is one of serenity, and to me was always vaguely reminiscent of Dali. It is a hard painting to ignore.

"He painted that one. It's called 'Love.' He really was a good artist and was on his way to becoming very successful... for a while. Then he went to Iraq, came back and went wacky," I said. "He was well known in Denver's art circles. I've known him all my life, and I've always admired his art. He had painted 'Love' better than twenty years ago. This one," I gestured to the north wall, "is after."

The painting I waved my hand for him to look at is on the opposite wall above a small table in a not so well lighted corner. It is in total contrast to 'Love.' A wall made of chrome is the backdrop and at the base of it, resting uneasily, is a coiled cobra, its mouth agape displaying rows of razor-sharp teeth. He is poised to strike, displaying his hood. Over the top of the wall is a single row of barbed wire, and on the other side, a tank with a gaunt man in an impeccable double-breasted navy suit standing beside it, wilting, as though he is weary. He and the snake are the focal points, both riveting to the eye. A full sun relentlessly beats down on the entire scene, but for some reason, the opposite effect of cold is what is felt. This painting is small – one foot by one – and because of the photographic realism, it sometimes catches the attention quicker than any other piece in the room.

"That one's called 'Is It Time Yet?' and he refused to tell me what it means. I have my own ideas, but I was always afraid to mention them to him. It's a tortured piece, isn't it?"

"Damn skippy." he murmured. "You should have a psychiatrist look at it. This is the work of one sick puppy."

"Yup, but it's a subtle sickness. Until you really look at it and take each element piece by piece, it's kinda pretty. Alex actually likes it, and most people don't see the pain unless they know about the artist. He did more pieces after this one, and they got progressively worse, more tortured."

"Is he seeing a therapist? I mean, I'm not a judge, but from what I can see, if he isn't, he really needs to."

"Last time I talked to him, he wasn't. He quit going. Said he didn't need it. The court had said he had to get help, but Frank's so lazy and defiant that I doubt he ever went back. I didn't push it," I said. "He hasn't seen Alex since birth and makes no effort to. So, my philosophy has been – if you don't bother me, I won't bother you. He doesn't even know where we live. Originally, I kept the paintings because I figured if he died, they might be worth something. I know, I know, I'm a calloused bitch." I continued. "But, you know, I feel sorry for him.

"He's like thousands of other guys and gals who go away to do what they think is right and are treated to government assisted training on how to be a serial killer. Then, when the enemy has or has not been vanquished, these unlucky souls are sent back to hearth and home and told to behave normally after all they have had to do in the name of God and country. Normal, after that, is just a tad skewed."

David shook his head. "Yeah, you are so right. But you're not a bitch. You're a realist." He turned his attention to the other four pieces, pale by comparison to Frank's, not nearly as eye catching, but pleasant in my bright living room.

"All of these are by currently unknown artist friends of mine. I keep them cause they're my heart. I could never part with any of them."

David nodded in agreement as he looked at my collection. Finally, we sat down on my flower-strewn sofa, awash in lilies and peonies. We didn't talk at first, just leaned back and enjoyed the coffee. I felt comfortable with this guy. He was movie-star handsome, but he had a flaw: a small gap between his front teeth. Funny, but somehow, it gave him vulnerability and made him approachable.

"Ok. Time to tell me about your family."

I was leaning on my elbow along the back of the sofa. I smirked at him, but he was not smiling. I stopped. He seemed to be chewing on the lower left inside of his lip, and as I watched, he chewed a tiny bit harder, ever so slightly. He sighed deeply.

"I read someplace that every family is, to a degree, dysfunctional. We were cursed with our share and the share of about two other families'. My father is – let's face it – rich. His money came from prudent investments, hard work, and computers. He was the original owner of Transcontinental Computing Systems – TCS. Sold to a corporation when I was in my first year of law school." He stopped to take a breath but quickly continued. "After that, Dad purchased Mouse Software, which he personally turned into a silicon giant. He and my mother live on an estate on Long Island."

"Whew! That is rich!" I said, shaking my head.

Telling about the enormous family fortune, David seemed almost apologetic. Not many Blacks could lay claim to the brand of wealth he described, unless they dunked a basketball or lobbed a football.

"Why do you sound as if he evicts single, welfare mothers when you mention how much money your Daddy has? I should think a large amount of wealth is a whole lot easier to accept than an equal amount of poverty. I've been on the poverty end. It ain't much fun," I said.

"Um-hm, I agree, but he has mountains of money, and he wouldn't help that single, welfare mother pay her rent. Particularly a Black woman. That's the problem I have with him. Gotta tell you, Nia, he's really a closet redneck. He'll let minorities work for his company, but they never advance any higher than third level manager. At home, all minorities were always niggers, wops, spics and whatnot. I never could deal," he sighed, wagging his head.

I didn't say anything, just sat and peered into my coffee cup. Finally, he said with a sigh, "Dad worked for every dime he had and always says the problem with other Black folks is they're lazy. 'Pull yourselves up by your bootstraps. White men know how to work,' he always says. We grew up like little white children, who never associated with any other people of color except our cook, Dora, and Mom's personal maid, Bettie. The only thing was, I was called nigger so much in school I thought it was a nickname. I only mentioned the name calling to Dad once. His comment was that I probably did something to make them call me that. Make them call me that! What a joke! My sister, Lisa, stayed there in Long Island until she married. She met this nice guy that the parents approved of: John, an upstanding, Italian fella who doesn't show his Sicilian heritage since he is blond and blue. Wealthy, but not as much as Dad. His parents resent Lisa. I got up and walked the day I graduated high school. Worked my way through college, never asked him for a dime. Granddad helped me a little, but for the most part, I've paid my own way since then. Haven't seen him in about ten years, and I can't say that I've missed him."

"What about your mother?" I asked innocently. I was starting to regret opening the family can of worms, because now, they were wriggling and squirming all over each other.

"Mom? What a scream. My mom lives in the shadow of my father, happy as long as he hands over her weekly check for power shopping." His tone was bitter, icy in his monologue. He continued, staring straight ahead at an invisible spot on the wall. "Her hobby is shopping. She loves to buy dresses for her countless functions and attends every one, even when he can't go with her. She wants to be the leading society dame of Long Island, but she forgets, conveniently, that she's Black. She makes it a point to go to every AIDS function, underprivileged children's wingding, and Catholic Church fundraiser. After she touches the little minority kids and AIDS babies, prays and gets her picture taken, she goes into the bathroom, washes her hands and arms in the hottest water available, scrubs them with antiseptic wipes, then lotions with Purell. She'd flip over backwards if she saw me here with you, enjoying myself with another person of color, and no cameras available to record my magnanimous attitude!"

We sat in silence, staring at the wall, the paintings, the ant crawling across my floor, anything but each other. The comfort level had dropped. I got up, found a three by five on my desk in the corner, scooped up the ant and put him out the front door. When I returned, I noticed the color was beginning to return to his face. He smiled.

"Want a dish of ice cream, another cup of coffee, a pinch of bicarb?" I asked.

"The third choice is probably the best. I think I ate and talked too much and now I'm seeing Marley's ghost. I'd better be getting home." He was rising from the sofa. I didn't want him to leave but I couldn't think of any way to stop him. We walked toward the front door.

"Thanks for all of your help today, David. I can honestly say that I don't know what I would have done without you." I smiled up at him, marveling at his deep gray eyes.

He was looking down at me with a slight smile curving his lips. "I know you must get tired of hearing this, but you are absolutely beautiful!" he murmured.

I blinked, looked over my shoulder and reached up to place my palm on his forehead. "You sure you're talking and looking at me? I'm far from beautiful."

"Would I have stopped for an ugly woman?" he said mischievously.

We stood giggling in the hallway, not too loudly so we wouldn't wake Alex. When our steam had run down, he took my hand, draped it over his shoulder, encircled my waist and lifted me so that my lips could meet his. Not only was he a joy to behold, but his kiss made my toenails curl, my ears tingle and my butt contract. I felt dizzy.

He set me back on my unsteady feet and whispered, "See you tomorrow, huh? I'll call you."

"Yeah. Give me a call when you get a chance. Make sure you call me and not the other chick you were so chivalrous to today. You know, the beautiful one," I murmured into his chest.

He gently pushed me away and grasped the upper part of my arms lightly. "Why do you say this? You're beautiful, very beautiful and I would really appreciate it if you'd stop denying it. I'm the one looking at you. Just say thank you and leave it at that."

His voice was a hint puckish, peeved, so I shrugged and said, "Okay, okay already! Thank you."

He reached into his back pocket, got his wallet out and pulled out what looked like a business card. Taking his pen out of his jacket pocket, he wrote something on it and handed it to me.

"Office number." He flipped the card to show me the back. "Cell number."

Taking his wallet and pen, I slid one of the cards out, wrote my number on the back and put them all in his hands. He looked at the number then said, "I'll call you around 11 tomorrow, come by and pick you two up, okay?"

I nodded. He gathered me up into his arms, kissed my forehead and said, "Bye." This was the guy of my dreams, and probably every other breathing female on terra firma. He honestly seemed to like me! I waved good-bye till his car was a dim shadow at the corner, then I turned and went into the house. It just doesn't get any better than this.

CHAPTER 6

I woke up Saturday with Alex's feet pressing hard against the lower part of my back. He had sneaked into my bed at some point during the night, and I was not in the least surprised. Periodically, he made the journey, never on a regular basis as he had in years past. He knew the rules: stay in your own bed except in the case of dire emergencies, up to and including prodigious nightmares. Alex could fabricate prodigious nightmares at the winking of an eye if it would get him out of his bed and into mine. Unfortunately, I'd heard the best of his repertoire, so he had to spend many a lonely night in his own bed, conjuring up boogie men, women and children that really didn't scare him but might have been, to a gullible mom, believable. It was a rare occurrence that produced something truly fearful. When his imagination failed him, wise child that he is, he knows I can't possibly keep my lids propped open all night. Hence, the size ones printing my back.

I gently moved them to the side and slid out of the bed. I

looked back at my sleeping son. His mischievous grin was dormant, a rivulet of drool making its way free of the right corner of his mouth. His long lashes caressed the tops of his cheeks, and thick curls spun around the lobes of his ears. He has the Carter complexion, the color as mellow and silky as milk chocolate, smooth as porcelain. When asleep, he truly resembles an angel, but just wait until the hunger for sleep is sated.

Leaning over, I kissed his cheek, and then went into the bathroom and turned the faucet, leaning on the counter until I figured the water had gone from icy to tepid. That was another fact of being a mom: water could never be hot, merely tepid to avoid scalding little fingers. In my house, it was not due to Alex, though. I needed a new water heater. Splashing water on my face, I groped for the towel, dried my face and finger combed the short strands of errant hair from my forehead.

The phone was ringing. I dashed to the kitchen to answer it before Alex woke up. All of my friends knew not to call my house before 10:00 on a Saturday. It was about 7:30, earlier than David had said he would call, but maybe he'd changed his mind.

"Hello?"

"Nia?" The voice was quiet yet rough.

"Uncle Harold?" I asked. "How are you and why, pray tell, are you calling me at this ungodly hour?"

He was silent for a long time.

"It's not good news, is it Uncle Harold. What happened?" I blurted.

"Hang on. I gotta get the rest of the file." Uncle Harold has been a detective at the University Station for about twenty years; he is Dad's brother and one of the most honest cops I know. He was back within moments.

"Well," he sighed deeply before continuing, "Frank won't be able to pay child support at all now. I'm sorry, sugar, he's dead. Looks like a bullet to the head."

I was breathless. Stunned to silence, it took a bit for the news to sink in. Uncle Harold waited patiently.

"What happened? Suicide?" I finally whispered.

But Frank had not killed himself. According to Uncle Harold, at about 12:00 p.m. Thursday, he'd received a call concerning the sighting of a body in the Cherry Creek Reservoir. Divers had begun to drag the lake with grappling hooks, but after making the initial appearance, Frank's corpse had sunk and then stubbornly eluded all efforts to be removed from its murky resting place. In the early hours of Friday morning, Frank had reappeared. He'd rose to the surface on the side of the lake the divers had yet to scour and scared two elderly fishermen into conniptions when they hooked him, thinking he was one of the lake's nasty carp. He'd been in the water quite some time, and the fish had fed bountifully. The coroner said Frank had been in the water at least two weeks, most likely secreted in the sludge created from a recipe of mud, plant life of indeterminate origin, the remains of wheat fields tilled long years prior, and assorted trash ranging from old car parts to abandoned swing sets, all found at the bottom of Cherry Creek Reservoir.

"How did you know it was Frank?"

"Had id in the pocket."

"Thanks for calling, Uncle Harold," I whispered. "I'll be down to the station soon. I'll need to positively identify him, won't I?"

"Ah...Nia, no." His voice was gentle. "Don't do that to yourself. I'll call his dad."

"No," I said firmly. "I'll do it."

"Ok," he sighed. "Come on down."

Involuntarily, shudders starting from my shoulders radiated down to my knees then back up. I felt cold all over. I thought back to my relationship with Frank.

Two weeks after I'd married him, I knew I'd made a major

mistake. Frank entered my life during a dark period, a time of loneliness and despair. I'd just finished college and was involved in the second outing in my search for the ideal career. I'd originally planned a lifetime of law enforcement alongside Uncle Harold and Adam, my brother – my idol – the cop. Mom had thrown a fit when I announced Criminology as my major in college, Music Education as my backup minor, with my plan to go to the police academy after I'd completed my four years.

"I don't need to worry about two of you maybe getting shot. Adam can more than likely handle the police life. You! You're too small! And besides, you're a girl!"

"Whew! Thanks for reminding me, 'cause I guess I haven't checked my panties lately. I'm not a 'girl,' Mom. I'm a woman, and what does my size have to do with it?" I spluttered.

"A small man could take you down!" she wailed.

"Don't worry, Mom. I'll make detective really quick."

She was right on a few points. I am a female, I am small, but in my favor, I have confidence and sheer grit, and I knew I'd make it to be a superb cop. Uncle Harold had helped me by getting them to waive the height requirement, although he constantly groused about how much he didn't want to. After college, I was treated to a comprehensive twenty-seven-week police academy program with fourteen weeks of field training, not at all strenuous; in fact I enjoyed every minute. It was a trip to the gym for free and I loved the workout. I was deadly with a gun, kept my police issue .38 with me at all times, became adept at defense and could take down a man twice my size, and before long, I passed all the tests and got my shield.

I'd been on the force exactly six days when a bullet sheared through the window of the cruiser I was in and took the top left side of my partner's head off. Strands of his hair, skull and brain matter decorated my uniform. He slumped to the right, turning the wheel as he leaned over, and the car bounced off of the curb and stopped. Derek was a big guy, six two or three, a solid 200 plus pounds of gristle and muscle, an eight-year veteran and specially chosen to ride with me. We'd gently argued that morning after check-in about who was going to drive, and after a coin toss, he'd won. Joking and jostling me, he'd gotten behind the wheel, driving straight to the King Soopers for doughnuts for him and a huge bear claw and coffee for me. After leaving the store, we had aimlessly stumbled on an early morning altercation between a husband and wife. The husband had thrown his wailing wife out of the house without a stitch on, and in an attempt to add injury to insult, had gone to their bedroom, and loaded his 30-06. He then stepped just outside of their front door and unloaded it in her direction, missing her but not our cruiser, which happened to be passing at that moment.

"Derek?" I whispered and swallowed a lump that felt like my tongue.

Traffic had come to a complete halt, people climbing out of their cars to look at the crazy man and his pitiful wife, the gawkers standing open mouthed, visions of shock, and less than a hundred yards from the man and his lethal weapon. I shook myself, gathered my wits, pushed Derek's limp body off of my shoulder, then looked through the gaping hole of the blown window. The man was calm, his body drunkenly swaying in the cold morning breeze, his wispy, silver shot hair twirling about his head, dirty plaid bathrobe rippling around his legs. He was unsteadily reloading his rifle. I hopped out of the cruiser.

"Sir, I must ask you to refrain from reloading your rifle." I held my shaking hand up to him, palm looking him in the face. "You are endangering your wife, this neighborhood, and me. Please put the gun down." I had my pistol unsnapped in its holster, had my right hand on the butt, but I'd yet to pull it out.

"Bitch deserves another hole in her ass!" He suddenly shouted; his voice slurred. "Gonna shoot her, then gonna shoot you!" he yelled.

"Put the gun down!" I shouted, but at that instant he raised the barrel mere inches and fired at his wife who had sat down on the grass ten feet from him, sobbing into her hands. The bullet hit her foot, instantly transforming it into something resembling a ham hock. I hesitated. She screamed which brought me out of my momentary stupor, and I pulled my gun and fired. The bullet hit him low in the fleshy part of his left shoulder, traveled sideways and right on through, missing his heart but clipping his spine squarely in the middle of his vertebrae. He crumpled to the ground screaming, destined to be carried by two large and two small wheels for the remainder of his life. I felt little pity for him.

We buried Derek with full honors. The morning after his funeral, I dressed in my blues, got into my ancient Mazda, and drove to my precinct, the University Station. Adam met me there. Adam is a foot and a half taller than I, lean and sinewy, and he always reminds me of a meerkat peering over the Serengeti.

"You need to go into another line of business, sissy." He told me without preamble. I didn't fight it, just walked in, and turned in my shield. The captain was relieved even though he tried to hide it, and Uncle Harold said it was for the best. I left the precinct without a backwards glance.

Mom never said she was happy I'd left, and I decided to go the route she and Dad had chosen for me. I enrolled back into college for the required certificate, a loose goal of teaching music beckoning in my future. When I'd finished boning up and had the new certificate, I set out to find a teaching position to no avail. When I did finally land one, it was less than ideal. I taught violin, viola, cello, bass and trumpet, and traveled between four different elementary schools. One principal was a pedophile who molested the children, eventually was found out and is now lifting weights in Canon City; another was an elderly matron who must have smoked whenever she wasn't talking and smelled so bad the children never got into trouble.

The other two were as normal as public-school principals could be.

During this time, I was attending the church I had been a member of for my entire life. New Light Baptist Church is the oldest African American church west of the Mississippi. Constructed of native Colorado granite, which had been quarried along the banks of the Platte River then hauled by freed slaves in horse drawn wagons back to 28th and Ogden, the church stood as a monument in the heart of the Black community. It had been the first brick building in the area. Somber in its display of religion, I always felt warm and safe once I'd sat down in the long pews of the main vestibule.

I remember the long Sundays. These are the first Sundays in New Light, the Sundays of baptisms and calls to give one's life to Jesus. I would sit in the bosom of my family, secure between my mother and sister, close to my father and brothers. Mrs. McToody, a name that brings a smile to my face even now, would be in her accustomed seat at the pride of the church, the magnificent, gilded organ. Her hands flamboyantly cleared the keyboard by a foot, and, with the aid of the delicate tiptoe of her feet on its pedals, she'd coax the organ's ethereal voice into "What a Fellowship." She is and has always been a large, florid woman, her dark complexion highlighted by implausible rounds of pink liberally applied to her cheeks. She has a tendency to wear dresses printed with large flowers, or if not printed, colors bright enough to tweak the imagination of a blind man. She warbled along, disrupting the beauty of the organ, her ruby lips mouthing "...leaning, leaning, leaning on the everlasting arms!" I would meekly sing along with Mrs. McToody and the rest of the congregation and feel safe and warm in the joy of love.

Frank was a year older than me and had been a New Light member for his entire life also. We possessed the same last name and many people in church and outside thought our families were related. He sat near the front, beside his parents, down the long pew from my family. As we got older, I began to lean not only on the arms of the Lord but also around the sides of my parents to catch a glimpse of him. He never noticed me.

When these scenes of life were replayed later, after my police stint and after he had graduated the Iraqi conflict, I once again began to lean to look at him. He was tall, slim, and Shemar Moore handsome. One Sunday, he noticed me and smiled. He stopped me on the front steps.

"I know you probably don't remember an old man like me, but I gotta say you've gotten even prettier. I didn't think it was possible."

My brown skin began to blush the color of a currant, and I was totally at a loss for words. Finally, "I think college made me grow up." Could I be more inane?

"Look. I gotta go meet a buddy of mine right now but write your number. Let's go to a movie or something."

He was smiling and I was grinning so big my hairline began to hurt.

"Sure," I said, trying to appear nonchalant.

For our first date and every one after, I would drive into Denver and pick him up. He did not own a car. Every date was Dutch treat, since he had little money and a few times, I had to pick up the tab. He was always short on cash. Mom and Dad were less than enthusiastic about these arrangements but kept their comments to themselves. We only dated for two months, and I stupidly asked him to marry me. He said, "Well, I guess so. I don't have anything better to do."

Any person with a shred of intelligence would have said, 'Don't do me any favors.' Instead of intelligence, I was mired in ignorance. We set a date and were married on my favorite holiday – St. Patrick's Day. My something new was a green garter. After a three-day honeymoon in Glenwood Springs, we moved into our new apartment on which I'd paid the security deposit and first month's rent and started our life together. I began to enjoy the driving routine from school to school I was engaged in, even began to see a glimmer of musical promise in a third-grade boy who enjoyed the violin and practiced without harassment. After a month or so of sporadic day labor, Frank went to work for a general contractor as a supervisor of the framing unit. He worked diligently for about six months, floated for the next three, and then quit when his acquired war syndromes began to wave hello to his struggling psyche. He fought long and hard, but one afternoon, he gave up, and although I knew he had problems, he refused to discuss them with me. I begged him to go over to Fitzsimmons and talk to one of the psychiatrists, which brought scowls and shouts of anger. He came in one night and announced that he had quit his job with the contractor's company and had taken a part-time position with a one-man printing and copying firm, for the enormous sum of $5.25 per hour.

He said, "I need a break."

I was standing at the sink, washing dishes since the dishwasher was broken. I was four months pregnant, upchucking ritualistically every morning, and, at the end of an extremely hot summer, I'd found out that the school district had too many music teachers, so I was the newest victim of LIFO – last in, first out. I'd applied to every temple of higher learning in the state, but my belly gave a hint of things to come, so the districts were less than anxious to hire me. I took Frank's news like a blow to the head and slowly slid down the face of the cabinets until my rump gently bounced on the linoleum.

"I have to do what makes me happy," he grumbled, then without offering a hand to help me up, turned and bounded upstairs. I was assaulted by the realities of our situation: I had no job; we had a baby on the way, and my husband had just taken a job that paid less than unemployment. I sat on the floor for a long time.

Frank turned in on himself. He forgot the meaning of

hygiene, never really bathing but instead, washing himself at the bathroom sink with a bar of soap and a warm washcloth. He stopped cutting his nails and hair and both began to grow to attenuated lengths. He would get his meager check and buy cans of imported chocolate and specialty coffees, never giving me a dime for rent, lights or food. I finally started substituting in three districts, not making much, and trying to get by. Finally, a week before Christmas, I answered a knock at the door. It was the landlady, her face written with the news she hated to give me.

"Nia, I'm really sorry," she began, "but I need for you guys to move. I haven't had any money from you for three months. I'm sorry, hon."

"I understand, Maybelle," I said. "You have to eat, too."

Frank and I packed our things, and in the middle of stuffing his duffel bag, he said, "I'm moving back to my parent's house. You can move back to yours. I'll find us an apartment and come get you in two weeks." I didn't protest but waited while my brothers stonily placed my items on their trucks and we drove away. I moved back in with Mom and Dad and those particular two weeks have never come. We never lived together again, and when Alex was born, my sister, T'ene, was my Lamaze coach. Frank finally came to the hospital to see us when Alex was two days old, perfunctorily held his son, stayed ten minutes, and then moved out the door.

"I gotta see a man. I'll see you two later. You did good, Nia."

Frank quit the print shop, and after a year, I lost track of him. Alex and I lived with Mom and Dad, and I saved every dime I could. I started as a junior level investigator at Shield and worked my way up to second in command. I had lost my desire to teach music, but crime is a cottage industry – always a job there. I also earned a fairly nice salary. I divorced Frank in absentia, although certified letters were sent to his parent's house. He didn't answer them and did not show up in court.

Child support was a mere formality, something I knew I would never get, but with the help of Mom and Dad, I was able to buy my small, suburban, two-car attached garage, with patio and basement, house.

My house is the first one Dad built, and he had kept up with the owners. There had only been one, and when the old lady died and the old man moved into a nursing home, Dad bought it back for sentimental reasons. He holds the note for me. We moved in on Alex's third birthday. The house truly is understated: three bedrooms, two baths, a den in which Dad built floor-to-ceiling bookcases on three walls to hold my antique mystery volumes, and a full basement. It's not the biggest house or the fanciest in our neighborhood, but I don't care. It is mine. I was now a woman with upward mobility – a SMOC: single mother, one child – and I was beginning to enjoy my life again.

After buying the house it took another year, but Frank popped up once again with a slimy attorney at his side. The story was that since I was doing quite well and since he was not and had not been working, I could afford to give him a stipend. His attorney was an old high school chum who took the case pro bono, and I'll never understand how the court system allowed him to float such a request through, since I'd never seen a dime of child support. Calls from him came regularly each month for his allowance, and because of those calls, I began to taste bile on a monthly basis. I got used to it though, and over the course of time, Frank became nothing more than a distasteful memory, an occasional apparition.

But unfortunately, spirits can come back to haunt, and here one came again, one of the prodigious nightmare variety.

CHAPTER 7

I sat down on the braided rug by my desk, hunched up my knees, pulled my nightshirt over them and wrapped my arms around them. I sat for a long time, leaning against the ottoman. My head swam with questions, mainly how Frank had gotten into Cherry Creek. I got up and called my mother.

"Hey, Mom." I said when I heard her velvet voice.

"What's wrong, honey?" she asked.

"I just got a call from Uncle Harold. He said Frank is dead," I mumbled.

"Honey, what are you talking about?" she asked, a hint of fear creeping into her voice.

"Frank's dead, Mom."

She was quiet then. "Can you drive up or do you want Dad to come get you?"

"I'll drive up. Give me an hour or so. I'll tell you what I know when I get up there. Bye."

I hung up. Alex was out cold, still drooling when I went back to my bedroom. I sat down, wiped his mouth with a tissue, lifted his head, and placed it in my lap. He sighed and wrapped his arms around my midsection.

"Wake up, monkey butt. Wanna go see Nana and Papa?"

"M'kay," he mumbled but didn't open his eyes. He twisted and scrunched his head further into my lap.

"Get up now and I'll make French toast." French toast was just about his most favorite meal, and I felt he deserved it.

"Cool, Mom," he mumbled and thrust his feet out in search of the floor. Stumbling to the bathroom, he said, "Thanks, Mom."

I went back to the kitchen, rooted around in the cabinet, found the griddle and put it on a burner. Setting the temperature, I turned when the phone began to ring.

"Hello."

"Hey, girlfriend." It was Laurinda. Her voice always sounded as though she was laughing, tripping and skittering like a mountain stream. I felt better for the first time that morning.

"Whuzzup!" I chirped, trying to match the cheer in her voice.

"How was the date?" she asked.

"Well, this is a guy that I would really like to hang on to. He's kind, great looking, likes Alex, smells good, and I really like just talking to him. Also, he's a BMW."

"He has a BMW?" she asked.

"Naw, he *is* a BMW – Black Man Working. That's enough for me to get goose bumps!"

Her laugh trickled through the phone.

"Girl, I know what you talkin' 'bout. He is truly an endangered species!" She paused with a giggle and said, "Let me stop. Brothers be tryin' every day, and more of 'em are makin' it now than ever before. Give me a brother every time!"

"I heard that!" I answered. I paused. "But, I got some other news this morning, and it really isn't good."

"What's wrong?"

"I think Frank is dead," I mumbled.

"And that's bad news? Humph, that Negro was one of the brothers workin' the other side of the fence...workin' to keep from workin'. Sorry, hon, if he really is dead."

"Yeah, I think he is a goner. I'm taking Alex up to Mom and Dad's then coming back down to the station to talk with Uncle Harold."

"If you want me to, I'll take Alex up to Evergreen. No prob."

"Thanks for the offer, but I'll take him. I need to decide if I'm telling him now or if I should wait. He really didn't know Frank."

"No loss to the little fella. All I got to say is: move on, girlfriend."

I hung up from her and decided to call David.

"Good morning," I said when I heard his voice. "Hope I didn't wake you."

"Nope. Got up early, went to the gym and worked out. Nice of you to call." I could hear the smile in his voice.

"Well," I began, "I may not be able to see you today."

"What's up?"

"I think my ex is dead." I was blunt. I felt like the town crier.

"Dead? Whoa, wait a minute! Step back and tell me what's up!"

I leaned my back against the counter and told him about the phone call from Uncle Harold. He listened without interrupting me. When I finished, he spoke up.

"What can I do to help?"

"Thanks, but I'm ok. I'm taking Alex up to Evergreen to stay with my Mom and Dad. Then I'll probably run down to the precinct and see Uncle Harold."

"Want me to come with you? Or better yet, I can take both of you to Evergreen," he volunteered.

"No, that's ok. Alex is about ready to go so I just thought

I'd give you a call before I left. I'll call when I get back."

"Well, call me if you need anything – anything at all. And hey! I forgot to give it to you. My home is..."

"Wait!" I said. "Let me get a pencil." I reached over and grabbed the one I always kept on a rubber band for grocery lists. Ripping off a piece of paper I was ready to write. "Go."

"303-700-9544. Got it?" he said.

"Got it. I'll call tomorrow."

"Call if you need anything. Anything, anytime, alright?"

"Thanks, David."

I hung up. Alex and I ate our breakfast, packed him a small bag, then piled into the car and drove to Evergreen. He was cheerful as usual, but I found myself speaking in quiet tones to Alex, I think because I felt bad about the loss of his father, even though he had never really been aware that he had a father. I knew the day would come that he would ask me about his dad – what type of person he had been, what had been his likes and dislikes, why had he left us – and I was scared about what my answers would be. The reality of Frank's death was not yet tangible, and my feelings of disgust for him were still open wounds.

So, my son and I cruised up I-25, caught 36, and headed to Nana and Papa's; me commenting on the varied splashings of green sliding along the hillsides in the form of pine, aspen, and elm and asking him why he had jumped into my bed the night before.

"I was cold, Mommy." He fidgeted and avoided my eyes.

"Cold, huh. It's almost summer, hon, and I know I put enough blankets on you."

"I just wanted to hug you." He looked up at me and smiled, turning back to look out the window before he saw the tears in my eyes. We chatted on, me now talking about our new car, instead of telling him that the man he did not know, who had donated sperm to my womb, was now a cold, lifeless object, lying on a slab in the morgue.

When we arrived at my parents', they were as gentle to Alex as I'd been, the ridges between their eyes more pronounced than usual. He tipped his head.

"Are you guys okay?" he asked, looking at the three of us quizzically.

I punched his shoulder to show him all was well. "Fine, honey."

Mom interrupted. "I called your uncle Bruk and he's bringing the boys up."

"Yea!" Alex shouted, pumping his fist in the air. The Boys are his cousins – Brian, Evan and David. Evan is the same age as Alex, and the other two are one and two years older. Evan lives on inline skates and jumps every wall, rail and curb in his neighborhood. Handsome and very quiet, he glows when he skates and his skills are truly awesome. Brian is our hopeful for the Olympics as a swimmer. Brian has a breaststroke that might make Michael Phelps train harder. He swims too well for his age group and competes with kids four years his senior. David is headed for the bright lights. He has been in plays and musicals all over the state since he was three; a natural actor when the eye of the camera or that of any audience focuses on his bright, whimsical face.

"Now you hang with Nana and Papa today, and I'll be back later, ok?"

"Ok, Mommy. See ya!" And with that, he turned on his heels and ran to find Zoë, Dad's terrier and the only one of the three dogs he could play with. The other two dogs, German Shepherds, were too big for him. He turned and yelled, "Mom, I forgot to call David. He's going to miss me!"

"I'll call and tell him you had another engagement, okay?"

"Thanks, Mom!" he yelled and ran away with the dog.

The three of us sat at the kitchen table and I told my parents what I knew about Frank's death.

"They found him in Cherry Creek. Shot, I think."

Mom gasped. "Do they know how it happened?" she asked.

"I don't know much yet, but I'll ask Uncle Harold," I said. I didn't want to tell them that I was planning to do the identification.

"I'll call Harold." Dad was up and grabbing the phone.

"No, don't do that Dad," I said, putting a hand on his arm. "I can take care of it. I've had to deal with stuff like this on my job and I know what to do. I've put it in my mind that he is just another insurance claim that I need to handle. I can make it through that way."

He hung the phone back up and looked at me. Gruffly, he said, "You call us if you need any help though, ok?"

I shook my head in affirmation. I was back in the car, driving down to Denver within a half hour. I planned to see Uncle Harold, see Frank, and after that, I was in a holding pattern.

When I arrived at the University Station, I found Uncle Harold in his office in the back, the usual neat piles on either corner. His pack of Pall Malls sat to his left, the picture of Aunt Glynn seemingly smiling in approval from the gilt frame at the right of his arm. Uncle Harold was an anomaly – neat in all of his work and surroundings but a varmint in dress and manner. He had worn his hair in a small, lint-ridden afro since at least 1965, and his cocoa complexion had always seemed to be a bit blue tinged; the corners of his mouth always crusty with the previous meal. His shirt was pressed but the omnipresent stains on his tie told me that he'd visited Chubby's, his favorite Mexican restaurant a few times since he'd changed it. Dark splotches painted his bulging, pregnant-like stomach, and his cuffs were grimy from scooting around on his reports after writing with the number 2 pencils he insisted on using. He has always written his reports in pencil, and then typed them for accuracy. He hugged me and kissed the top of my head, the smell of cigarettes more of a comfort than an impediment. He sighed and told me to sit down.

"There's nothing you can do for Frank now, Nia. He's gone."

"They do need identification, though, right?" I asked.

"Well, like I told you – his father and mother can come down and do it."

"I'll go." I volunteered.

"He's not a pretty sight, sugar. He was in the water for a while from the looks of him. Sure you can handle it?"

I nodded.

"Ok." He sighed and rose from his chair.

We drove in silence to the morgue, traffic swirling around us like a tide pool. We didn't speak until we arrived in the front of the non-descript building, labeled Denver County Coroner.

He turned to look at me and tried again. "You don't have to do this, you know."

"I know, but better me than the Carters. Old Mr. is in no shape, and I'm sure Myrlie will pass out the minute she hears. You didn't call them yet, did you?" I asked.

"Naw. Thought I'd wait a while. Let's go."

"I'll do it," I mumbled.

Uncle Harold just looked at me. Then he said, "Suit yourself," got out and came around to my door. As my feet hit the pavement, I realized that my knees were knocking and my hands were shaking, but I plunged my fists into my pockets so he couldn't see how nervous I was. I'd seen dead bodies before, some in ragged shape depending on the way that they had died, but I'd never had to identify anyone I'd loved, and I had loved Frank at one time, so I knew this would be difficult.

"Feel yourself getting shaky, just stick out your hand and I'll hold on to you," Uncle Harold said as he closed the car door.

"Thanks," I mumbled.

I don't remember walking into the morgue, don't remember speaking to the people who worked there, but I can remember the canned, winter odor of the rooms we passed through and the cool, almost clammy feel of the exam room. Frank lay covered with a sheet on a gurney near the door, and the attendant pushed him more to the center under better lighting.

"We can do this on the TV if you want," he told me.

"No. That's ok. I'm here now," I whispered.

He gently lifted the sheet from Frank's face and I looked down on someone I had known for my entire life and at the same time, someone whose face was totally foreign to me.

Uncle Harold had been right. Many a fish had nibbled at Frank. His body was a bloated mass held together by a pair of stained jeans and the remains of a t-shirt. His nose was partially gone, and both ears looked like half chewed graham crackers. The overstuffed, cracking skin on his face, which was a rather dark greenish, chalky color, had little nicks and cuts where flesh had been. One eyelid was gone and the milky orb stared up as though amazed at the fluorescent lights above his head. His chewed lips were partially open and he looked as though he was about to speak.

But Frank was done with vocabulary now. All words from him were frozen.

"That's Frank," I whispered. "That's my husband." Without being able to take my eyes off of the wrecked face, I asked the morgue attendant, "How did he die?"

"There appears to be a bullet hole behind his right ear. Looks like a small caliber, maybe a .22. Entrance but no exit. We'll autopsy this afternoon and be able to tell you more then."

"Okay."

I just stood there, looking at Frank. After a while, taking my elbow, Uncle Harold led me back out to the brilliant sunshine and fresh air, and gently pushed me into the car. The ride back to the station was as silent as the ride out, with the exception of 'You ok?' from Uncle Harold. I think I nodded. I couldn't get Frank's ravaged face out of my eyes. I'd close them and see him, then open them and see his painted image on my mind's canvas. I shook my head and, as though I'd just awakened then, realized that we were sitting in front of University Station. Uncle Harold had swiveled in his seat and was staring at me.

"I'll have one of the guys take you home," he murmured.

"No, that's ok. I can make it."

"One of them will follow you back, and no argument."

When I was back in my car, I broke down. Sobs rumbled up from my chest and hit my teeth, spittle splattering the steering wheel until I plunged a tissue into my mouth. He was gone. He was not coming back, and I would never again look down the pew at his handsome, Shemar Moore face.

CHAPTER 8

Once I was home, I couldn't sit still. The house got a cleaning of the spring variety, from scrubbing the bathroom floors on my knees, to washing all of the windows. Took my mind off of Frank at least temporarily.

I'd always wondered how I'd feel when someone told me Frank was dead, and I'd always sworn I would grin real big and say, 'Good riddance.' But now that it had actually happened, the tears began to flow again, and I sobbed and hung my head in sorrow for the knowledge of a truly wasted life. When I'd pulled myself together, I looked John and Myrlie's address up on the computer. While dialing the number, I nearly lost my resolve and wanted to hang up, but I knew that I couldn't. I called and spoke to John Carter. It took him a few minutes to remember me. After exchanging pleasantries, I took the bull by the horns and crashed his world in. I told him about Frank. He took the news with a silent reserve, his voice softer than I'd ever heard it. He murmured that he would tell the rest of his family, then with a vague word of thanks, hung the phone up so softly, I thought we were still connected.

After contacting Mr. and Mrs. Carter, I felt obliged to go over to see them. After taking a quick shower and changing into a pair of khaki slacks and a beige dress tee shirt, I grabbed my keys and drove to the Carter's home on Ironton Street. The drive took about a half hour and every light seemed to present me with an opportunity to turn around and go home.

But I knew I couldn't do that.

I hadn't entered that house for over six years, yet I could see that time had been locked in a bottle once I walked through the front door. The old, blonde spinet still crouched to the left of the entrance, its top surface a landscape hidden by frames and doilies. To the right on the wall was Carl, Frank's nephew, the same photo in the same frame; seven-year-old face peering out as ageless as it had been six years hence. To his left was his brother Chase, red shirt slightly faded after all the years of hanging in full view of the sun. The white sofa was smothered in the same clear vinyl cover, now a bit yellowed and cracked with age. Its shiny surface reflected the oak coffee table and the 25-inch Zenith in the corner, on top of which was a picture of Frank when he was proclaimed all-city for football in his last year of high school. He was smiling his small, wan smile, dressed in a grey suit and tie, holding the plaque in one hand, the other shaking the hand of Denver's mayor. The picture bore not a hint of resemblance to the man I had seen early that day. In this house, nothing had changed, at least not anything that could be seen.

Myrlie was sitting with her head in her hands, but when I came in, she rose and came crying into my arms.

"This would never have happened to Frank if he'd stayed with you," she sobbed.

"Hold on, Myrlie. We'll get through this," I whispered. I held her frail, shrugging form gently. She wore a full, white slip and a pair of hose, her body sagging as though supremely fatigued. Only she and John, Frank's father, showed the effects of the years. They were the Dorian Grays to all the items in the room, absorbing the ages of all the grandchildren, cousins, aunts and uncles in the pictures. Both of their faces were mapped with lines and furrows, tried by the hardships of lives of manual labor. John had worked for the landscaping department of Denver Public Schools for over forty-five years, planting a lifetime's worth of flowers, shrubbery, trees and lawns beautifying the elementary, middle and high schools of the city. His job had been back-breaking work – lifting trees, bending over to unroll landscape tarps, digging and weeding. Myrlie had been a maid since before Frank was born, her job taking her into a number of elite residences.

They had inexplicably switched churches after Frank and I had divorced, some said, because Frank and I had divorced. I'd not seen them in as many years. Try as I might, I couldn't swallow the tiny bone of disgust lodged in my throat, caused by the fact that neither of them had reached out a hand of support or kinship to their grandson or me. Alex had never seen nor did he know either of them.

John came over and took my hands in his large, rough ones. His mahogany skin was dull and slightly gray; his eyes rimmed with red. "How are you, Nia?"

"As well as can be expected. I really am sorry, John."

"Ah, shoot," he snorted, "I knew and so did you, that if Frank didn't get help, somethin' bad was gonna happen. Well, I guess it's happened." He paused. "I called Bennett's and they're gonna take care of everything. He said he would make the calls and we could come on down and make the arrangements. Would you go to the bedroom with Myrlie and help her get dressed so we can go?"

"Sure, John. I'll help her."

I took Myrlie by the hand and led her to her bedroom. She sobbed lightly and seemed not to know me, looking into my face with wide eyes, without a hint of recognition. In her youth, judging by pictures, she had been extremely beautiful. Now, she was like a dishrag, her beauty wrung out by the trials of life and the last few years of dealing with her son. I guided her head into the dark, brown, dress John had laid out for her, zipped the back and eased her down so she could sit on the edge of the bed. When I slipped the dark shoes on her feet she murmured, "Nia, he shouldn't have been messin' with those people. I tol' him!"

"Who was he messing with, Myrlie?" I looked up into her brown eyes. I hadn't told her that Frank had been shot, but she seemed to know. She turned her face away and stared at the wall.

"Who, Myrlie?" I said insistently.

"It don't matter no more," she whispered. She got up from the bed and started out the door.

I followed her down the hall. "Myrlie, if you know anything, tell me so I can tell Uncle Harold. We might be able to find out who...who did this to him." I hesitated to say murder.

"It don't *matter* no more," she stubbornly repeated. John stood in the center of the room looking at his wife, shaking his head. Myrlie shut me out and went into her husband's arms. They walked out and I trailed behind, pulling the door shut behind me, testing the handle to make certain it was locked.

"I'll drive you over, Mr. Carter," I offered.

"Oh, thank you, Nia. I really don't even feel like driving."

John assisted her into my car, and I got in on the driver's side, started the engine and pulled away. We drove to Bennett's Funeral Home, one of two Black mortuaries in Denver. Everyone in the Black community knew Pop Bennett. He'd been putting away Denver's African American population for over fifty years, and each patron – rich or poor, upstanding or lowlife – was treated with the same degree of respect. Passing under the white plaster portico, I remembered all the times I had gone through those doors to attend services for

Black folks I hadn't really known. Many of those involved with cases I'd had through Shield, had been prepared in the basement of Bennett's. Pop often offered his services to the city for just the cost of an inexpensive coffin when a Black vagrant had died on the streets without benefit of family.

I sat through the cheap coffin and expensive urn choosing, (at my advice and after conferring with Pop, what was left of Frank was to be cremated) the music selection and the program wording. During the entire ordeal, the bulk of my job was holding and issuing tissues to Myrlie. It was decided to inter Frank the following Thursday, and two hours later, Pop and John shook hands and we led Myrlie back to the car. It was now full dark, and the drive back to their house was punctuated by a sniff now and again from both of them. Myrlie was dry, her day's quota of tears poured into countless tissues. Unfortunately, the stock would be replenished that night as she slept, and when dawn broke, she would be faced once again with the reality that her only son no longer would lean over to kiss her sunken cheeks or break her heart. John told me to go on and he would help his wife in.

At the door, he turned and said, "Thank you, Nia. We'll see you Thursday."

I drove back home, opened the garage and just sat in the car to get myself together. I couldn't put a finger on what I was feeling, but I knew it wasn't abject sorrow. After a day of being privy to crying over Frank, I now felt slightly calloused about the lack of emotion. Finally, I got out and went inside. I put my purse on the kitchen counter and called Mom and Dad. I asked about Alex, who was fine, and told them about the trip to the mortuary. Both offered their condolences and after asking them to keep Alex until Tuesday, we said our goodbyes and rang off.

I slept badly that night, not from grief but from the question of who had killed Frank, since obviously he had been murdered. My head felt as though it was filled with cotton when I woke up Sunday, and I had sit for a while on the side of the bed before I could stand, then stumble to the bathroom. After washing my face, I went to the kitchen, opened the refrigerator and poured a glass of orange juice. It helped clear my head. I had no intention of going to church. House of memories.

Picking up the phone, I dialed Adam's cell, since he worked most Sundays and would be out on patrol. Obviously, Uncle Harold had told him what had happened, and he was looking at the caller id because he answered, "You ok?"

It was good to hear his voice. He asked me how I was coping.

"I'm hangin'. Nothing else I can do."

"You know I feel bad for you, Sissy, but there's not a lot you can do. He's dead. End of story."

"I know," I sighed. "But he was the father of my son."

"He was the *sperm* donor of your son. He was never the father of your son. You talk to his parents?"

"Yeah, I went by there yesterday and took them to Bennett's for arrangements," I told him.

"Damn, girl! You didn't need to do that. Uncle Harold told me you were the one who identified him. Why didn't you call me?"

"I..." my voice trailed off.

"Never mind," he grunted. "I'll be there in about a half hour. Want a doughnut?"

"Umm-hmm," I mumbled.

"Make coffee." And he hung up.

After putting coffee into the filter, I poured the water and flipped the switch to turn on the coffee maker, got up and went to take a shower. I soaped top to bottom, washed my hair, rinsed and got out of the shower and into my heavy terry robe. Wrapping my hair in a big towel, I went to my room, lotioned, dug out underwear, a pair of grey athletic shorts and a t-shirt, and got dressed. Adam was sitting at the table, cup of coffee and a box of Krispy Kreme in front of him when I walked into the kitchen. He had a key to my house and always let himself in.

"Thanks for coming." I walked over and got a mug from the cabinet.

"No prob."

I put a spoon of sugar in my mug, poured in some half-and-half, poured in coffee then sat across from him.

"So, Uncle Harold filled you in?" I asked after a sip.

"Yep."

"Do they know anymore after the autopsy?"

"Yep." Adam could sometimes be stingy with words.

"Was he murdered?" I asked.

"Shot with a .22, which was still inside."

"Brother." I shook my head.

Adam sipped his coffee and took a bite from his doughnut before speaking again. "I don't know why you are even getting upset about this, Nia. That bastard never did a thing for you or Alex. Forget about him! He's dead and all I can say is good riddance!"

"I loved him once, Adam. Try to remember that," I whined.

Adam didn't bother to answer. He got up and said abruptly, "I gotta go. Call me if you need anything." He leaned over, pulled the towel from my hair and kissed me on top of my head. "Go comb your hair."

And he left.

Reaching for my purse, which I had left on the counter, I sifted through the jumble, found David's card and dialed his home number.

Caller id was working overtime, because he answered, "You ok?"

"Yeah, I'm alright."

"Is Al still with your parents?"

"Um-hm. They'll keep him as long as I need them to. You want to go somewhere today?"

"Absolutely. Where did you have in mind?" he asked.

"Someplace mindless. Maybe a movie." I answered.

"Well, I've been wanting to go see *Captain Marvel*."

"Naw. Bruk would kill me if I went without him." The word 'kill' made me pause.

David sensed it and continued, "Well, then we need to go see *Knives Out*."

"Oh, okay. That sounds good. What time?"

"I'll check the showings and come get you in an hour, how's that? We can go to lunch."

"That'll work. See you in an hour."

I hung up and went to my bedroom to dry my hair and get dressed. I decided to wear a bright colored outfit so I would look nice for David and maybe brighten my spirits. A touch of lipstick and I was ready. I went into the living room and sat staring at the wall, hoping David would show up soon so I wouldn't have to be alone with myself for too long. Luckily, the doorbell rang before I had time to churn up tears.

"Ready to go?" he asked after softly pecking my mouth with a kiss.

"Ready."

We went to lunch at Mama Mia's in Park Meadows and I ate very little. David knew that I was not at my best so he didn't push. The movie must have been great because everyone in the theater seemed to thoroughly enjoy it, but I had too much on my mind to find the joy. I kept going over the fact that Frank had been murdered. Who had killed him and why? Frank was scum to me, but who else had that opinion of him? I simply could not concentrate on a funny movie with so many serious questions roiling about in my head.

David dropped me off and I did not invite him in, which was a bit of a disappointment to him, I knew, but I just didn't even feel like talking.

"Going to work tomorrow?" he asked.

"Naw. I think I'll keep Alex out of school and hang out with

Mom and Dad in Evergreen."

"Ok." That's all he said.

"Oh, David!" I pulled his arm around me and let the tears come.

I looked up at him and changed my mind. "Could you come in for a while?"

"Sure," he said.

Once we were in the house, sitting on the sofa with a couple of cups of coffee, which David had made, I started to tell him about the identification.

"I have known Frank nearly all of my life and just seeing him like that was surreal." I sipped my coffee.

"Why did you have to do it?" he asked.

"Oh, I just felt like his parents wouldn't be able to handle it. I think I was right because I told Mr., and he said he couldn't have taken it."

"Still. If you had told me you were going, I would have gone with you. Do you want me to go to the funeral with you?"

"No," I told him. "I think I'll go alone. They're cremating him, so I won't have to see him again. It's just..."

"What? I think what it is, is that you don't love him anymore, but you're feeling like you let him down, aren't you?"

I looked up and into his dark eyes. I hadn't realized it until then, but David was right. I felt as though I had let Frank down. I knew all along that he had problems, but I didn't try hard enough to help him, and now I didn't have a chance.

"You know, I think you're right."

I put my cup on the table and stood. "I may not have been able to help him, but I will help Uncle Harold find out who did this to him."

David stood too and took me by my shoulders. He looked at me and said, "Don't do anything you will regret. I don't mean to sound cruel, but he is dead, and you have your son to think about."

"Oh no, don't worry about that. My older brother is a cop, and I was a cop, you know..."

He nodded.

"And I still have contacts in the department, so I just want to keep up with the investigation. That's all."

"Well, just so that is all you do."

He hugged me close. He had on light cologne that smelled so clean and fresh, and his chest felt so solid. I could feel the muscles in his arms, and I was like a small child, leaning on my dad for support. This was a man I wanted to be with for a long, long time and I didn't want to jeopardize this relationship for one that was absolutely over.

"I will," I whispered into his shirt.

"Ok," he said, pulling away and looking down on me again, "Do you want me to stay?"

"No, that's okay. I'm alright now, but thanks."

Nodding, he took my hand and we walked to the door. "It still goes. If you need me, call. Anytime, night or day, and I will be here. If you feel like talking, call. I will always listen."

He kissed my forehead and I clung to him for a minute, not wanting to let his strength out of the door, but then he let me go and walked out.

"Thanks!" I waved and he turned and smiled, opened the door of his car, got in and drove away. I watched him until his lights turned the corner, then I closed the door.

CHAPTER 9

When he opened his eyes, he could see sunlight filtering through a dark web. He was on his back, his left arm numb from the weight of the woman lying on it; her long, black hair the source of his dimmed vision. Sliding the arm she had draped over his chest away, he swept her hair from his eyes, pulled his arm free then swung his legs to the floor. He tried to stand but had to sit back down and wait until his head stopped spinning and the queasiness had washed over him. One too many gins.

He looked back at the woman. She was totally naked. Her eyes were closed, the lids rimmed in smudge rubbed from the thick layer of mascara she had worn, the lashes resembling fuzzy spider legs. Her legs were splayed to either side of the bed, the dark crest of her pubic hair staining the vortex of her thighs. Her olive skin had paled ivory, the opposite end of the spectrum from her hair, a study in black and white. Had it not been for the blood pooled in her concave stomach, the flecks of it decorating her like glitter, she would have been totally monochromatic.

A butcher knife stood at attention in the center of her sternum.

He looked at her without a shred of emotion. She was an empty vessel, a husk, no more interesting than the shell after the peas have been removed for the pot. They had left a bar in the city of Đồng Xoài, where he had picked her up and come to her small bungalow on the edge of town. The short walk had done nothing to sober them up, a situation further exacerbated by the pint bottle of gin she had pulled from her voluminous handbag midway through their walk. When they reached the door, she extracted her keys, turned her back on him, pressed her buttocks firmly into his crotch and began a slow, circular grind, which – although he was thoroughly besotted – made his extremities stand up and take notice. She unlocked the door and he held her shoulders to keep her in position. Giggling, she pulled away and dragging him past the minuscule front room, they fell on the covers of her double bed.

The room was little more than a closet, the bed commanding most of the space; the floor carpeted with dirty underwear, skirts and pants. The fetid odor of unwashed body sullenly hung in the air. He paid no heed to the squalor. Sucking at her mouth and neck, pausing only while she pulled his shirt over his head, his hands groped for flesh. She had undone his pants and was seeking inside his shorts. Shaking his butt to relieve himself of his pants, he shucked her blouse then proceeded to unclasp her bra. When both were nearly naked, he still wore his socks, they began to copulate violently.

After he was temporarily sated, he got up and padded across the room in search of his pants, which he'd kicked across the room in his haste, for a cigarette. Suddenly, she began to giggle. The sound escalated to a laugh, then a guffaw.

'What'er you laughin' at?" he growled.

"It dương vật!" she squawked.

He looked down. His member had drooped and sagged,

resembling an empty sausage casing.

"What did you say?" he yelled.

"Your little peenie!" She was giggling behind her hand.

'Shut-up!" he yelled.

"Những vớ!" she trilled, then translated, "Your socks!"

"Shut-up, you bitch!!"

Her giggle danced around the room.

Angrily glancing into the tiny kitchen, he saw a large butcher knife glinting among the dirty dishes. He grabbed it and rushed back to the room. Thrusting the blade deep into her stomach, he pulled it upward, toward her sternum, and then pushed down. Blood sprayed him, her, walls and ceiling. Her eyes flew open, she fell back on the bed, and her mouth formed a surprised "O", but she didn't utter a sound. He pushed so intensely, the blade went through, severed her spine then stuck in the mattress. She slowly closed her mouth, but her eyes were open, startled that she was dead. Then, they slid shut like the curtain going down at the end of a play. Her hands had closed on the knife hilt.

He staggered to the opposite side of the bed where he had been before and lay down beside her. The motion of his body caused her to release the blade, her hand coming up and flopping over his chest. Moving into her warm body, he pushed his shoulder under her and fell into a drunken sleep.

Now, he was gathering his clothes to depart for camp. He walked into the bathroom and rinsed the blood from his face, arms and upper body, using a pair of panties hanging on a suspended clothesline to dry himself. Walking back into the room, he collected his clothes as he stepped over hers. Gingerly sliding into his shorts, he shook a cigarette from the partially crushed pack nestled in his pants. Matches were found in a change dish on her dresser. He dressed slowly, bumping the ashes from his unfiltered Lucky Strike into the change dish, and staring at her on the bed. Smoke lazily curled around his head, glowing saffron in the rays of the morning sun. It was 7:45 a.m., and he knew if he hurried he would be able to slip back into camp before First Lieutenant Carlson knew he was gone. Buttoning his shirt, he took a final look around and smirked. He'd be in the jungle with his friends by the time she was found.

If she was found.

Ron would be there to greet him. What a pal! What a buddy! They looked alike enough to be brothers. They looked like Gary Cooper, tall and rangy. Their thick hair was the same dark brown, with slight waving, and their eyes were the same deep blue, the color of tanzanite. Both were boyishly handsome and had a look of innocence which, when they smiled, was attractive to many women. Their similarities were only in appearance. Ron was a deeply religious man, truly kind and innocent, and his friend was deeply evil and had lost his innocence many years before. Why they were friends was a mystery, marginally explained by the old cliché – opposites attract.

Few citizens were out on the street that Sunday morning. The air was soggy; a hint of fuel wafting on the breeze, at times almost overpowering. Hopping into his jeep, he navigated the wet fields, hoping he could remember the way back to the camp, deep in the jungle. Sounds of battle assaulted him as he drove deeper into the jungle, but he continued. The fear of battle was outweighed by the fear of Lt. Carlson, so he kept moving, Birds chirped and jumped at the sound of the engine, fluttering skyward in surprise and fear. He focused on a solitary red and brown bird in his path, quickly realizing that it was not a bird, but a human hand. Looking up, he saw smoke and then heard the cries of death. He killed the engine and listened to the gunfire overriding the screams. Falling to the ground, he crawled through the grass to look through the trees at the fighting. He could see that the Vietcong outnumbered his troop; slashing, shooting and killing the Americans with what appeared to be happiness. As he watched from the safety of the jungle, his comrades were attacked one after another. He waited until the enemy had put the entire troop down, started fires in many of the tents and vehicles, then marched out of the encampment.

His entire company was either dead or dying.

Creeping from cover, he crept through looking at the men, some bloodied and broken beyond recognition, their heads smashed by the boots of the Vietcong. Others had died from bullet wounds or bayonet thrusts. He had made it nearly to his tent, when a grenade thrown by the retreating enemy exploded to his left. The concussion knocked him off of his feet, and when he dazedly looked down, he saw a two-inch rip in his left arm. Blood streamed from the wound, and he knew he needed to staunch the flow. Clutching his arm and pinning it to his side, he stumbled to the medic's tent, pushed in and made his way to a first aid box that was laying open on the floor. He got the gauze, and using his teeth to pull, wrapped it around his arm at the top, tightened it, and formed a tourniquet. When the blood slowed, he wiped to see how bad the wound really was. It was a deep trench near his elbow and shallow near his shoulder, as though the shrapnel had hit his lower arm then traveled up and out. He also had one small wound on his left cheek, but luckily, that was all. He was amazed that he had not sustained any more damage. He cleaned his arm, then clumsily wrapped gauze from his elbow to the tourniquet at his shoulder, pulling it tight to close the wound. Satisfied that he would live, he left the tent.

"Help me," a man whimpered, and he squinted through the smoke and saw that the man's entire left side from the waist down was a bloody puddle of gore and gristle. It was Lt. Carlson. He jerked away and began to search for Ron. Ron was finally found, lying on his back in a small patch of grass. His face was a puttied mass of gore, nearly unrecognizable. One lock of his hair curled over the remainder of his left eye as though offering protection.

"Ron!" He whispered. He cradled his friend's bloodied head, and surprisingly, he felt near tears.

Then a thought hit him. No one else was alive. Ron was dead. The woman was dead. He smiled.

Looking at Ron, he removed his friend's dog tags. Swiping his own tags from his neck, he placed them around Ron's. Gently laying his friend back down on the blood-soaked grass; he jumped to his feet and ran to their tent. Smoke forced him to reach into his pocket to find his penlight. He flicked it on and looked down through the dim light with the aid of the thin, pointing beam, and stumbled to the sleeping quarters. His luck was holding since everyone in the tent was dead, so picking his way through the bodies on the floor, he reached his bunk that was next to Ron's. He reached into his shaving kit and grabbed the money he'd won in a poker game two nights before, reached under Ron's pillow and pulled out the worn and well-read bible his friend had cherished. Opening it to II Kings 4, he looked at the money Ron's only relative, blind, old Aunt Judith, had sent him, ostensibly to buy her a trinket. It was $100.00, a good sum, but he knew that Aunt Judith's eighty-year-old fingers held the purse strings to a fortune in Adobe Wells, Colorado. Ron meant the world to her. If he could survive the war and get to Colorado, he would have a new and very good life. Smiling to himself, he scurried out the door, bible clutched in his hands.

Saluting Ron as he passed, he strolled back to his vehicle and continued into his new life.

CHAPTER 10

Amid the chaos created by one of the worst military conflicts America had sustained, the new Ronald Goddard was just one more survivor to add to the roll call of the lucky. When he emerged from the tent, the strong fumes of burning gas, oil and human flesh stung his eyes. In the distance, the tympani of the bombs hitting and the symphony of the shells being spit out of the anti-aircraft guns accompanied by the screams and cries from the dying assaulted his ears. Đồng Xoài was under attack. He moved around and over the unfortunates unable to save themselves, extricating his leg a second time when another man grabbed and tried to hang on.

Covering his mouth and wiping his eyes, he stumbled back to the clearing where he had left his jeep. He drove back to Đồng Xoài, and decided during the trip that he had no intention of ever returning to the service. Pushing into the bar, he nearly ran into the heavy set bartender who sat on a stool drinking a beer. He was the only occupant in the darkened room.

"Chào bạn." The bartender grunted. "Hell out there."

"Chào bạn, Phong. Got another one of those?" Goddard asked.

Hoisting his bulk from the stool, the bartender ambled around the counter, reached into the cooler, and came up with a sweating bottle, thrust his hand back and retrieved the opener, pulled the lid off and handed it to Goddard. He then sat down on the stool behind the counter.

"On the house."

"Cám ơn." Goddard swigged down a large gulp, closed his eyes and felt calm swirling through his system. After he had downed most of the bottle he turned back to his companion.

"I am glad to be alive." He said to Phong. "Nearly didn't make it."

"I don't remember your name. What unit you from?" Phong asked.

"Umm...name's Goddard. I was with the 51st. Probably gone now," Goddard lied. He looked around the room. "You have anywhere I can get cleaned up and maybe get some more clothes?"

"Sure. Back there is the men's room," he jerked his thumb over his shoulder, "and there's some pants and a work shirt that one of the janitors left hanging on a nail in the supplies closet, if you don't mind wearing them. Don't think you could fit into my stuff." He smiled like a benevolent Buddha. Outside of the building, the fighting was continuing.

"Much obliged." Taking the final draw of his beer, Goddard walked in the direction indicated. When he reached the closet, he pulled the clothes out, examined them and determined they were better than his current attire. Once he was in the small badly lit bathroom, he stripped, removed his bandage and examined the wound. It didn't appear to be as bad as he had thought. He threw cold water on his arm until the blood had been cleaned off, then washed his body with the bar of soap on the rim of the sink. He dried with the rough towels piled in the corner. After re-bandaging his arm with gauze he found in the medicine chest on the wall, he used the soap to wash his underwear and socks, then wrung them as dry as he could in one of the towels. He wrapped another towel around his middle and walked back out to the bar.

"Gotta cigarette?" he asked his host.

A crumpled pack of Camels lay on the counter. Phong tapped one out and handed it to his guest along with a couple of stick matches. Goddard nodded thanks and went back to the bathroom. Sitting on the closed lid of the toilet, he contemplated his good fortune. If he could bottle luck, he would rule the world.

"I mean," he thought as he puffed the cigarette, "what are the chances? What are the chances that I kill a whore and get away with it, get a new identity, and make it out scot free?"

Puffing, he grinned and let his thoughts drift to the fact that he was now a new man, ready to go to some podunk, Colorado town and become richer than he ever dreamed possible.

Salinas, California was a great place to grow up if you were John Steinbeck, or rich and white. Poor and white only got the dried scraps of tortillas and the leftover fish heads; never sat at the table in the big dining room, only served the owners; and rarely were they able to earn enough to buy the sugar beet farm, just pull the produce out of the musty, brown, dirt in the hot California sun, alongside people who had immigrated long after the Mayflower had deposited its passengers on the continent.

Goddard had been born in a house with a dirt floor and only two rooms which housed his sickly mother, lazy father, and three siblings, with a stinking outhouse fifty yards from the back door. His mother had lost her health and hope it seemed at the same time, when his unborn sister had died halfway out of her belly. She had sent his father to get the doctor that they could never pay, and somehow, along the path to the doc's, he stopped to pass the time with the farmer down the road and totally forgot that his wife was bleeding on the straw mattress and near death. By the time Goddard ran to get the physician, she was unconscious, the child half out of her womb, choked by the cord of life.

The doctor had removed the child, cleaned the small body, and wrapped it in a rag for burial and gone home, leaving Goddard with instructions for his mother's care. The younger children had taken the mattress out to the back of the house and burned it. Goddard and the doctor had, with the help of his sister Sue, cleaned their mother, changed her clothes and put her in the bed on the other side of the room. She was conscious but dazed, and kept asking the doctor when he was going to deliver the baby, unable to accept the fact that the child was dead. Goddard took the small, limp bundle, placed it in an old gunny sack, and dug a deep hole in the back yard beneath the old maple tree, its leaves turning gold with the promise of fall. He gently placed the bundle in the hole, said a small prayer and turned the earth back in.

He was twelve years old and it was the last time he cried or prayed. He buried his conscience with his dead sister and vowed to never again give God the time of day.

Hope had shriveled in his soul when his sister died. Back in the house, he fixed a bowl of thin oatmeal for his mother and fed it to her spoon by spoon between her questions. He fed her, wiped her mouth and sat by the bed until she fell asleep. Then, he put more wood on the fire, pumped a pail of water which he poured into the cook pot, added the last of the oatmeal and fed his siblings. His father came in at about 8:00 p.m., just as they were licking the remnants from the wooden bowls.

"Y'all save me any?" his father asked in the southern drawl he had never been able to get rid of. He seemed to have forgotten what he had gone out for early that afternoon.

Goddard looked at his father and shook his head. He was tired and knew that he had to get up before five to go to work at the sugar beet farm down the road. He wanted to get there early so he would have time to beg food off of the cook (she pitied him and his brothers and sisters), and take it back so the kids would eat that day. She would give him enough for himself, his mother, Ralphie, Sarah and Sue, and tell him to make sure to hide the rest so his father wouldn't get it. His father would do alright on his own, since he always caught a ride to the next town, and charmed the señoritas with his good looks and southern manner. He always managed to find enough to eat, but never did he bring anything home to his family. He only came back to sleep occasionally and to force himself on his wife.

Early the next morning, Goddard got into his worn overalls, slicked his hair down, and went outside to get a pail of water. He brought it in, placed it on the table and turned in a slow circle, looking at each of his family members. Sue was eleven, small like their mother, but unlike their mother, feisty and able to fight life. Sue would be okay, and she would make sure Ralphie and little Sarah would eat. He went over to his parent's bed and only spent a glance on his worthless father. Goddard knew that he would never change. Then, he stared at the pale face of his mother; lines of worry carving years into her mouth and brow. She was only twenty-eight years old and looked fifty. He gently touched her hair, and made that the gesture of his goodbye.

He left Salinas that day, putting his family, the poverty, and all memories behind him. He never returned.

When his underwear was nearly dry, he stepped into them and put his damp socks on. Putting on the borrowed outfit, which was a few sizes too large, he wrapped his dirty uniform in a towel, put it under his arm and left the bathroom. When he got back into the bar, Phong was propped on the stool by the front door, staring out the window. He turned when he heard Goddard enter the room then went back to gazing at the commotion outside. Sirens were screaming like pigs at the slaughter, but the walls of the building muted the sounds of yelling, horn honking and thundering feet on the boardwalk.

"Looks like the clock has finally wound down. End of the world, I tell ya." He made his observation to the window and those outside who could not hear him, but if they had, they might have agreed.

"Naw. It's just war, but if God has his way this'll do it." Goddard surmised.

"Well, if that's the case," the bartender said as he rolled off of the stool, "may as well toast with the good stuff." He lumbered behind the bar and took down a dusty bottle of Chivas. Palming two shot glasses, he filled both to the brim, handing one to his companion.

"May you knock the bottom out of hell and bounce back up 'fore the devil knows you been there," Goddard said as they clinked glasses.

"Yup," said Phong.

They sat and watched the melee outside until Goddard finally said, "Well, I need to get moving. Need to get to Saigon."

"Hum...I'm not getting any business, so I was gonna close up. I'm heading home and planned to go that way in the morning if you want a ride. Lots of transport up the coast"

"Well, yeah. Thanks."

He helped Phong put chairs on the tables, then when his host wasn't looking, stole a beer and slid it into the pocket of his borrowed pants. Phong came back into the room swinging a set of keys. After turning out the barroom lights, he locked the front door and nodded for Goddard to follow him out the back. He turned out the lights in the back room then locked the door behind him. A dilapidated old Ford pickup sat hunched on the sandy back lot, looking like a beat up dog. It was twenty years or more old, was missing both fenders and had terminal cancer on the passenger side. When the two climbed into the front seat which had stuffing hanging out of it like the guts of the dying soldiers Goddard had seen back at his camp, Phong inserted the key, and surprisingly the engine turned over without complaint. Taking a back road, they slid out of town and away from the battle.

During the ride, Goddard tearfully told Phong that he was leaving the Marines since his best friend had died in his arms. He just wanted to get as far away as he could from all that the service stood for. What he didn't tell Phong was that he was only looking for a place to hide out until the war was over and he could make his way to Colorado to claim his "inheritance."

Phong was a man with a soft heart. His only brother had died in a freak accident – one that the Navy could have prevented – so he held service to the U.S. in low regard. He wanted, unfortunately, to help this man who had witnessed the horror of war.

"I have a cousin who works the rice fields near Saigon. We drive over there tomorrow. He can get you a job."

"Oh, man, thanks!" Goddard knew this would be an excellent idea. The U.S. was throwing everything they could at Vietnam now; every American male who could shoulder a rifle would be needed to fight. If he stayed in Saigon, it would be obvious that he was not serving the country and his disloyalty would stick out like a turd in a punchbowl.

When he was sixteen, he'd been on the run from the law after breaking into an elderly couple's home, beating the man nearly senseless and stealing every bit of money and anything else that he could carry. At seventeen, he lied to get into the Marines, his wide shoulders and six foot four frame giving him the appearance of being older. But now, after nearly a year, he felt that he had given the service as much time as needed and besides, no more breaking and entering. If he could last out the war, he had real money waiting for him in Colorado. He decided that he would stay the night with Phong and go over to the rice fields in the morning.

Luck.

If he could only bottle it!

CHAPTER 11

Working in the rice fields brought back memories of digging sugar beets in Salinas. Goddard didn't mind it though. He had settled in to his new life with relative ease. Phong's cousin, An Dung, had no trouble getting a job for him since so many of the young men had gone to fight and jobs were plentiful. They lived about ten miles outside of Saigon, and he was accepted. He lived in a hut with An Dung and his two dogs. Life was simple. The two men had a routine: working in the fields harvesting from 5:00 a.m. to about 2:00 p.m., going back to the hut, washing in the small creek that pulsed in front of the door, eating a dinner of fish and fruit then heading down the road to the juke joint to drink and amuse themselves.

There, they found the women.

Women with olive complexions were Goddard's weakness. He loved the dark smooth skin, the lilting talk and the sumptuous hips. Buy them a drink or two and they were his for the night. When his urges required more than regular sex, he paid them more than the drinks and they did whatever was asked. He was insatiable and his needs were far left of the scale of sanity.

Only once, on a hot night in September had he nearly slipped. He had drunk too much and the woman he had paid for the night was reluctant to perform the crude acts that he had in mind. He had grabbed her by the throat, held her down and raped her viciously. When he finally let her go, she was trembling and crying, screaming that she would tell her brothers.

"Say anything," he growled, "and I'll kill you!"

He had grown bigger and stronger and the woman knew very well that he truly would kill her. She ran from the hut, and Goddard was a bit nervous. Her brothers were as vicious as he was, and he wasn't certain he could fight all of them. He packed his meager belongings and hiked to the city. There, he caught up with a battalion of Army soldiers and told them about his near death outside of Đồng Xoài. He lied about hiding out in the jungle and finally getting to Saigon. Taken before the officer of the unit, he showed his tags and told his tale. The officer knew of the battle, and was quick to believe his story, treating him like a hero. They drove him to the nearest Marine battalion, where he nervously retold his lie, but again, he was believed. They arranged transport for him for the next day. A new uniform was provided, and he breathed a sigh of relief, knowing he was going home.

Twenty-four hours later he was on a cargo plane bound for Los Angeles, California. When he arrived, he stuck out his thumb. He had no trouble hitching rides to Colorado since he told the story of the massacre of his platoon to every driver who stopped to help him. He was careful not to expound on the story for fear that he might meet a soldier who was familiar with his unit.

Goddard arrived in Denver on September 23, 1966, and was in Adobe Wells the next day. At first glance, Adobe Wells was a major disappointment for a man who had dreamed of a large metropolis. It was not a metropolis and was a bit nondescript. The main street was the center of downtown, and consisted of a large bank and grocery store, doctor's office, dentist, dry goods, and hardware store. At the end of the block was a car dealership across from the bus station. The steel mill south of town, which employed fifty percent of the citizens, dominated the town. This fact lifted Goddard's spirits, knowing that the size of the plant and the powerful influence it had in the community translated into big bucks.

Bidding his ride goodbye, he walked to the bus station and stood with other returning servicemen. A young Hispanic, dressed in Army fatigues sidled up to him.

"Just getting home?" he asked, offering Goddard a cigarette.

"Yeah." Goddard accepted the smoke with a nod. The soldier flicked a Zippo with 'Hanoi' stamped on the side and Goddard took the light. He puffed deeply.

"I'm sure glad to be back. Name's Martinez. Tito Martinez." Tito stuck out his hand and he and Goddard shook.

"Ron Goddard," he murmured cautiously, trying to see if the name struck a chord.

Tito did not appear to know the name. During his trip west, Goddard had decided that if he ran into anyone who knew the real Goddard, he would tell them that he had been hit in the face with shrapnel during a skirmish but had been fortunate to have received excellent plastic surgery, which would account for the different look. He and Ron had looked enough alike to be brothers – same height and build, same hair color – and he knew much about the town of Adobe Wells, gleaned from Ron's incessant chattering. He was glad he had listened occasionally. If he got something wrong, he decided that he could tell those who asked that his memory was dimmed from the concussion he had suffered when he had been hit.

Goddard and Tito stood together, waiting for a cab, one of

which could be seen slowly moving down the street. The street was fairly empty, a few women dragging kids along behind them, shopping at the grocer's, and a handful of men laying bricks, building what appeared to be a new store. It was 3:30 in the afternoon, so most of the citizens were probably at work. Six other servicemen stood with them at the bus stop. Finally, the cab got to them. The driver poked his head out and asked where they were going.

"Fifth and Oswego," Tito stated, grabbing the door handle.

"I need to go to Judith Goddard's house, if you know where that is." Goddard told him as he followed Tito into the cab.

"Sure. Everyone knows where Miz Goddard lives. You a relative?" The driver was staring into the backseat at Goddard through the mirror.

"Yeah. I'm her nephew, Ronald."

The cabbie spun around in his seat and Goddard felt a clutching in his heart.

"Hey!" the cabbie shouted. "Word around town was that you were dead!"

"Naw," Goddard's voice was a bit shaky. He started reciting his lie, scared that maybe his story wouldn't ring true. "I was lost in the jungle near Saigon. Took a lot of shrapnel and got a blow to the head. I was in the hospital for quite a bit."

"Well, I'll be. Your aunt will sure be glad to see you! Umm...I mean, she sure will be glad you're safe and sound!"

"Well, I sure will be glad to see her. It's been a long time." He sat back in the seat and fingered his dog tags.

He perked up a little and his eyes began to glow as he rode down the unimpressive main street at the end of which stood the jewel – Proteus Steel. The only way to describe it was huge.

The cab driver pointed to it and said, "Miz Goddard still owns Proteus, but she doesn't go in like she used to. She's been pretty sick these last few years, but I think she'll get better, soon as you get there!" He chuckled and shook his head.

Tito was dropped off first on a residential street a few blocks from Main. The houses all looked pretty much the same, clapboard and picket fences, with small yards and well-kept lawns and flowers. It was a street that could be duplicated in many small, American towns, and bespoke of comfortable families. The driver accepted payment for the ride, and murmuring thanks, Tito got out and turned back to Goddard. "You know where I live, man. Let's go for a beer real soon, ok?"

"Sounds good to me."

The two men shook hands then left Tito standing in front of the small frame house.

"Miz Goddard lives on the other side of town. Big, 'ol ranch."

They drove past the steel mill, dwarfed by the sheer size, turned left on and traveled over a low hill. Goddard could see that, although Adobe Wells seemed small, it was not as tiny as he'd first assumed. Homes stretched in front of him, and he could see a few large buildings, probably schools.

"Not bad," he thought.

Capping another hill and sliding down the other side, they saw the Goddard ranch, lying in a verdant valley, an intricate wrought iron arch proclaiming the name. The drive to the main house was nearly a mile from the gate.

Whitewashed, pillared and two storied, the main house sat like a mother hen with her chicks surrounding her. Sitting on what had to be at least fifteen acres, it was an anomaly; an exceptional display of architecture that did not fit the country attitude of the town of Adobe Wells. Red mountains loomed behind the house, and as they drew closer, Goddard could see that the main entrance faced the Sangre de Cristos. The cabbie navigated the circular drive and stopped in front of the stairs leading up to the double doors of the entrance.

Goddard got out of the car and turned to pay the cabbie.

"On the house. You're the nephew and besides – you

fought hard for us over there. Thank you, and call whenever you need a ride."

Tipping his hat, he drove away. Goddard was a bit nervous, but he climbed the stairs and rang the bell, which echo deep within. A butler dressed in a black suit opened the door before Goddard's hand had returned to his pocket. When Goddard gave his name, the man's eyes widened then teared, an ear-to-ear grin splitting his face. He clutched Goddard's hand.

"So happy to see you, sir!" He vigorously pumped the young man's hand. "She will be overjoyed! Please wait here and I will go fetch the mistress." Smiling, he nearly ran toward the back of the house.

The room in which he stood had an extremely high ceiling, the focal point a circular stairway trailing up to the second story. At the top of the landing was a large, stained glass window depicting an old vision of Adobe Wells, similar to the Cliff Dwellings in Manitou, Colorado; the afternoon shadows casting the blue of the sky, green of the cactus and yellowed beige of the buildings in soft pools on the white marble floor. Sparsely furnished, it was an enormous room, the far corners unseen in the waning light. Through a door in the main living room to the left, the hearth took up an entire wall, the stones which comprised it smooth and grey. When Goddard peeked in, he saw white walls unadorned with the exception of a floor to ceiling bookcase directly across from the fireplace. Circling the hearth was a sizable duo of sofas, crouched on either side of a low, round wooden table, in the center of which stood a bronze statue of a horse with a Native American atop. On the entrance wall was a wide, tall window with many individual panes, the heavy brocade drape partially open. Looking up once more, Goddard gasped at the sight of a chandelier constructed entirely of antlers. At the tip of each of the larger points was a light. So profuse were the antlers that, had the chandelier been lit, it would have illuminated the entire room.

It was an elegant room that required none of the usual clutter found in most homes to provide beauty. Looking around, Goddard knew he had struck the veritable mother lode. A slight shuffling could be heard coming from the back of the house. Goddard stepped a few feet over and looked down the hall.

Judith Goddard must have been a tall woman in her youth, close to six feet. She was now slightly stooped and walked with a cane and the aid of the butler, but her bearing was that of a woman who was in charge of her surroundings. Steel gray hair was pulled back and gathered up in a short, thick ponytail with a black ribbon at the back of her neck, and she wore a dark green dress, which nearly touched the floor. She wore dark glasses to shield her sightless eyes, and the face behind the glasses was wrinkled and pale but strength was apparent in her high cheekbones and straight lips. She had a striking face.

"Ronnie?" The voice was small and almost a surprise, coming from such a commanding presence.

Goddard knew that if he was to become lord of the manor, cement his future and have all his dreams come true, it was all hinged on his greeting.

"Hello, Aunt Judith."

Tears crept from beneath the glasses, following the deep trails cut by her wrinkles. She reached up and grasped his face in her hands, pulled him close and gently kissed his cheek.

He was home.

CHAPTER 12

Adobe Wells proved to be all that Goddard had dreamed and more. Actually, the money proved to be all that and more. Aunt Judith never questioned his identity. She accepted her nephew back with open arms, had his old room opened and aired and reestablished the relationship that had been postponed when the war intervened. She opened a bank account for him then outfitted it with enough money for a new convertible and wardrobe. Gloved servants in the dining room served their meals, many of which consisted of steak carved from beef raised on her ranch. The table could accommodate nearly fifty. Afternoons, he was the gracious nephew who took her for walks around the ranch and told her the status of her cattle and gardens.

She only became suspicious once, when she noticed after a few weeks that he was not the chatterbox she had known prior to his enlistment. Goddard, ever the man with the right answer, told her that the war caused his reticence; that he had seen so many horrors he had been transformed into an introvert. The answer satisfied her.

He was golden; had everything his heart desired and then some.

He spent most weekdays in the company of her plant manager, learning about the life of steel and the vast holdings of his aunt. She was an extraordinarily wealthy woman. In addition to the steel mill and the 1,000+ acre ranch, Aunt Judith owned a hotel in Colorado Springs and one in Denver, both luxurious and profitable. It was Aunt Judith's wish that Goddard would take over her businesses in the event of her death, which pleased him.

Although his life was now better than he could ever have imagined, Goddard knew that in order to preserve it, he always needed to be on his guard. His main tenet was, no matter what, 'Don't shit where you eat.' The needs and desires that were an integral part of his personality were taken care of by driving to Denver most Thursday nights to spend the weekend in the seamy parts of town. Tito would always accompany him. They would settle in for drinking, gambling and women. He made it a point to find a new woman (sometimes more than one) each weekend. He had always had a penchant for gambling, and Tito acted as friend and bodyguard, helping find the card games as well as the necessary bedmates. Pulling Goddard out of fights, which were invariably his fault, also proved to be one of Tito's duties. For his loyalty, Goddard paid him well. Tito was given the task of driving the convertible home Saturday night to be ready for church Sunday morning, since Goddard was never in shape to get behind the wheel after his weekend.

Goddard would have found it more enjoyable to stay in Denver instead of attending church on Sunday morning. Services were held at 8:00 and 11:00 a.m., and Aunt Judith attended both, arriving back at her ranch for the big meal of the day – lunch – at precisely 12:20 p.m. Goddard endured the head burn of too many vodkas, gins or beers, making him rise from his seat sometimes as many as five times during each service to purge in the bathroom, and feeling, in general, that he would vastly prefer death. But his love of money was stronger than his fervent death wish, so every Sunday found him sitting beside his aunt in their reserved pew box, mouthing "Amazing Grace" along with the other voices in the sanctuary. She thought he was a saved Christian, and he made it a point to keep the charade alive. He told her about the bible that he had saved when he made his exodus, and the admission made her sob. He comforted her with a smile on his face that she could not see.

The church was recruiting young men to become deacons, and at Aunt Judith's urging, Goddard was one of the first to volunteer. Although he had little formal schooling, he had taught himself to read well and used the bible as one of his lesson books. The book provided the words but he had no desire to dwell on the meaning of them. He had read Hemingway and learned more from his writings, although the task was accomplished as ends to a means in the same way as becoming a deacon and reading the Good Book – it cemented his bond with Aunt Judith. Once he became a deacon, he was forced to give up a weekend a month for bible study and church duties, but he gritted his teeth and forged on.

Edith Martin was the only daughter of a wealthy businessman in the next county. Reasonably pretty, she had her pick of the sons of the other rich men in Colorado, and there were many, but she met Goddard at one of Aunt Judith's dinner parties and fell in love. In Aunt Judith's mind, an alliance between Edith and Ronald would be ideal, since they were both young and wealthy. She found ways to push them together, which Ronald realized from the very beginning, but since Edith was rich and not too hard on the eyes, the direction that his aunt moved him in was okay in his book. Two fortunes are always better than one.

Edith hungered for Ronald. He charmed her on every

occasion, asking the cook to prepare special meals when she came to dinner, and when he had his needs and couldn't get to Denver, the cook packed a picnic lunch and he would take her to a secluded spot in the Black Forest. There, the lunch would be laid out on a white tablecloth, and after the food was consumed, Goddard would indulge his desires with Edith. It was not hard to get her to spread her legs on their first date, alone there on the smooth blanket, which covered the fallen pine needles. She was very willing.

After six months of courtship, a date was set for their wedding. Aunt Judith was more alive than she had been for twenty years, and the preparations were all she indulged in, driving to Denver in the company of Edith and her mother for the decorations and fittings of the wedding gown. On Saturday, June 14, 1969, Ronald Goddard and Edith Martin said their 'I do's' in the garden at the ranch under a gazebo festooned with garlands of ivy entwined around pink and white roses. The happy couple cruised from New York to Bermuda, spending two weeks enjoying tropical surf and sun. When they returned, Ronald and his bride moved into the new wing that had been added for the two of them in the Goddard house.

Nearly two years passed and Ronald became restless. Acting the part of loyal nephew to his aunt and husband to his insipid wife was difficult but endurable, and all had become second nature. Goddard actually found it rather enjoyable, the honing of his Janus personality. What gave him fits, kept him awake at night and ruined many a poker hand, was that he didn't own it all. His money, his lifestyle, every diversion that gave him happiness was ultimately under the iron thumb of his aunt. Aunt Judith would not die. She suffered from a slight heart complaint, but her doctors assured her nephew that it was minor and her pills were sufficient to keep the ailment at bay. Frequently tired, she always rallied and attended church. The pastor would come on Sunday evenings only on the rare occasion when she was unable to rise from her bed and enter the Lord's house for the regular schedule. Her other outings consisted of consultations with her business manager and Goddard, held at the steel mill. Most of the time she was content to stay at home, accepting visits from her close friends. She refused to die and relinquish the reins.

Aunt Judith had updated her will within the first month of her nephew's return, stating that all of her worldly goods would be an 85/15 split. Goddard would receive the eighty-five percent and the remainder would be given to the workers at Proteus and her servants. Separate gifts and endowments had been reserved for the Colorado Historical Society and Colorado College to fund the women's dormitory, built in 1935 that bore her name. His wife would come into her inheritance when her father died and stood to receive twenty-five percent of a fortune valued in the millions.

The fifteen made Goddard furious, but it was the eighty-five that was on his mind every time he pushed his aunt in her wheelchair out to the stables, and when he rode with her to the plant in her black limousine. He wanted his eighty-five and on Christmas night, after the guests had bid goodbye, the servants had cleaned up the remnants of the party and turned off the lights downstairs, he led his aunt to the elevator, installed at his insistence when it became apparent that climbing the flight to her room was a trial. When the elevator arrived at the second floor, he opened the door and helped her walk the short distance to her room. At the door, he kissed her good night and wished her a Merry Christmas.

Once he was back in his rooms, Goddard waited. Judith had drunk too much Christmas cheer and was out cold in her separate rooms. She had started to drink, had become a closet drunk, when she realized that her husband only wanted her for sex and absolutely nothing more. Goddard waited until there were no sounds of wakefulness in the big house. He then waited another hour to be certain. Then, he left his chamber, tiptoed down the hall to his aunt's room and silently opened the door. Light from the window illuminated her sleeping face. On her bedside were her pills.

Reaching around her head, he smoothly picked up the extra pillow and slowly lowered it to her face. The struggle was fleeting and in no time, she lay still. Placing the pillow back in its original spot, he straightened the covers a bit then gazed into the dulling surfaces of her eyes. They were startled and he smiled when he realized that it was the first time that he had seen them.

"Thanks, auntie!"

Sliding the lids of her eyes closed, he saluted, turned and went back to his own room.

His "aunt's" death changed everything for Ronald Goddard. He could see that steel manufacturing was going to take a fall and began to diversify his portfolio. He put his money into aerospace and technology, banking on the growth of the country following the war and was handsomely rewarded for his efforts. Proteus became one of the lesser concerns in his portfolio, although he kept the offices as his base of operations. He also bought huge tracts of land in and around Denver and a large construction company, confident that the capital would grow in population and industry. Again, he was correct. He doubled his wealth in ten years. Goddard became one of the richest men in Colorado.

Edith had died from a fall in 1973, orchestrated by her husband and executed by his bodyguard. Her father had died in 1972, leaving her a fortune and making her husband very happy. Edith had endured the years of deceit, lies and neglect from her husband, but because of her status in society, all of her tears were shed alone, behind the doors of her bedroom, clutching a bottle of Courvoisier. She would not stand for a divorce. Her husband had used her for sex for less than a year after their marriage, returning to his drives to Denver and sometimes down to New Mexico. He was always careful that none of his numerous escapades hit the news.

Edith was triumphant on a single occasion: when she forced her husband to remove tangible proof of his escapades – an illegitimate child. Immediately after the birth, the indiscretion was whisked away, adopted into a suitable family. She would not have her standing in society sullied by his sordid affair. Rumors were whispered, but Goddard was a rich man, a leader in his community. They were only rumors, and his wealth deflected the bounce back of the filth in his life; armor in the form of a designer suit.

Goddard had never believed in the doctrines of Christianity, but he came to respect the power afforded a bible-carrying individual in the eyes of the great-unwashed masses. His community was exceedingly religious, and he found that by just attending church regularly, imparting donations to the needy and directing his minions to help them, he became known as a Christian and by association, a good and honorable man. In 1979 he met a young woman on one of his New Mexico outings and fell into more lust than he had previously, a lust that – in his mind – was conceived as love. She was a beautiful brunette with a stunning figure and blue green eyes the color of the turquoise stones that abounded on the ranch. She wanted to live in town, so he built a new home and appointed Tito and his wife as caretakers of the ranch. Tito had served him well for so many years and deserved the perk.

The riches Goddard had so wished for were put to use, and, since money could buy anything, he used it to oil the necessary wheels to get elected first as city councilman and over the years, he segued into the post of mayor. His biography was professionally written and the lies were never in dispute. He was Ronald Goddard, Judith Goddard's nephew and only living relative, for goodness sake, and there were none who would dare question his veracity.

CHAPTER 13

I arrived at New Light at 10:15 on Thursday. Alex and I had spent the last few days in Evergreen with Mom and Dad, and I had left him with them and driven down to the church. My brothers and T'ene had all volunteered to come with me, to give support, but for some reason, I wanted to go alone. I needed to blow away the specter of Frank by myself, no accompaniment. I got there early to see if John needed help with Myrlie. The day was crisp and beautiful, the sun smiling joyously as though it were providing warmth for a wedding. But its glow was not temperate, and the sight of the church brought me back to why I was there. I slid into the foyer and made a sharp left to go to the restroom. I made my way down a long, poorly lit hall. At the fork at the end of the hall, left was the bathroom and to the right, the door was open. On display was the next center of attraction after Frank's show – an elderly, African American woman, laid out in what appeared to be a New Light Baptist Church Mother's dress, a uniform worn by all of the octogenarian females of the church. It was a white suit, devoid of decoration save her blue bow pin, a sure sign of her stature.

Looking closer at her face, I realized it was old lady Grace Marshall, one who had been a member so long, she had been my mother and father's Sunday school teacher when they were in school. I'd always thought she had resembled someone from *Night of the Living Dead*, owing to the liberal dusting of pale powder she always insisted on wearing on her charcoal skin. Seeing her now, she looked more alive since Pop's crew had taken over the makeup kit. Since Frank's service had threatened to be small, Pop must have decided to kill two birds with one stone and put both of them away that afternoon. Saying good-bye to old lady Marshall with a salute, I turned and went to the bathroom.

When I returned to the foyer, I assessed the mourners. My former sister-in-law, Rachel, stood in the foyer with her husband, James, a rail-thin man whose face resembled Abraham Lincoln, had Lincoln been Black. With them were their two handsome sons, Chase and Carl, both teenagers, but not gawky as most young people their age, nor as crane-like as their father. They had an air of self-assurance, secure in their good looks and bearing. Neither Rachel nor James spoke to me, but both boys came over and gave me hugs.

"Well, you two have certainly grown since those pictures in your grandma's house. How're you doing?" I said.

"Hi Aunt Nia," Chase said.

"Okay, Aunt Nia. It's good to see you," Carl said.

"It's good to see the two of you. Sorry it's a sad time, though," I said. I turned to Rachel. She is a female version of Frank, looking as much like him as a twin; could have been mistaken for him had her hair been shorter. There is not a flicker of femininity about her. She was always considered to be a "handsome" woman.

"It's good to see you Rachel. How have you been?"

"Fine," she answered through tight lips. She was still a bitch.

"How are you, James?" I said, turning to her husband.

"Fine," he said with a clipped tone. He was still stupid.

Having gotten the cordialities out of the way, I smiled, slipped by them and walked toward the chapel. I looked back, and Rachel was scolding the two boys. Both lifted their hands and waved. I smiled. She and James deserved every headache they were bound to receive from every young woman who would chase that duo.

I rounded the corner and came face to face with Frank.

Pop must have talked to John, gotten a picture of Frank and enlarged it to nearly life size. It was his service picture, shot from above the waist, his brown jacket festooned with medals. He wore an expression of calm reserve, secure that he was a good soldier and proud to be an American. Frank had served his country well and the red, white and blue flag waving behind his head was a testament to his loyalty. I had a copy of the picture at home in a box under my bed, sharing space with other photos that I didn't want to discard but would never display. Alex had never seen it.

Leaving the picture behind, I walked into the chapel. It was filled with people from the church that Frank and I had known all of our lives, and also with a contingent of faces that I was not familiar with. John, a sobbing Myrlie, Reverend Panticott and Ms. Evers occupied the front pew of the chapel. The Rev and Ms. Evers had been an item since I was twelve, and since his wife had died the previous month, they now were free to be inseparable. She lightly held his elbow as he tried to comfort Myrlie. He turned, saw me and pleadingly beckoned.

"Help us out here, Nia, please?" he urgently whispered. "I need to get up there on the podium."

I took his place beside Myrlie. Ms. Evers was a corpulent matron whose first husband had been the pastor of Living Waters church, our Baptist rival around the corner from New Light. She always wore a belt regardless of the outfit; cinched tight around her middle, which brought attention to her obvious pride – her huge bubble butt. Bruk always joked that all she needed to do was reach over her shoulder to get something out of her back pocket, her butt was so high. Her face was the cool color of my father's leather jacket, dark and smooth. She smiled transparently then slid over a cheek's length as though I had cooties. It was more than enough room for me to sit. I held Myrlie's hand as the Rev began his sermon.

"Man...born of woman...has but a short time...to live..." He actually said that. He chanted the eulogy in sing song, using wide gestures to drive home his point. Choruses of "Amen" echoed throughout the sanctuary.

"We...do not know...the time...or the place." Each phrase was emphasized by his little hops, as though the words were too hot for him to stand. Reverend Panticott was the epitome of the African American preacher, and his sermons were delivered in the same manner as Frank's eulogy, full of fire, brimstone and warning. I found myself echoing the "Amen" that concluded his sentences.

Blah, blah, blah, ad nauseam. "Amen." Rev did basically the same sermon each funeral, varying little from man to woman, boy to girl. I knew he wouldn't say anything original about Frank so I zoned. I began to think about what Myrlie had said. Who were the folks Frank had taken up with? Since I hadn't seen him in a few years, I couldn't guess. I wondered if William might have a clue. William Franklin was one of Frank's buddies from the old days. He and a handful of others had most likely stayed in touch with Frank through all the bad times. I looked around the church and sure enough, there they all sat: William, Joe Deckers, Isaac "Gerber" Jackson, Steve Butcher and Dallas Fears. All were attentively looking up at Rev. Panticott, nodding each time he shouted. Their lips chanted "Amen!!"

All but Isaac Jackson. He was looking at me.

"Meet me outside," he mouthed.

I nodded. Pressing Myrlie's wet hand into John's, I

murmured, "Excuse me," and made my way down the aisle behind Isaac.

"You're lookin' good, Nia," Isaac gasped between sucks off of his cigarette. We were standing in the alley west of the church. The hearse and family cars gleamed in the rays of the sun, the drivers standing at attention beside the front doors. I could see the facade of the front of the church reflected in their sunglasses.

Isaac was always a skittish fellow, even when he and Frank were in school. Heavy smoking, drinking, and the occasional joint did nothing to mellow his movements. Tall and gaunt, his black suit hung from his frame like a glove on a scarecrow. He was what was known as "high yella" – light enough to pass for white in white society, but Black people could tell he was just extremely fair. When he was a kid, his nickname had been Gerber, in homage to hair the color of strained carrots. It had mellowed to the deep rust tones of an old pipe, glowing above his small, well-defined features, sculpted nose, thin lips, and honey-colored eyes. His mother and father, Suzy Mae and Fenton Jackson, were both as dark as a couple of tires and just about as round, and the rumor was that he had been adopted. No one knew for sure, and after so many years, it really didn't matter.

"Sure's a rough way to see you again," he murmured in ghetto slang after a deep draw. "Frank din' deserve to go out like that."

"What was he into, Isaac?" I asked.

His eyes darted first into mine them back down to the searing tip of his cigarette. An involuntary shudder rippled through his affected calm.

"Don' know," he said and averted his eyes.

"Look. You and I both know Frank was killed. You remember my Uncle Harold? He's looking for all the information he can to find out who did this." I was begging Isaac. "Call him and tell him whatever you know."

"An' end up like Frank? Ah don' think so!" he snorted.

"Uncle Harold will protect you."

"Yeah, right. You was always book smart, Nia. But ya never knew what went on out here in the streets. Fugheddit. I don' know nuttin'."

Throwing his cigarette butt to the ground, he stamped on it viciously, and then stalked down the alley, back up the stairs into the church. I stood for a moment looking at the cars and listening to "What a Fellowship" on the organ, then turned and followed him back inside.

Frank was entombed at Fort Logan with full military honors.

His urn was placed in a wall alongside others who had honorably served their country. The reverend said a few more words and with the brass tones of 'Taps' ringing in our ears, we turned and made our way back to our cars.

"Will you be coming back to the house, Nia?" It was Myrlie. The burial of her son signified closure, seeming to bring her out of the stupor she had been in and back to reality.

"I'm sorry, but I really can't. I need to get Alex from my Mom and Dad's."

"How are your parents?" Not a word about her grandson.

"Oh, they're fine. Alex is well, too. Look, I gotta fly. I'll be in touch." And before she could utter another word and make me add her name to the Fort Logan rolls, I turned and walk/ran to my car. Isaac was there, waiting for me.

"Whuzzup?" He was lounging against my car, the ever-present cigarette hanging from his lips.

"Nothing to it. Care to enlighten me yet?"

"Meet me at the Drop Zone in Thornton at 6:00," he said and immediately walked away.

The Drop Zone is an upscale coffee shop franchise with probably twenty-five locations in and around the metro area. It struck me as incongruous that Isaac even knew the one in Thornton existed, much less wanted to meet there. Thornton is a quiet, middle-class, mostly white area, unaccustomed to the wildlife Isaac seemed to hang with. I decided not to speculate on what he had to tell me yet and went to my parents to get Alex. When I drove up, he was in the front yard, peddling his Big Wheel with ferocious intent, his face a mask of determination, trying to beat his opponent, Zoë. Zoë's tongue was hanging out as she flew alongside my son. They came to a screeching halt at the edge of the porch, Zoë stood for two beats then jumped, barking, landing on top of him.

I suddenly felt glad that Alex had his grandparents. I knew that he would always be happy and safe with them. Dad had been the father that Alex did not have, and he loved him as if he were one of his own sons. To Mom, Alex was the favored grandchild, even though she denied it. Both of them would give up their own lives for their grandson. I couldn't specifically say why I was determined to find out who killed his father, but I was. Frank had been a failure as a husband and a father, but Alex had his genes, he was a part of the man, and I felt that I might be letting my son down if I didn't solve this homicide. It might be dangerous, but I had to do it for my son.

"No, Zoë!" Alex shouted. "I won, not you! Get offa me!" Zoë continued to lick, slobber and nip at him.

"Hey, you two!" I called, walking up to them.

"Mom save me! I'm training for the Olympics and Zoë keeps cheating!" He was grinning from ear to ear as he ran up, the dog jaunting along beside him.

I leaned over and kissed him before sweeping him up into my arms. "Where's Nana?" I asked.

"She's in the house. C'mon Zoë!" He wriggled from my arms, jumped down and ran for the house.

Mom was in the kitchen creating a peanut butter, banana and jelly sandwich for Alex. She had her back to us and said, "C'mon in. Do you want a sandwich, Katherine?"

"Uh-huh," I mumbled.

Mom was the only one who called me Katherine. Katherine was both of our middle names. Dad had chosen it. They had switched off, child after child, in their naming exercises, and since I was the last, Dad had named me. Mom made that concession with him, and I was Nia Katherine, Taye had Joel as his middle, and the only one she regretted was Fynn. He was saddled with Clarence, the name of Dad's favorite uncle.

"How was it?" She asked as she turned away from the sandwich to get plates. She started making another pbbj for me.

"Well, Myrlie finally came out of her stupor long enough to ask about you and Dad, but she never did inquire about the Sea Monkey." I shot a glance at Alex who was rolling around on the floor with the dog. He was oblivious to us. Since he had learned to spell, we'd had to resort to other ways of talking about him.

Mom shook her head. "Those people."

She was too kind to say anything derogatory about them, so we sat down to our sandwiches and said nothing more about the funeral or the Carters.

"Mom, could you watch Alex tonight? Lucy Gervin was there, and she asked me to come have a drink with her and her husband tonight. I'll be back to pick him up early, but I need to go and talk to her." Sure, it was a lie, but I wasn't about to tell her I was meeting with Isaac. She would remember how he was as a teen, and she'd never approved of him. She was a mom. She would worry.

CHAPTER 14

I almost didn't recognize Isaac. He was sitting in a back corner of the coffee shop, a mug cuddled in both of his hands. He wore a pale cream polo that appeared to be silk or something equally as soft. Dark brown, tassely loafers protruded from beneath the legs of olive-colored Dockers. From where I stood, they all seemed to fit his frame. He looked like a wealthy frat brother, not a down-on-his-luck, dope-dealing loser. He couldn't give up his smokes, though. An ecigarette was firmly planted between his fingers, the vapors spouting up and swirling in the breeze of the overhead fan.

"Well, I'm glad you were smoking, or I wouldn't have known you," I said, sliding into the booth.

"I have to tell you. I'm not what you think I am." The voice was not even Isaac's. There were no Ebonics, and his inflections were crisp and enunciated.

"No shit, Sherlock. Your name *is* still Isaac though, isn't it?" I asked.

"Yes, Nia, I'm Isaac," he said, as though tired. "I work for the government now."

"Shut up!" I motioned to the waitress. "Could you bring me a cup of the house brew? Little cream, two sugars?"

She walked away and I focused once again on Isaac. "Okay, I'm ready to hear the fairy tale."

Isaac told me how he'd left Colorado and gone to Washington, D.C. to college when all of us thought he had moved to California to go to college but instead to hang with the druggies. He said he'd been very impressed by his cousin who had landed a job as a secretary for the FBI. He wanted at that time to be an agent but didn't think that would sit too well with the brothas, so he was ashamed to let anyone know. He turned out to be an excellent candidate.

"I went to college, studied criminology, got good marks, and did the Quantico strut to become a DEA agent. Nobody here in Denver, not even Moms and Pops knew where I'd gone." He took a long drag off of his cigarette. "Always thought I was still in California, drugging it up and faking it in school. Mom'd send me money, the government would forward my mail, and when I came home, she and Pops saw me just as everyone else in the community did – an anorexic pothead. It bothered them, I know, that I wasn't working, using my degree in Sociology, to do anything, but they never said a thing. Thought I was suicidal and didn't want to give me the shove over the edge. Thing was, I have been the eyes and ears of the illegal drug community, a real cottage industry, and I report everything back to the boys in Washington."

He told me that he had taken an exceptional interest in Frank and many other veterans when they returned to the states from their war duties. Frank was not the only one who came back with a drug problem.

"Frank had a drug problem?" I asked, idiotically.

"Yeah. Frank had the usual war problems: smoked more pot than anyone, sniffed when he could get it and loved crack. Didn't you think it a little odd when he quit his job and went to work for that printer?"

"Yeah, but..."

"He still left the house and stayed away for the same amount of time he did while he was working full time, didn't he?"

"Oh, crap." I looked up dully when the waitress returned and put down my cup. "I'd gotten to the point where I was just happy he wasn't hanging around the house all day."

"He would come meet all of us – me, Dallas, Steve, the rest of the guys. We'd sit around, smoke and shoot the shit. Frank was always the one who was holding. I started getting closer to him and found out who was his source. Remember after you guys divorced how a month later, he moved to Florida?"

"I knew, but I only saw him once after the divorce was final," I murmured.

"Yeah, well, you know he moved to Florida to deal?"

"Yeah. But I didn't know it was to deal."

"I went down to visit him and keep tabs on his deals. Frank was good. He should have gone into something legitimate with his brains, but...oh well. He had a nice little Porsche, and he was working his way up the drug ladder. Y'know, I felt a little guilty spying on him, but he was going too far."

"I was paying him a hundred a month and when I forgot, he had his sorry butt on the phone asking for it. And he had a Porsche?" I squeaked.

"Well, yeah. It was an older model..." Isaac said in Frank's defense.

"Still, Isaac. Alex and I could have used that money. Who was he working for?"

"He was with some big time 'playas.' Real money. Nationwide network."

"Did they kill him?" I whispered.

"Yeah, that's my guess. I'd gotten close, and Frank was getting sloppy. I think they thought he was exposing them. There were these two cleaning women – sisters. Pretty blondes, one named Darlene and the other, Carla. The Moran sisters. They both cleaned the De Soliel Hotel where the big boss held a lot of meetings."

I interrupted him. "The De Soliel? That's where I sent his check every month."

"Well, they both did a few tricks in the hotel along with working as maids, but of the two of them, Darlene was slickest. Saw and heard just enough. Met Frank and fell in 'love,'" he said with sarcasm, "and I think she told him things about the business that she'd heard while eavesdropping. They got married."

"Married!?" I grit my teeth and swallowed the lump of anger that had formed in my throat. "That shitheel scumbag! He was getting money from me and got *married*?"

Isaac's eyebrow lifted slightly. "She turned up face down in her bathtub," he continued after a drag off of the ecig, "and then it looks like they went looking for Frank. Guess they found him." He laid his cigarette down, took a long sip of his coffee and stared into the cup. We sat in silence, every so often sipping off of our mugs, each lost in our own thoughts.

"So, what now?" I finally asked.

"Well, I'll be fading back to Florida to follow another lead. May be able to get to the head of the hydra after all." He leaned over the table to me. "Nia, I only tell you all this because you're curious. I know how many questions you've asked these last few days. Now, can you leave it alone?"

"Yeah, well, I guess I can. Thanks, Isaac," I whispered.

We finished our coffee and he walked me out to my car. There was a brand-new Porsche parked beside my car and a beautiful, shiny, pale yellow older car, something from the forties, parked two down from mine. I was thinking about the fact that I was struggling to get a vehicle to transport Alex and I from place to place and his dead dad had owned a Porsche. Didn't matter that it was old. It was a *Porsche*.

"It really is good to see you. You're still a cutie!" Isaac

smiled and pinched my cheek. I smiled back.

"You're not so bad yourself once you get clothes that fit. Take care, Isaac, and thanks." I pecked him on the cheek, got into the car and drove back to Evergreen to pick up my son. When I arrived, the porch light was the only beacon shining in the house, so I knocked cautiously, and moments later, the door opened to the face of my dad.

"Hi, Papa," I whispered as I stretched to kiss his cheek.

"He's asleep. I ran his little butt off today," he chuckled. Dad was wearing one of his old uniform shirts as he usually did. Since retirement, he kept himself busy fixing up around the house and he wouldn't wear a "good" shirt unless he was going down to the church to do bookkeeping in their business office.

We tiptoed back to the bedroom reserved for my son. He lay on top of the covers, one of Mom's afghans bunched up around his small form, curled around a stuffed whale Mom had sewn for him when he was two. Dad had built his bed to resemble a pickup truck the color of his own, bright blue with white stripes. The mattress rested in the bed of the truck, and the cab was a toy bin. Alex loved the piece of furniture and had cried fiercely when he'd been forced to leave it here at his grandparents because it was too big to fit in his room at our house. Scooping him up, Dad carried him to my car, placing him in the center of the back seat and fastened the seat belt. I followed him out after I'd peeked in and given Mom a peck on her cheek. She slept peacefully and I could see no point in waking her.

"Call me when you two get home. How was the funeral?"

"Sad. Myrlie took it hard, but she is still such a cow." Dad frowned. "She didn't even ask about Alex. He's her grandson and she makes no effort to know him."

"Don't let it worry you now, honey. She doesn't know what she's missing." He smiled down at Alex.

I climbed in and kissed his cheek through the open

window as he leaned down. "Thanks, Dad. I'll call you when we get home."

Within forty-five minutes, I was pulling into the garage, clicking off the headlights, gathering my purse and Alex's toys. I opened the kitchen door, dropped the booty on the table, then went back to get my son. He was sleeping soundly, little baby snores escaping him when I slid him to the side and removed his safety belt. He was almost too heavy for me to carry, but the mom in me simply couldn't wake him and make him walk in. He settled into the crook of my arm, sighed serenely then, with his head lolling against my shoulder, I took him into the house, down the hall and placed him on his bed. He didn't stir as I removed his clothes and shoes, pulled back the covers and placed him under them. I got a washcloth from the bathroom and swabbed his face because I knew Zoë had liberally washed it during their playtime. Kissing him, I murmured that I loved him, turned on his night light and slipped out of the room. Returning to the kitchen, I locked the door, walked down the hall and set the burglar alarm, looking for the reassuring red light and listening for the three beeps.

The phone rang, and I glanced at my watch to check the time. It was a bit late for someone to be calling, but I rushed to get it before it woke Alex.

"Hello?" I whispered.

"Nia?" It was Myrlie. "I'm sorry to call so late, but I just needed to talk a bit."

I was shocked. "Sure, Myrlie. What's on your mind?"

She sighed. "Oh, nothing really. I just had a few of Frank's things that I thought you might want to keep. Maybe to give to Frank's son."

Not my son, but Frank's. Crap! Cut the lady some slack. She was a grieving mother. "What kinds of things?"

"Oh, just a couple of the toys he played with when he was little, the suit he was baptized in, some paintings he did and sent to me, stuff like that." She was barely whispering, a little whimper escaping as she told me about the articles.

What the hell did I want with one of Frank's old suits? Alex would never wear it. "Sure. I'll come over and pick them up, just tell me when."

Hypocrite.

"Oh, anytime. I put them into a box here by the door, so you can stop in and get them whenever you're in town."

"Umm, ok. I'll do that." I had a feeling that giving me Frank's things, stuff that I'd beeline straight to the Goodwill, led to door number two, the real reason she was calling. I didn't say anything, just waited to give her time to unload.

"Frank looked real good last time I saw him, but I know he was doing things he knew he shouldn't. John and I taught him to do better than he was doing, but he got off-track somehow. He just got off-track." Her voice trailed off and she gave another of her deep sighs. "He got tied up with some people who looked good on the outside, but inside, they was rotten. Looked like children of the Lord, but...um-um, they was evil. Evil, I tell you, Nia."

Her voice had raised an octave. She was agitated, and I asked, "Who, Myrlie? Who was Frank with? When did you last see him?"

As suddenly as she had lost her composure, she regained it. "Oh, Nia. I don't need to burden you. Come by whenever and get the stuff. Kiss li'l Alex for me."

And she was gone. She hadn't said goodbye, but surprisingly, she had remembered her grandson's name. I shook my head as I hung up the phone, did my evening bathroom ritual, and climbed under the covers. I called Dad to reassure him that we had made it home safely, then lay back on my pillow. A fingertip of dread stroked my heart, and it was the last thing I thought of before closing my eyes and drifting to sleep.

At first, I thought the phone was ringing really loudly, then I realized that it was the burglar alarm. Panicking, I jumped out of bed, grabbed my robe and ran down the hall to Alex's room.

"Mama?" He was awake with fear draining color from his face. With one arm, I swooped him up, ran back down the hall and into my bedroom, grabbing for the phone as I ran by it, but before I could dial, it rang.

"ADT, ma'am. We noticed your alarm was going off," a calm male voice said.

"Yes, it did! I think someone tried to break in. Please notify the police," I had to yell over the loud ringing of the alarm. I ran into my closet and shut the door.

"Done." he said. "They should be arriving soon. What is your password, just to be sure?"

I told him.

"Ok, Ms. Carter. Do you want me to stay on the line with you until they arrive?"

"Oh, thank you! Yes, please," I said. Alex had tightly wrapped around me, his breath ragged as though he had been running. My baby was scared. I stroked his face and shushed into his ear.

"Did you hear any noises?" he asked.

"No. Can't hear anything over this noise," I yelled.

Finally, I thought I heard the doorbell, and a then a voice shouted over the din of the alarm, "Police!"

"They're here." I said into the phone. I tried to put Alex down, but he clung to me like a cat in a high tree. Opening the door, I tiptoed down the hall and peeked out the little viewer and saw Jake Ritter, a cop who had been Adam's partner for a few years. I sighed, flicked on the hall light, turned the alarm off and opened the door. The silence was as deafening as the siren had been.

"Oh, Jake!" Alex and I both tumbled into his arms.

"Nia! Nia, what happened?" Jake said as he caught us.

"Just a second." Handing him Alex, we all moved into the hallway, and I told the dispatcher at ADT, "Thank you. I'm okay now."

"No problem, Ma'am. Anytime." And he hung up.

"Jake, thank you."

He had turned to his partner and told him to go check the outside. I put the phone down on the counter in the kitchen and took Alex out of his arms. Alex seemed calmer now that his friend, Officer Jake was in the house.

"Mommy, is everything okay now?" His eyes looked deeply into mine.

"It's okay, baby. Jake wouldn't let anything happen to us."

Jake had gone to the back of the house, checking the windows as he went. I had closed the front door and gone to sit on the sofa in the living room. Jake returned after a few minutes and went to the front door to let his partner in. Both of them went into the kitchen. After nearly five minutes, they came into the living room.

"Well, Nia, someone did try to get into your kitchen door. Did you close the garage door after you put your car in?"

"Well, yes, I did," I stuttered.

"Locked the door leading into the house?"

"Of course!"

"Well, it was opened just enough to set off the alarm. The lock was forced. The alarm must have been what scared him away."

Oh my God! Someone had tried to break into my house! The full weight of the implication hit me, and I leaned back into the cushions. Jake sat down and put his arm around my shoulders.

"It's ok, Nia. Be glad you have an alarm," Jake said, patting my shoulder. "I'll get it shored up to last through the night, and in the morning, you can call a locksmith."

I looked at my watch. It was 3:15 a.m. "It's morning. Too early to call them?" I asked Jake.

"Ya think?" he said. "Go back to bed and I'll take care of it."

Right. Go back to bed. I was up for the night, but I shook my head and got up to take Alex back to his room. Halfway to his room, I changed my mind and put him in my bed. I went to his room and got his stuffed monkey. When I returned, he was sitting up, big eyed.

"Thanks, Mommy." He took the toy, curled it around in his arms and went back to sleep. I kissed him and returned to the living room.

"Ok, hon. We nailed it shut. You'll have to go out the front door to get out, but I brought the garage door opener in for you. I'd also get a new one of those with a dual frequency remote opener and a worm drill and see if the alarm people can wire it with the rest of the house." Jake handed me the little, black control box.

"Thanks Jake. I'll remember and call in the morning for that, too. I'm glad it was you who came out." I kissed his cheek and we walked to the door.

"We checked all of the windows and doors. You set the alarm again as soon as we leave, ok?"

"I will, don't worry." I said goodbye to both of them, shut the door, set the alarm and went from window to window and door to door to make sure all was secure. Dad had bought the alarm system for me and made sure every opening was wired. He was always afraid for his daughter, the single mom, who lived alone. I had pooh-poohed his worries but consented to the installation. Now I was glad that I had. I checked on Alex who was fast asleep, grabbed my afghan off of the cedar chest, went to the family room and turned on the television. After about two minutes of mindless channel surfing, I settled on TCM. The *Road to Morocco* had just come on and the guide stated that another '*Road*' show was coming on after. Oh well. I decided that I would be spending the night with Bing and Bob. I curled up and settled in with my eyes on the TV and my ears on any mysterious sounds. This had been a day like no other, and given the circumstances, sleep was the furthest thing from my mind.

CHAPTER 15

Myrlie and John were having trouble accepting their son's death, but life and work must go on. The day after the funeral, John arose at 5:00 as he'd done for most of his life, went into the kitchen, rinsed the ancient percolator, filled the basket with Folgers, then lit the burner and put it on to boil. Stopping by the linen closet in the hall, he got clean towels then peeked into the bedroom at his wife. Myrlie slept with her arm stretched over his side of the bed, snoring gently. He knew she was destined for another day of sorrow, and his heart ached with the reality that he could not prevent it. Sighing, he went to the bathroom for his shower.

The shower masked the sound of a key turning in the lock of the backdoor. The intruder slid in, mouse quiet, knowing his destination. Lifting the lid of the igloo shaped sugar bowl on the small tile table in the kitchen, he sifted white powder into the container then stirred it into the sweet crystals with the spoon on the side. Replacing the lid, he turned and was out of the door, closing it as silently as it had opened. In the bathroom, John turned off the water, dried himself off, and put on his robe. He went back to the kitchen and his fresh pot of coffee. From the cabinet above the sink, he selected two mugs. Two teaspoons of sugar from the igloo were placed in each cup and after pouring one for both he and Myrlie, he stirred each and took them into the bedroom.

"Wake up, girl. Coffee's ready."

Myrlie mumbled unintelligibly then slowly sat up.

"Time to get movin', baby. Mrs. Tucker will need her floors vacuumed and her toilets cleaned, since you haven't been there for a while. If you want, I'll come help you." He sat on the side of the bed and gave her a mug.

After taking a sip, she looked at him. "Naw, she said, shaking her head, "I'll go it alone. I can handle it." She took another swallow from her mug, then swung her legs over the side of the bed and got up. Slipping into her robe, she moved slowly down the hall to the bathroom to shower and get ready for work.

"I'll drop you off, so you don't have to catch the bus, okay?"

"'K."

John shook his head, put his cup on the nightstand, got his work clothes from the closet and began to dress for work. When his boots were on, he went outside, got the paper off of the walkway and waved to the departing paperboy, busily riding down the street on his bike. The sun was just peeking over the horizon and the thought crossed John's mind that his son would never see another sunrise. Shaking his head, he returned inside, closed the door and read the first few pages of the Post while waiting for his wife to complete her morning rituals and join him. Picking up his cup, he walked down the hall, got Myrlie's now empty cup from the bathroom, went back to the kitchen, refilled his then hers, complete with sweetener for both.

"Coffee's on the bed side table." He called as he sat it down then returned to the living room and his paper. Five minutes later, Myrlie joined him.

"Ready?"

"Um-hm. You gonna get lunch at school? I forgot to make you one."

"Yep. Today should be a hamburger day. I'm putting the tarps down over at Gilbert, so I'll drop in there."

At the mention of their son's former school, John saw tears twinkle in Myrlie's eyes, which she quickly brushed away.

"Lord, I feel like I never went to bed, I'm so tired," Myrlie murmured as she gathered her things.

"Me too," he said tiredly. "Too much sadness." John shook his head and he and his wife slowly drifted out the backdoor and to the garage. They wordlessly got into the car, and John put the key into the ignition then prepared to open the garage door.

But his hand never picked up the remote.

His eyes closed and he slumped to his side, his head gently bumping into his wife's, both seeping into unconsciousness. Their executioner entered the side door, reached past John, took the remote and closed the garage door. He then turned the key to the ignition and started the car. Silently closing the door behind him, he took a deep breath, checked his watch, then continued his run in the direction of Colorado Boulevard, in route to DIA, and his next destination.

CHAPTER 16

I had not seen David nearly as much as I would have liked, but we had talked every day at least twice and had gotten to know each other well. I called him the moment I had a chance when I got into the office Friday at about 10.

"Is Mr. Dillon in?" I asked his secretary.

"Oh, he's not in right now, Ms. Carter. Shall I leave a message?"

"If you would, Crystal. I'd appreciate it." After I hung up from Crystal, I called the alarm company and a locksmith and scheduled to have both of them meet me at home at 5:00. I then cleaned up accounts and did busy work until about 12:30, one ear attuned to the phone. I was rising from my desk to go get something for lunch when it rang.

"Good afternoon. This is Nia."

"Good afternoon." David sounded as luscious on the phone as he did in person. "So, are things going better?"

"Oh, yeah. Feeling better and ready to deal."

He asked, "So, what's up for tonight?"

"How about grilled salmon, snow peas, dilled potatoes and sherbet for dessert?"

"I'll be there by...6:30?"

"Sounds good. You bring the sherbet." I rang off. Talking to David made me feel better.

I must have reread the same file twenty times I was so tired and preoccupied. By 3:00, I decided to pack up and go home. Ellen came ambling over just as I was placing my cell phone into my backpack.

"Calling it a day?" she asked.

"I'm so disjointed, I can't work. I keep thinking about David, then I actually feel guilty, and I think about Frank. He's dead, and I need to put thoughts about him aside." I slumped back into my chair. I hadn't told her or anyone else about the near break in the night before. No sense in getting everyone in a tizzy.

She said, gently, "There's nothing you can do about Frank, Nia. He is dead. He never did too much good for you anyway, now did he?"

"He gave me Alex."

Ellen didn't have an answer for that. We sat for a minute or so, leaning back in our chairs, each engulfed in her own thoughts. Finally, Ellen said, "You know, Jason didn't expect you in today anyway, so you really should go on home."

"Yeah. Guess I'll go pick the little guy up. I'll see you Monday."

I zipped the mouth of my backpack closed, slung it over my shoulder and left. There were still many unanswered questions having to do with Frank: his death, the drugs and of all people, Isaac. Something about Isaac was gnawing at me, but I couldn't put my finger on what it was. I pointed the nose of the car to Inverness and turned right. Summer was going to be a doozy. It was already feeling warm and dry. Easing down the Drive, I was startled by a woman driving a red Mercedes convertible who came from the far-right lane directly across my path and into the far left lane, without benefit of a signal.

"Cow!" I shouted. She'd almost hit my passenger door. I caught a glimpse of yellow, tortured and frizzed hair, and a smear of red lips. "Get out of the Clairol bottle!" I yelled. She flipped me off and kept moving.

Alex was out on the playground, concentrating on hitting a high sailing, large, blue ball with a hugely oversized, yellow bat. Both ball and bat looked as though they belonged in a cartoon with only one item missing – a cross-eyed umpire to call the plays. Alex swung high as the ball arched low and he missed by at least two feet. Oh well. Alex saw me and ran to the car. In a blaze of words he squealed, "Didja see that, Mom? Didja see it, huh? I almost hit it! I'll get it next time. Didja see?"

Optimism is the balm of the ego. Though he had been a mile off of even allowing the ball to feel a breeze from the bat, he steadfastly believed in the promise of the future.

"I saw it, honey! What a shot! You're great; you're really great, but c'mon now and get your stuff. Let's go home."

Alex chattered all the way home about his burgeoning baseball career, and I didn't have the heart to tell him his chances of making it to the all-star game were slim to none. Allow him his euphoria. He might be the one to break the curse. I stopped by the store to pick up some salmon and fresh dill, since I'd committed to that particular meal. The next stop was Macy's, and with Alex firmly attached to my left hand, I bee lined to the Godiva chocolate counter. Laying my hands on a 1/4-pound Gold Ballotin, I made my way to the check stand.

"Survival equipment?" The cashier was a pretty high school girl, dressed in a T-shirt dress of neon green. Her smile was a quirky up turning of the corners of her mouth.

"It's been one of those months, and the catharsis is a premium box of chocolates. This was one time Hershey's was just not enough," I told her.

"Been there, done that. Go home, soak in the tub and if

little man will let you, eat the whole box," she whispered as she passed me my change.

We arrived at the house just as the locksmith was driving up. I parked the car in the driveway, gathered up our stuff and met him on the walk. Greeting him and asking to see his identification, we all walked to the house. He followed me into the kitchen, and I gave him instructions to put a new door lock and key lock deadbolt on both of the entrance doors. The doorbell rang as I was heading out of the kitchen and when I looked out the peep hole, I saw the man from ADT. When I opened the door, he got an id check, too.

Both men had completed the work within a half hour. The garage door opener was reprogrammed, and the ADT man gave me the new dual frequency opener. The locksmith gave me two new keys. I wrote two checks, told them thank you and goodbye. Alex had hunkered down in front of the set to watch Pooh Corner on Disney, and I got into the bath. Leaving the door open so he could come in if he got lonely, I laid back in the hot, bubbly water. The phone rang.

"I'll get it, Mommy!" Alex yelled.

"Let it ring, honey!" I yelled back. I didn't want him answering the phone, just in case. After the call about Frank, I just didn't want him to get it, but he must not have heard me.

"It's for you, Mommy!" he handed me the phone then ran back to Pooh.

"Hello?" I answered cautiously.

"Hey, kid," Uncle Harold growled. "Got a minute?"

"Oh, hey, Uncle Harold. Sure. What's up?"

"Myrlie and John were found dead today. Looks like suicide. Carbon monoxide."

I gasped. "W-w-hat happened?"

"Found 'em this morning in their garage. They'd been there a while and it looks like John turned the car on without opening the garage door. Then he and Myrlie just went to sleep. Asphyxiation looks like the cause, but we won't know till the coroner gets done. Usually, folks are kinda cherry-pink when they go out like that, but those two looked almost normal." As soon as he said it, he knew he shouldn't have. I knew he could feel my curiosity perk up.

"Do you think they were murdered?" I asked.

"Oh, Nia, don't go off on that, please!" he grunted. "I'm only telling you they're dead because their family may need help with the funerals and all."

"No, Uncle Harold. I can't do that again. I just can't." I was shaking my head as though he could see me.

"Ok, girlie. I'm actually glad to hear you say that. Stay out of it."

"I will, but you gotta admit, this is too weird. So soon after Frank dying."

"Yeah, well, let it be weird for me and the guys on the force, not you. I'll keep you in the loop."

"Well, thanks for that at least."

He rang off. I sat there in the cooling water. John and Myrlie dead. That was just crazy, and too much of a coincidence for my taste. Try as I might to get away from it, I had a notion gnawing at the base of my skull. When I'd gotten into the tub, I just couldn't get Frank to lie still. Now his parents were squirming in my mind alongside him. Something was wrong, and no matter what Uncle Harold said, the three deaths were intertwined. To get to the bottom of the whole thing, I knew I had to find out what Frank had been doing just prior to his death.

Why had Myrlie called me? Who were the people Frank hung with, and were they his friends? Enemies? Lackeys? Was he a lackey, or were those people his employers? Isaac said he was dealing drugs, using Florida as his home base, but Florida had plenty of drug dealers, plying their trade on the sunny beaches, the hotels – heck, even during the Jai-Alai matches, and every day probably saw a few of the scummy fellows dumped into the Atlantic or the Everglades. Did someone bring Frank all the way back to Colorado to kill him? That was impossible. Not logical that he was killed in Florida then carted back up here and dumped in Cherry Creek. No. He had to have come to Colorado under his own steam, either because he was summoned or running away.

Although Frank had never been to my house to grace me with his presence, about ten months prior, he'd begun calling every month to inquire about his monthly stipend. I always cussed him out, dishing it up freely at the sound of his voice. He had become a zealot about the call, his punctuality almost religious. Always on the tenth regardless of the day it fell on. He would ask about Alex, always saying, 'How's my son?' I don't think he even remembered Alex's name. Then he would inquire if the check was in the mail. Knowing he would be calling on that date, I got to the point that I would leave the house to avoid speaking directly to him, instead allowing the answering machine to be privy to his begging. He left about five calls until I relented, called him back, cussed him out and told him the check had been sent. Why did he still call if he was making all that drug money? A hundred bucks was, in the great scheme of things, probably just a drop in the proverbial bucket. I jumped out of the tub and into my terry robe.

"Alex?" I called.

"Um-hmm." He was enormously preoccupied.

"You still watching Disney?"

"Um-hmm." I could hear the stuffed actors singing lustily about keeping your head out of trashcan liners.

"Ok. I'm going to be on the phone for a while, so stay out of trouble. I called Uncle Harold. At the first wheeze I said, "Hi, Uncle Harold. How long did the coroner say Frank had been in Cherry Creek?"

"Nia!" he hollered then sputtered a phlegmy cough. Uncle Harold could do with leaving the Pall-Malls alone for a while. "Why the hell are you calling asking about Frank now? He's dead! His parents are dead! They were sad over him and shit happens, Nia! Get over it!"

"All right, all right! I know, Uncle Harold. Don't blow a gasket!" I barked. "But I wanted to find out just that one thing."

"Hang on," he grunted, put the receiver down and I assumed he had opened his door because the office cacophony assaulted my ears. I waited nearly five minutes. Finally, he returned, still huffing.

"He'd been there about three weeks, just like Jake said, near as he could tell. What's it to ya?" he asked.

"I just wondered. Frank always called for his check, and from what Isaac told me, he was a big-time drug dealer in Florida. Why would he need my piddley Benjamin?"

Uncle Harold exploded. "What the hell you doin' talking to Isaac Jackson? I'm supposed to talk to those people! That man is trouble, Nia. Keep your nose out of it!" he bellowed.

"Please, Uncle Harold. Don't yell at me," I whined. "It's just strange, that's all. What caliber bullet was it they found in his head?"

"22." He calmed a little. "He had a hard head. Bullet must've bounced around something fierce, dentin' everything, but it was still there."

"Did the coroner think he had been weighted to stay down so long?"

"Looked like it. Had the remnants of a rope around his ankle. Why do you want to know all of this, Nia? Would you please stop tryin' to go detective on me?" he pleaded.

"I'm not, Uncle Harold, but I do have police training and I'm getting those things-don't-add-up prickles shimmying up the back of my neck."

"Let us get the shimmies, sweetie. We're better equipped, and since its obvious Frank was into something that got him killed, they could just as soon do the same for you. Stay out of it!"

I thought about the attempted break in. "I will, don't

worry. Just keep me informed, and don't give up on it, please Uncle Harold?"

His voice softened. "I will, sweetie, but remember he had been down there a long time. There was no evidence on the shore after all this time, so we really have little to go on."

"Talk to all of his friends: William Franklin, Dallas Fears, Steve Butcher, Joe Deckers. And call Isaac Jackson. One of those guys is bound to know something, so ask 'em."

"Already did, and nobody knows anything. Stay out of it, Nia," he repeated.

"Alright!" But I wasn't ready to throw in the towel. I knew he was probably right, but that little alien of suspicion still wiggled at my neck. It was time to get down to it and find out what was really going on.

I owed it to the man.

CHAPTER 17

By the time David arrived, I'd run every imaginable scenario through my mind twice. I was still so disjointed all I'd accomplished was shredding lettuce for the salad. Good thing I was grilling fish, not preparing a big meal. I'd just started peeling potatoes as the doorbell rang.

"I'll get it!" Alex yelled as he sprinted for the door.

"Hey, big fella!" David laughed. It felt good to hear his voice. Moments later, he swung around the corner, Alex slung under his right arm like a burlap bag, a bottle of zinfandel and a King Soopers grocery bag in his left hand. He had changed from his corporate uniform into a black t-shirt, black jeans, and black cowboy boots. He looked like the good guy riding in on his horse. Black, of course. The man was movie material.

"Hey," he said.

"Hey yourself," I whispered.

He put the zinfandel in the fridge, the sherbet in the freezer, turned and sauntered over, Alex still attached like a barnacle. His lips grazed my jaw and he winked. I realized in that flashing moment that I loved the guy.

"Need help?" he asked, setting Alex on the floor. Seizing his opportunity, Alex punched him in the butt. He grinned and made to grab the child, but Alex feinted away.

"You can get the tomatoes out of the fridge and finish making the salad, if you want. I only have one more potato to peel, so we'll eat soon."

"I'm goin' watch TV, Mom," Alex yelled and streaked to the family room.

"Want to talk about it?" David asked, opening the refrigerator door.

"May as well," I said. "Frank's parents were found dead this morning."

He stopped moving around the kitchen and looked at me. "Dead? What happened to them?"

"They were found dead in their garage. Engine had run till the gas ran out, so Uncle Harold and the boys think it was suicide."

"And you?"

"Ah, c'mon, David." I turned to face him. "We just buried Frank and now they're dead, too? Isn't that just a little too pat? I mean really." I shook my head and went back to peeling.

"Well, yeah, I agree with you to a certain extent. It is a bit strange, but it doesn't mean they were killed, hon. They were distraught over their son's death."

"Yeah, right. And I'm an astronaut."

We worked together in silence. He knew I had a lot on my mind, so he made the salad without another word. I boiled and seasoned the potatoes as he cooked the salmon outside on the grill, we soon sat down to dinner. Alex was the only one talking during the meal. His youth was a shield against the brooding silence of his mother. The understanding murmurings David uttered in response to his questions were sufficient to keep his mouth flapping, full of food at times, and his attitude content. I could feel the weight of David's gaze on my forehead but refused to acknowledge by lifting my eyes from my plate.

David was born to be a dad. He possessed the talent necessary to keep the child swathed in the belief that everything he said was of utmost importance, that the world was still spinning in harmony. He instinctively knew how to make all the appropriate sounds to ensure that Alex was never cognizant of disharmony at the table. But it was obvious David had a portion of his brain cells relegated to the task of cracking the barrier I'd erected while eating my dinner. When we'd finished eating and Alex had slowed down in his narratives, I got up, cleared the table, went to the kitchen and began doing dishes.

"Need help?" It was David, leaning on the doorframe.

"Nah. I'll get this cleaned up. Go ahead and sit down. I'll be back in in a little while." I stared at the sudsy water as though an oracle inhabited the bubbles, waiting to illuminate me on The Meaning of Life.

"Later then." And he left the room. I knew what he meant. He intended to draw me out, make me talk about what was weighing me down. Sighing, I drowned the seer and washed the pots and pans. Fifteen minutes later, I wiped my hands, turned out the lights and went to the living room. Alex was sprawled in the middle of the floor, an oversized tablet of newsprint cradled between his elbows, busily drawing what appeared to be either Spiderman or a charging Tyrannosaurus Rex. Although it was hard to determine the subject of his current masterpiece, it is apparent Alex is destined to receive the legacy of his father – a talent for art. Of all the things Frank could bequeath to him, this skill was the most appreciated. He had the artist's manner of etching lines, shading and duplicating on paper what he saw, and usually after careful examination, the subject matter emerged and could indeed be deciphered.

"What 'cha drawing, fella?" I asked.

"Ah, Mom. It's Zoë, jumping up to catch a ball. See, there are her paws and look how she's grinning." As he pointed out the details, Zoë did indeed leap to capture the circle of a ball. Alex was more Picasso than Rockwell at this point but I hoped his abilities would progress.

"Honey, I can see its Zoë. She looks good!" I left him shading the fur on her back and adding more detail and went to stand beside David. He was reading the National Geographic I'd received that day, pretending to be engrossed. He pointed to a picture of a man with Mongolian features and said, "This could have been what Genghis Khan looked like. Interesting article. You need to read it."

"Yes, Master. Fascinating." I was feeling better and wanted him to see it. He put the magazine down.

"Now?" he asked.

I sat down beside him and said, "You know I told you I sent a hundred a month to the charity in Florida, right?" His eyebrows arched quizzically, and I mouthed "Frank," and pointed to Alex. He caught on and shook his head in affirmation.

"Well, I found out that the charity was getting other funds from a mission in Columbia, dedicated to supplying medical prescriptions...

"Drugs," I mouthed.

"...Probably big dollars."

"And..." he said.

"And it's just that I can't imagine why they always called for my little moola. They were doing things that must have paid a lot more than my little stipend, so why call to ask for it? And another thing. The mama bear called me and alluded that she'd seen baby bear recently. I hadn't heard a thing about him being in town from anybody. Something's not right." I curled my legs beneath me and leaned back on the sofa. David leaned forward, staring at the floor.

"Anyone," he corrected.

"Hmm?" I said.

"Well, you could be right, Nia. Something's funky, but how are you going to find out what happened? Let Uncle Harold get to the bottom of this, and I know you'll think it cliché for me to say, but it is his job."

I sat stewing in silence for a minute. "I can't stand it!" I jumped up from the sofa as though I'd been bitten. Alex looked up from his work.

"You okay, Mommy?" His face was etched with concern.

"I'm okay, sweetie. Go back to your picture."

His eyes floated from my face to David's. David nodded and mouthed, "It's okay," and he went back to his drawing. I crumpled back down on the sofa.

"I'm going to Florida." I announced. David's mouth fell open and Alex said, "O-o-oh! Disneyworld!"

"No Disneyworld. I'm leaving you with Nana and Papa, buddy."

"Ahh, gee. That's not fair!"

"Uh-uh!" I shook my head and crumpled my eyebrows at him.

"And who do you plan to leave me with?" David asked. I looked at him dumbly. "You go, I go," he said. I could tell by the look on his face that he was going, no matter what I said.

CHAPTER 18

When I walked out of the Miami Airport Sunday morning, the air felt like a wet towel wrapped around my face. Coming from Colorado, this level of humidity was like meeting an irate boxer. It had hit me in the face with a sucker punch, leaving me gasping, as thick as pudding to my unaccustomed lungs. The plan was to find out as much as possible about Darlene Carter, nee Moran, by talking to her sister, and get out. Convincing David to let me go had not been an easy task, and making him swear a vow of silence to not tell Mom and Dad the real reason I was going was even harder. Although I'd hated to lie, I'd told them it was for my job, and they believed me. I'd often gone on trips for work, so they didn't question a trip to Florida. Khari gave me the okay to use one of his stand-by tickets since there was no way I could afford the full cost to Miami. David was not convinced that I'd be reasonably safe even though I'd had self-defense training, so there he stood beside me, silk t-shirt clinging to his frame, sweat trailing down his face.

"Whew! I'd forgotten how pleasant the air is in these parts."

He was drenched, and I knew my face had to mirror his. Every available pore on every available spot on my body was spitting sweat. My arms were soaked and leaden, my legs felt like spaghetti, and I pictured crawly things already nesting in my privates.

"If you'd stayed home, you'd be dry," I remarked, my sarcasm as thick as the air.

"I couldn't let you come down here alone. Lying to your mom and dad is one thing. Letting you do the crazy alone is another."

"Cute."

He raised his arm and waved to a waiting cab and we climbed in, collapsing on the back seat.

"Marriott?" the cabby asked in a heavily Cuban-accented voice. David looked at me and gritted his teeth. "Nope. The De Soliel Hotel on South Dixie Highway." Shrugging his shoulders, the driver flicked the switch to start charging for the ride.

Thank goodness, he had the air conditioning turned up full bore, which helped us to dry out a tad. Sitting in the cab gave me an almost watery, goldfish view of the towering palms and the coastline dotted with boats of every size from yachts to cruise ships. The sun filtered through the palm fronds, flickering in tune to the island music blasting out of the taxi's radio.

We rode without talking until David piped up, as I knew he would. "What do you think you will accomplish by coming down here?" he asked for the umpteenth time.

"I want to talk to the management of the De Soliel 'cause the housekeeper worked there. She was Frank's wife, and they might know something about her eavesdropping. We'll go to the Marriott as soon as I talk to them, promise. You can wait in the cab, please?" I pleaded. His answer was to turn and stare out the window.

When Ricky Ricardo had rounded up his band, the De Soliel had probably been a class hotel. Now, it was a decaying queen, her patina of respectability painted in garish tones to hide the wrinkles of time. The front desk still wore a deco sunburst, though some of the rays were the verdigris color brass assumes when polish is hard to come by. To the left of the lobby was an antique elevator wheezing its way from floor to floor, the door repeating the sunburst, a few of the rays broken away from the sun. The walls were painted the drab green found in veteran's hospitals and other depressing institutions, but the floor was covered in a thickly veined marble, a pale, almost white, mint color, easily the most beautiful feature in the room.

"Hi there!" I said as I walked to the desk displaying my most tourist-cheerful smile. "I'm looking for the manager, please."

"He not here." The clerk was as old as the desk he leaned behind, a Cuban refugee who'd probably been in this country longer than I'd been alive. It made me sweat just to look at him. He wore a threadbare tweed suit, skinny little tie, and a heavily starched white shirt. The U-neck of a wife beater shone through the front. His head was carpeted with a woven, seedy toupee that made me wonder how he could be so vain in the heat. Had he been younger, his attitude would have been considered surly, but as it stood, he was just weary with being a gatekeeper.

"I'm actually trying to get a little information on an employee of the hotel, Darlene Moran? I'd like to try to locate her, if possible."

"You not from here, are you?" he said in his slight accent, waving the air in front of his nose. I scrunched my armpits closer to my body, sure my perspiration was ganging up on my deodorant, and I was beginning to offend.

"How can you tell?" I asked nonchalantly.

"Natives don' sweat so much. You look like you jus' got out of the shower."

"Well, yeah. You're right. I'm from New York, down here to locate Ms. Moran. There's a finder's fee if you could give me a little info."

The flicker of greed was in his eyes and gone in an instant. "Ya got money for Darlene? If ya do, ya too late. She dead."

I feigned shock. "Dead? You telling me I came all the way down here for nothing?" Leaning on the counter with my elbows for support, I allowed the weight of the air to rest on me. I kept my arms close to my sides.

"She has sister who work here, though. Mebbe she could use the money. I give ya her name and address for tha' finder's fee?" His eyes were shining in anticipation.

"Well...alright then," I said, extending twenty dollars. "But..." I said, jerking the money back, "I need her name and address first!"

"Carla. Carla Moran. 112 E. Astilbe NE, Apartment #2," he blurted.

"You know that one by heart. Go there much?"

"Carla's a friendly girl. Like Darlene was," he admitted, feigning shyness and licking his lips as he whisked the money into his pocket.

"Cool. Thanks. Hope I find her there, 'cause I definitely know where to find you." I smiled, turned and left.

I trudged back out to the front of the building, where David waited in the cab.

"You go to the Marriott and I'll meet you there in about an hour."

His bland gaze told me that he didn't believe me.

"I promise!"

Turning to the cab driver, he said, "Take us to the rental car agency."

With that, he slumped back on the seat. We got a little white Passat that had great air conditioning.

"*Now* can I go see Carla?" I asked.

"Yup. On the way. Then...we go to the Marriott."

112 Astilbe NE was a two-story apartment building in the heart of a depressed area. A stuccoed affair, it had once been painted white but now was more the color of bad dentures. The windows were hidden from the midday sun by shutters whose drab coat of peeling paint further added to the deteriorating exterior. Although it was obvious the lawn and garden had not been privy to the benefits of care in at least a decade, Mother Nature still fought the battle for beauty. Roses climbed one side of the building casting hues of pink, red, and yellow, and underfoot violas, primrose, and the namesake Astilbe colored the drab walkway. Number 2 was at the top of a cracked uneven staircase, an awning shading the door. I knocked once. No answer. I tapped a bit harder and waited. If, as the desk clerk had indicated, Carla was a party girl, she was more than likely sleeping off the effects of the night before. The third time I rapped till my knuckles stung.

"I'm comin'! Jus' hol' on!"

The husky voice did not prepare me for the diminutive lady who opened the door. She looked like a Madame Alexander doll and was not much bigger than one from the Portrait Collection. A perfectly proportioned midget, she was no more than three feet tall. When she looked up into my face, I was startled because she resembled the dolls to such a degree she could have posed for the sculptor. Pouty, full lips, round, naturally rouged cheeks and big, china blue eyes, red around the rim, probably from lack of sleep. Her hair, though tangled and suffering from serious bedhead, seemed to be true platinum, and she would have been a beauty had she not been wearing the scowl.

"Whaddaya want?" her gravelly voice inquired.

I stuttered, "My name is Nia Carter, and I'm trying to get some information on Darlene Moran. I may have some money for her."

"Money?" Her attitude was suspicious tinged with greed, but also sad. It was obvious the memory of her sister's death was swirling back to her. "Darlene's dead. Been dead a month now," she mumbled.

"I know and I'm sorry, but I came to try to get a little information. Look, I don't mean you any harm, but I really would like to ask you a few questions about her and her husband, Frank Carter."

"This about Frank?" Her eyebrows rose. "He got out of town so quick, he didn't even wait to bury her," she said, shaking her head. "C'mon in."

Her apartment, as neat as could be, resembled the bedroom of a teenage girl, delicate and frilly. The walls were a pale salmon, and each available seat had a ruffle. The low coffee table held a vase of pink and white silk roses, and the pictures on the wall were cheap-framed prints of lovers in meaningful embraces, peering deeply into each other's eyes. I got nauseous just looking around. However, over a small bookcase was an unexpected, beautifully framed surprise in the form of a very good reproduction of Dali's "The Rose."

"Pretty room," I murmured.

She pointed to a seat, and as I sat, I saw her light the reason for her husky voice – unfiltered Pall Malls. Uncle Harold had smoked those as long as I could remember and I realized she sounded just like him.

"Thanks. Glad you like it." Her attitude totally softened after she took her first puff. She sat on the frilly ottoman and said, "I guess you know I'm Carla Moran, Darlene's sister."

"Um...yes. Pleased to meet you."

She suddenly said, "Darlene and Frank, believe it or not, were in love. Both of them were trying to get something out of this shitty life. He met her where we both worked, the De Soliel Hotel, and they hit it off from day one. Darlene tol' me everything, even how he was in bed. Hmmm..." She puffed, exhaled, and waved the smoke from in front of her face. "He married her a week after they met."

"That's nice," I murmured.

She threw me a glance, puffed again and continued talking. "He was good to her; they were good to each other, an' she always tol' me how much she loved him. They got an apartment right below me, and you'd hear 'em down there gigglin' and laughin' like a couple of kids. Only thing was – he worked for some rough folks. Drug folks. Frank coulda done better, and he was ready t' try, but the guy he worked with didn't want t' let him. Said Frank was too good a dealer." She took another drag of her cigarette then got up and slowly began pacing the length of the small room. Finally, she sat.

"Do you know who he worked for?"

"I don't know his name, but he's not what he said he was to Frank. I've screwed the guy. Goes by the name of Gerber. I think he's a cop, and he scored more drugs than Frank ever could."

A thrill rippled down my spine. Isaac.

"Do you know where he stays?" I asked.

"When he's in town, stays in a high rise downtown. Real nice."

"Okay. Thanks for the info, Carla. I'll put you down for the money my company was saving for Darlene."

"Drop the act, honey," she drawled. "Frank kept a picture of you and the kid in his wallet. His wife and son were the only things he said he couldn't part with from his ol' life."

"Oh!" I chirped. "You knew who I was when I walked in then?"

"After I cleared the sleep outta my eyes, yeah. I gotta tell you, girlie. You be careful. That Gerber's a mean sonofabitch. He sends a lot of stuff to your state. Colorado, right?"

I nodded.

"Frank was dealin' with some guy out of Mud Hut...Clay... Pebble? Oh hell, I can't remember the name of the city. But it's in Colorado. Frank said the place where the guy lived was near a zoo, and the house was new and huge. Big house. Said it looked like a castle. Big, pink castle. Made me think of rocks and Cinderella," she finished.

We sat in silence, her staring at me with those big blue eyes. She got up and started pacing again, tapping her fingertips on her bottom lip. Suddenly, she stopped.

"I got it!" she croaked. "The guy he was dealing with was named Goddard. I guess he's a big man in Mud Hut. Lotsa moola. Frank had the goods on him and was workin' an angle. He said he was makin' the guy pay."

Blackmail.

"Did Frank or Darlene tell you about it?"

"Darlene. Sisters don't have no secrets, least ways, me an' Darlene didn't."

I asked her, "Aren't you afraid? I mean, you've told me a lot, and Gerber might know you know. I wouldn't want him to come back on you."

She leaned on the arm of the ruffle-skirted, pale pink sofa. "Darlene died right downstairs in that bathtub," she whispered. "Frank found her. I'd heard someone go into their apartment a few hours before, but I just thought it was her or Frank. When he came cryin' up here to me, I thought he was drunk. He kept sayin', 'Gerber! Why, Gerber, why?' Before he called the cops he made me swear not to say anything 'cause I could get it jus' like Darlene."

"You didn't say anything?"

"Naw, but Frank told me he was goin' to get Gerber." She stamped out the cigarette and immediately lit another. "Gerber's back in town now. Saw 'em down at the hotel the other day. Asked me to do a friend of his, but I tol' 'em I was busy. I'm waitin' to get him back in that big ol' bed on the third floor of the De Soliel. I have a surprise for 'em." She grinned. A nasty, scary, smirk of a grin.

"Well, thanks again, Carla. I'd best be going now." I turned to leave and she followed me. "Please be careful," I told her.

"Don't you worry about me," she said. "You be careful. Like I said, that Gerber's a mean, snake of a man. I may be small, but I can take care of myself. You got your son to think about. Tell Frank I said hi when you get back. Tell 'em I understand why he left."

I turned back to her and gently said, "Carla, Frank is dead, too. I guess Gerber caught up to him. I'm trying to find out for sure."

The little lady looked as though she would crumple but then she visibly stiffened her spine and looked into my face. "I kinda knew it. No other way for it to end. Well," she sighed, "you let it go now. Nobody left for him to hurt 'cept you and your kid. Stay out of it."

Same thing Uncle Harold had told me. On impulse, I hugged her quickly then let myself out. When I got back into the car I glanced up to the second floor at her small frame standing looking at me and I waved. She waved back, and I felt sorry that she had lost both her sister and a friend in such a short span of time.

"Now are we going to the hotel?" David asked when I'd settled in.

"Driver, take us back to the airport," I said.

"Wha'?" David's mouth hung open. "That's it?"

"I told you, you should have stayed home. I also told you this was going to be a quick trip. Found out all I needed and now we can go home. Tell you what. We'll go to dinner at one of those Miami Vice-ish restaurants and you can look for Crockett and Tubbs."

"Those are reruns," he murmured dryly. "That program went off twenty years ago."

"Well, heck. Phillip Michael Thomas didn't have a job when they went off. Maybe he's still down here preening for the girlies? Worth a shot!"

No answer.

He grunted and we were rolling. David glanced at me,

shook his head and turned back to staring out the window. The restaurant was all bright neon and klieg, an announcement to the buying public.

"Let's just hope their food's not as high as their light bill," I told David as we walked up the curving staircase. A window overlooking the brightly lit street was where the hostess seated us almost immediately. People of all shapes, sizes and persuasions roamed the boulevard, each with a look of affected nonchalance coupled with a discreet air of 'Look at me. I'm somebody!' By sheer weight of numbers, they covered the street. It reminded me of New York, had Manhattan given way to beachfronts. Although it was beautiful, it was just a bit much for my country attitude. I wondered how Frank had fared.

"So, what's the verdict? Find the murderer?" David gnawed on a breadstick for nourishment. My stomach realized with a rush we hadn't eaten since we'd left my mother's over eight hours ago, and now I was famished.

"As a matter of fact, I now am reasonably sure I know who the murderer is."

He nearly choked on the dry crust. "Nia, c'mon! This is getting to be too much!"

"Oh, stop! I'm safe. He doesn't know I'm on to him."

"Who is it?" David demanded.

"Honey, you must think I'm out of my mind. No way I tell you."

"Nia, look. I'm starting to get used to you. I don't want to lose you and neither does Alex."

"I don't want to lose me even more than either of you do, so don't worry! I know what I'm doing. Here's the waiter. Let's order."

The waiter had slinked up, and his I-don't-care attitude should have told me to scram, but instead I foolishly ordered prawns in a butter sauce on a bed of wild rice. Had to maintain my cholesterol. David wisely ordered a spinach salad. We sat in silence after the waiter had taken the order, but I knew it was only a matter of time before David would start to grill me again.

"Okay, so what did she tell you?" He was not about to give up.

"She said Frank and Darlene were really in love. Oh, and she didn't fall for the insurance money story. She'd seen a picture of Alex and I. Knew who I was almost immediately." I told him about Goddard, Adobe Wells, and everything else that Carla had said. His eyes grew and he glanced around the room then settled his attention back on me. When I'd finished talking, he plucked another breadstick out of the pile, leaned on his elbows and studied me, every few seconds bringing the breadstick to his mouth and taking a nibble.

"What?" I yelped. David just shook his head. I regretted having told him anything.

The waiter returned with our meal, and I immediately also regretted my food choice. Four yellowed prawns rested on a bed of honey colored rice, adorned by a sprig of parsley. Nothing more. I could see a trip to the Burger King in my near future. David fared much better. His salad was the size of half a football, pleasingly crisp, and decorated with a variety of garnishes including croutons, egg, bacon bits and garbanzos.

"You had better hope she is the only one in Florida who knows you're here," he said as I snatched a garbanzo and popped it into my mouth. I speared one of the prawns.

"Aw, c'mon," I drawled, waving a crustacean decorated with a thick line of poop down his back, "I really should go to see the mouse. Mickey and I had a thing going the last time I was here. I only hope he remembers those romantic evenings on the deck of the Mark Twain. It's so sad when a good love goes bad," I sighed.

David finally smiled. "I do worry about you," he murmured.

Cleaning the poop out of the prawn, I swished it around in my water glass. It's naked, oleo-free back dripped, and I popped it into my mouth. The prawns were pretty flavorless without the sauce, but I cleaned the others in succession and ate without enjoyment. I knew there was no way I would put a morsel of the strange rice into my mouth, so I picked up a breadstick and began to nibble, watching David enjoy his meal. He offered me a forkful, but I declined. I could tell he was in a thoughtful, no more talk mood, so I let him finish his meal, pay the bill and we left the restaurant.

"We could stay the night, I guess if you'd like," I offered.

"Nah. Let's go on home."

We made our way back to the airport.

During our trip home, I mulled over the information I'd collected. I knew I had to find a way to prove what Carla had said about Isaac. Isaac was DEA, as invulnerable as an FBI agent. The thought that he'd killed Frank, a man he'd known since childhood and one Frank had trusted so completely, made my stomach bubble. I leaned the seat back a bit further and thought about Frank. He actually must have cared about us, if he still carried a picture of Alex and me in his wallet. I'd spitefully enclosed the photo one month in his check. It had been taken in a studio at Christmas, the year that Alex was about six months old. In the background was a roaring fire, and I sat with Alex in my lap in a big wingback chair. At my feet were presents of all shapes and sizes with big ribbons tied around each. It was the typical homespun holiday scene, and I'd sent it to make him jealous of what he was missing. I guess he knew what he was missing, but maybe he just couldn't do anything about it. Maybe, in his own way, he did love us but simply didn't possess the means of showing it. He'd lost his life, but in remaining distant, he'd lost a more important life: his son's.

I looked over at David. He'd dozed off, head canted to the left, chin slumping almost to his chest. A thin line of drool had made a shiny path down the side of his mouth and I realized once again while seeing him in such a vulnerable state, that I loved him, and it spiked my heart. Even though we had only known each other a short time, he had been hinting at loving me, but the commitment thing seemed to rear its head when he tried to say the words 'I love you.' On down the road, if all went well, I would need to find a way to ask David for his hand in marriage and assure him it was all his idea. This time, asking was worth it. Alex needed and deserved a good dad. Father's Days had come and gone for six years and it was time someone else had the privilege of receiving his paper plates affixed with gift-wrap ties besides Dad and I.

Wiping the trail from David's mouth with a tissue, I leaned my head toward his, kissed his cheek, pushed the mysteries of life into a remote cavern in my brain, and joined him in restful sleep.

Our plane landed at DIA at 11:30 p.m. and knowing we both needed sleep and had lost nearly a day, David perfunctorily kissed me goodnight in the car when we arrived at my house, watched me walk to and open the door, then waved goodbye and went home. Alex had made plans to stay with Nana and Papa over the weekend, so I'd left him in Evergreen to enjoy another day or so of Zoë's companionship. I checked the house, set the alarm and my bed was a welcomed haven. Within moments, I slept.

It was odd getting up, taking a shower during which, the curtain remained closed, dressing without being interrupted, getting both feet into my pantyhose, drinking an entire cup of coffee, and getting to see the bottom of the cup. Alex loved coffee, and since I drank half coffee, half milk, he always finished my cup. God, I missed him! He only had less than a week of school left, and then he'd be in daycare. He was anxious to begin his daycare adventure, but I dreaded it. Sighing, I rinsed my cup, completed mascaraing and went back to my bedroom. My cell phone rang. I saw from the caller id that it was Mom.

"Hi, darling," she said when I answered.

"Back at 'cha. How's my boy?"

"Oh, he's fine. Your dad and I were thinking we might get away for a week or so. We'd like to take him with us as company for Zoë. It would give you a break that I think you sorely need. What do you say?"

I rolled the thought around in my mind for a bit. If Alex was with them, I would be able to look a bit deeper into the murders. He would be safe with them.

"You know, Mom. That's not a bad idea. I can get him out of school next week, since the end of the school year is Thursday, and he's already missed a week anyway. I actually could use a little more non-Mom time. Where are you going?"

"Oh, you know your dad. He plans as he rolls along."

"Sounds good to me. Oh, and I'm back home. Come down here before you hit the road so I can kiss him goodbye again. I'll look for you tonight."

"You're at home?"

"Yeah, I only had one meeting so I decided to come home,"

"Well, ok then."

"Oh, and I changed the locks on the house, so I'll leave a spare key at the post office with Mr. Miller. Remember him?"

"Um-hmm, I remember him. Big old fella with a full beard?"

"Yup. He's a good guy," I said.

"Why did you change the locks?" she asked, as I knew she would.

"There have been a few break-ins in the neighborhood, and I just want to be sure we're safe." I was getting too good at this lying business.

"Alright, then. See ya tonight. Love ya," she said, and rang off.

"Love you, too."

I wasn't too productive during the morning – too tired – and afternoon found me doodling Adobe Wells on my to-do pad. Logging onto the Internet, I Googled a search of hotels, motels and bed and breakfasts in the town. Opting for the bed and breakfast listings, I found what I was looking for. There was a thumbnail picture of the proprietors posed in front of a sweet little place quaintly named The Red Apple Inn. They looked like Ma and Pa Claus, waiting for the elves to get home. I decided: why let their hospitality go to waste? The weather was beautiful; my son would be safe with Nana and Papa. What better time to go in search of a murderer?

CHAPTER 19

I called the Red Apple and made arrangements for two rooms. I loved David but didn't think our sleeping in the same bed was a move I was ready for, since I already had too many little puppies chasing their tails in my head already. Sex had been a word absent from my vocabulary and sleeping quarters for better than six years, and though I knew it was a habit akin to getting back on a bicycle, I wasn't sure I could ride aimlessly. After hanging up from Martha Grainger, who was thrilled to accommodate us, I called David.

"Hey! How are you doing?"

"M-m-m, I'm fine. Little busy. How are you?" he asked, a bit absentmindedly. "What's up?"

"Well, I was calling to find out if you could stop by tonight, okay? Just for a few minutes. Mom and Dad are coming down to get a few things for Al."

"Sure. I'd like to meet them. What time?"

"Oh, about 7:00. Whenever."

I didn't say anything else.

"So...what's up?" he sounded wary.

"How 'bout we get away for the weekend?" I began.

"What are you planning now?" he asked, suspicion tingeing his voice. This guy was just too perceptive.

"Well, you know Alex is with Mom and Dad and they're going out of town, I figured we could drive down to Adobe Wells. They have the sweetest little bed and breakfast, and there are caves with petroglyphs and..."

"And – remind me – Adobe Wells is where Carla was talking about!" he interrupted. "No, Nia. NO!"

"But David, there has to be some..."

"NO!"

"But Isaac is in Miami..."

"Uh-uh, babe. We're not going, so just get it out of your head!"

Silence. "Well, okay," I finally said with a sigh. "'WE' don't have to go. I'll go alone."

I could hear him puffing. I waited. When enough time had elapsed and his breath had slowed, I said, "See you tonight and then would you pick me up at about 7:00 Saturday morning, please honey?"

"Nia," he whined, "after this, will you stop?"

"I stop if and when I find out who killed Frank. And I have to find out soon. I'm going to Adobe Wells this weekend. It's something I have to do, David, and I'm sorry but you just have to try to understand. Please, honey? Try?"

He sighed. "Alright, babe. I'll be there." And he hung up.

By the time I got home, Mom had gone in and prepared her very special deep fried catfish, potato salad, green salad, collard greens, and corn bread. Dessert was deep dish peach cobbler.

"Hoo, doggies!" I exclaimed when I walked in. "Girl, you been busy! Did you cook all of this since you've been here?"

"Oh no, sweetie. I cooked the greens and the cobbler at home and the rest since I've been here."

"Oh, Mom, you didn't have to do this. I was going to cook for you and Dad."

"Now you know it's not a problem. Go on in there with Dad and Alex."

"Oh! I forgot to tell you." I said as I got to the door. "David is coming over. I wanted you to meet him."

"Well, see? I didn't cook this special meal for nothing. Hope he likes catfish."

"I'm sure he'll like *your* catfish. He's a big boy who doesn't look like he misses many meals. I hope you guys like *him*."

"Well, I know Alex sure does. He talks about him all the time." Mom said, chuckling.

"I really like him, too."

"Lord knows I'm glad. You need somebody, and so does my little monkey." She was shaking her head and clucking under her breath.

"Oh, hush! You sound like an old hen!"

Dad and Alex were in the living room, Dad hunkered down on the floor beside Alex, the newsprint pad between them. They were taking turns adding to a new masterpiece.

I poked Dad in the ribs. "You better get up from there, old fella, before you hurt your back."

"You better get away from me, girl, before I hurt *you*."

I bent over and kissed them both on top of their heads. How are you, my man?" I asked Alex.

"Oh I'm fine, Mom. Look at these pictures of Zoë that Papa and I drew." Their model was jumping first to the sofa, then to the chair.

"I know you better get that hound off of my furniture," I told him.

"C'mere, Zoë." She hopped from the chair, landing squarely on his back. I left them in a giggling heap and went to my room to change. The doorbell rang as I was pulling on a pair of jeans.

"I'll get it!" Alex yelled.

By the time I'd slipped my feet into a pair of slides and returned to the living room, Alex had introduced his grandparents to David. He was smiling and shaking hands with Dad. My mother said, "Nice to meet you. I hope you're hungry, 'cause I made dinner."

"Oh, yeah! I can always eat." David licked his lips.

Mom told him, "I hope you like catfish."

"Catfish?"

Mom nodded.

"Deep fried?"

She nodded again.

"Booyah! I haven't had deep fried catfish in years. Bring it on!"

Alex had shimmied up his back like a monkey heading for bananas in a tree.

"Then let's eat!" Mom went back to the kitchen for the food. I walked past David and gave him a little peck on the cheek.

"Hi," I said.

"Hi yourself."

Dinner was delicious. I thought David would never put his fork down. I think it was a combination of his hunger and the fact that the meal was scrumptious, and either way, Mom nodded to me with a look of approval at my choice of men. After dinner, the boys went into the living room and Mom and I went to Alex's room to pack his bag.

"You guys keep me informed of your whereabouts, ok?" I was folding a tee shirt to put into his duffle.

"Oh, don't worry. We'll call."

"Call me on my cell phone anytime."

"Will do."

Dad bellowed from the front room. "C'mon, old woman. I want to get on the road before it gets too dark."

I zipped the mouth of the bag shut, handed it to her, and we walked arm in arm back to the boys. We all walked to the door and down the walkway. I kissed Alex's little cheek and told him, "Be good to Nana and Papa, Alex, because if I hear bad reports, you'll be old enough to drive before you get to go with them again."

"I'll be good, Mom," he solemnly nodded. "Do I have to go to school?"

"No, sweetie. Mrs. Roache said you can stay away until the next school year if you want, but you had better keep up with the summer reading. I put your *Little Bear* book in your bag, and Papa will get you more if you ask real nice."

Dad shook his head and pulled Alex off of David's back, where he had climbed while we all stood in the doorway. I kissed Mom, Dad and finally Alex, waved goodbye and went back into the house. David was in the living room, sitting on the couch and thumbing through a magazine. I plopped down beside him.

"Want a beer?" I asked.

"Sounds good."

Getting one for myself, I opened both, walked back in, handed him his and plopped down beside him. After a great dinner, nothing tastes better than a cold one.

"So...what do you think about my detecting?" I asked after a swig.

He sighed, drank some from his bottle, and said, "It does concern me that you don't seem to have a fear of anything. I worry that something could happen to you while you're doing all this investigating. Sounds corny, but can you be a little careful?"

"I am careful. And remember: I was a cop. I know how far to go, but this is important to me. And it's not because I loved Frank so much. I don't and haven't loved him for a long time – a very, long time – but I need to get to the bottom of this. You understand, don't you?"

He nodded in resignation, pulled me to him and kissed my forehead. I looked into his grey eyes as they closed. His kiss was soft and filled with longing. He wrapped his arms around me, and I melted into the warmth of his embrace.

His hands roamed over my back. They slowly moved over me, stopping at my breasts. He gently squeezed them, then began to kiss each one alternately. I nearly moaned with longing. His mouth moved back to mine, and we held each other as though we couldn't let go. I could no more remove my lips from his than I could move a building. His kisses were gentle, then fierce and I kissed him deeply, as though it was lifegiving. We came up for air and held each other, and he whispered, "Where is this going?"

"I don't want you to drop me if I say I can't sleep with you yet," I whispered. "I'm kinda scared of that, but I don't feel ready."

He didn't speak for a minute, and I really thought he was going to get up and walk out. We held each other and did not talk. Finally, he pulled my head down to his chest.

"Not going to lie and say I like that idea, but I'll reluctantly abide by it."

CHAPTER 20

David had kissed me passionately before he left, and I longed to pull him back in the door and race him to my bedroom. But I didn't.

Saturday dawned bright and clear, lemony sunshine coloring my kitchen, causing a glow in my coffee cup. At 6:45, the front bell sounded and I smiled into the last milky spoonfuls, glad that he had come, even though he really didn't want to.

"Good morning, glow worm!" I said cheerfully.

"Hi," he mumbled. Obviously, my brightness was not rubbing off.

"Would you like a cup of coffee?" I said to his back as he walked into the kitchen.

"On my way to get my own."

"Whew, you give some folks that proverbial inch, they walk the entire mile." I quipped. He turned and faced me.

"Let's not start this enterprise off on the wrong foot. I'm not happy about any of this, but, I love you, and a man in love

173

can do – well, some stupid stuff. However, don't push your luck. I am still bigger than you!" He turned and strode into the kitchen.

He said he loved me!

I couldn't stop smiling as we drove down to Adobe Wells. I tried to read my new James Patterson novel, but every few minutes I would sneak a glance at his profile as he intently watched the road while driving. He seemed so absorbed that I didn't have the heart to interrupt his reverie. I started staring out the window at the line of mountains that grew in size with each mile we traveled.

I've always loved heading south down the black ribbon trail of the Valley Highway, known by non-natives as I-25. When I was a little girl, my family made this drive at least once a month to Adobe Wells, to visit my great-aunt Patricia. My great-grandmother, Julia Marie Shaw, had been a cook and had owned what was referred to as a rooming house since the fifties. She had left her daughter, Grandma Angel, and great-grandfather Titus in Arkansas, and with other Black immigrants, went in search of a better life than the one offered in the south.

When she arrived, she made use of her skills as a cook. She knocked on the door of what would become her residence and applied as a cook and housekeeper that she'd seen advertised on the blackboard outside of the grocer's. Her skill in the culinary arts was phenomenal, and, after she had secured the job, Mama Shaw began her reign in the kitchen. Her first night there, she cooked the owner and boarders a meal of ham, black-eyed peas seasoned with generous slabs of pork, corn bread, peas and carrots, and a dessert of Apple Brown Betty. Every diner was said to have smacked their lips and licked the tin plates clean. From then on, she cooked for the railroad and steel workers living in the house, and any others who had heard about the goodness of her food. She saved every spare cent, requiring little to live on since she had a place to stay and food to eat. Her other duties were reasonably light: general housekeeping, laundry and changing the bed linens weekly. She soon had many friends and devoted her free time to her newfound church and reading, a rare ability for most Blacks at that time. Her employer, James Meekin, a blustery but kind ironworker was nearly as fond of her as he was of her cooking, treating her fair and with unheard of respect. After working for him for nearly a year, he came to her and announced that he was moving to Central City to mine for gold.

"There's still a fortune locked in those hills," he told her, "and I intend to get me some!"

Timidly, she asked him what he would do about the boarding house.

"Well, I'll probably be selling it."

She decided to make her bid.

"I'd like to buy it from you, if you don't mind."

"How much ya willin' to pay?"

Mama Shaw bid low, but within a price range that she thought he might go for. He pondered the sum, then his desire to be shut of Adobe Wells and move on to real money got the best of him. He told her yes. He would never know that she had saved nearly twice as much as she'd bid. He migrated to the mountains, sunk his money and his pick in a mine, squandered the funds she'd paid him and died in a mine accident later that year. With the help of her daughters, great-grandfather Titus, who had followed her later, and the members of her church, Mama Shaw had renovated the house and began collecting rent. Whites, Blacks, Hispanics and Asians had quietly lived side by side in her home, and after Grandma Angel had married and moved back to the south, and great granddad died in 1985, she kept the house and continued to rent the rooms. Great Aunt Pat, Grandma Angel's daughter, stayed and helped her, doing all of the cleaning but leaving the cooking to Mama Shaw. Everyone knew her and Aunt Pat, and even when Pat left to marry Uncle Jimmy, she still did not give up the house.

Unfortunately, in 1990, she fell one evening on the ice while going to church. Breaking her hip, she was confined to bed and Aunt Pat moved her into her own house. A cousin ran the rooming house, but it was not the same as when Mama Shaw had been in charge. Reluctantly, she sold the building to the church, and settled down to a life of sitting in the sun in the front room of Aunt Pat's house, which is where they found her asleep in death. We made the trip at least once a year to visit Aunt Pat, Uncle Jimmy and their son and daughter, Aunt Stacy and Uncle Jamie.

I dozed and didn't wake until I heard David say, "Hungry?"

"Umm..." I mumbled, rubbing my eyes. It was about 9:30, and we were on the outskirts of Adobe Wells. "I guess I am if you are. Get off on Manitou and head east." We were at the exit to W. Manitou Street, and I knew of a little restaurant at the cross street of Broadway and Cholla Avenues, just hamburgers and such, but I hit it every time I came to Adobe because they were the best.

David nosed the car up the exit ramp, got into the turn lane and made the light. After a few blocks, the little restaurant, a squat building that resembled an old-fashioned schoolhouse, could be seen nestled between two stately oak trees that were probably planted when Harrison Guthrie Mendenhall had founded the city. Inside, the air fluttered soothingly from the movement of a large ceiling fan, the luscious smell of charbroiled burgers mingling with the tart, cinnamony scent of apple pie. The waitress was a tall, rapier thin blonde with long, blood red nails. Her face was laced with a spidery web of wrinkles, decorated with an icing of thick makeup. The eyes were plastered with a shade of blue not seen since Elvis was a hottie. Pinned to her chest was a name tag which read 'Wilma.' She unbelievably wore stiletto heels and spoke in an enunciated whisper.

"What can I get you?" she murmured, smiling at David.

David and I ordered burgers with home fries and big, strawberry malteds. She smiled and the wrinkles around her mouth seemed to protest.

"Dessert?" she queried.

"Apple pie!" I chirped. She tortured the wrinkles once more and swished away to the kitchen.

David looked after her and whispered, "She's quite the looker, eh?"

"Be nice."

Within about five minutes she returned with our food. "Gee." David remarked after a big bite of burger washed down with a slurp of malted. "No one can ever accuse us of watching our cholesterol. Lunch for breakfast! Tomorrow, kiddo, we run!"

"Ok!" I burped.

After our meal was done, David paid the bill, gave the waitress a tip and his best smile and we walked to the car. I looked around.

"David?" I asked. "Want to go see where my great-grandma's rooming house used to be?"

"Sure." I'd told him about Mama Shaw as we drove up the hill to East Dorado Avenue.

"That's pretty fascinating. Are there many Black people in Adobe Wells?" he asked as we drove.

"Hmm...not that many. Mom grew up down here, went all the way through Mendenhall High School, and she was one of about twenty Black kids in the entire Adobe Wells school district. She did say that the kids were all pretty nice; said she was never called any names."

The site of Mama Shaw's home was now blanketed by a field of emerald lawn, large enough to play a ferocious game of croquet. The grass flowed down the hill like topping on a double dip of ice cream. When we were kids, Mama Shaw's had been the apex, topping a bevy of small Victorian gingerbread dwellings all of which were now gone. The area was now crowned by a home standing tall and insolent like a cabochon of pink pearl ornamented by flashing diamonds. It was an ultra-modern castle composed of pale pink, adobe-like brick complemented by a bevy of windows of different shapes and sizes, one set at the focal point: an octagonal, two-story chamber which must have served as a living or great room. Stylized spires and turrets poked into the sky, like fingers in the whipped cream of clouds. It was the size of an office building. The view from the upper rooms must have been really fantastic. It must have been breathtaking to look west at the panorama of the Rocky Mountains, and south, the glistening peaks of the Sangre de Cristos. The only items that remained from Mama Shaw's time were the magnificent trees – elm, maple, pine and aspen – which stood about in pairs or in threes, as though huddled and asking what had happened to the neighborhood.

"That's Mama Shaw's house?" David asked.

"Are you kidding?" I croaked. "That's where Mama Shaw's house *was*. They must have torn hers down. Whew! I haven't been down here in a while!"

"Nice neighborhood," he murmured.

The street wound up the hill to a fork with the fabulous house in the middle; a trail to the left wound around the front of the house and one right, wending past to the back.

"Go left," I murmured as David cut the wheel. "Go slow."

Doing as asked, we crept past the mailbox, a brick and glass sculpture with Mama Shaw's address and the name of the owners discreetly embellished on the side in inch high calligraphy letters: 2543 East Dorado Avenue and above that, GODDARD. We continued the equivalent of about a block in a normal neighborhood without looking at each other until we came to a street sign. In white letters on a field of green it proclaimed: ZOO, One Mile.

David whispered, "Ok...I think we have finally entered the Twilight Zone."

CHAPTER 21

I could tell David was turning the house, the zoo, and the city over in his head just as I was. Carla had said Mud Hut and what is a mud hut made of? Why, adobe, of course. She also said it was near the zoo. This had to be the Goddard she spoke of. We drove out of the neighborhood and down the hill. I realized we were close to the restaurant we had eaten in earlier.

"Pull in." I urged David.

"Why?" He asked dryly. "So you can go in there and start pumping the help?"

"Yup!"

"Nope. Time to go home." He started to pass the restaurant and I grabbed his hand, causing the wheel to jerk to the right. Luckily, we were alone on the street. He pulled into the lot, turned and glared at me.

"It's just that...well, maybe they know something about the Goddards. It can't hurt," I whined.

He was exasperated, I could tell. "Nia, when will you stop?"

"Soon as I find out what I need to." And I hopped out of the car, watching him from the corner of my eye as I rounded the front end. He shook his head and got out. Inside, the homey aroma greeted my nostrils as I greeted the waitress.

"Back so soon?" Wilma was pouring ice water into a customer's glass from a big silver pitcher. Her red nails looked like falling drops of blood.

"Well, we were headed to our hotel and decided to get another couple of pieces of pie for the road," I lied. Again, David shook his head, reached for his wallet, and looked at the floor.

"Well, pull up a stool and I'll cut you a couple of slices," she rasped.

"We were sightseeing around the area and came upon a big pink and glass house up on the hill..."

She interrupted me. "Oh, yes! That's the Goddard house. A simply wonderful, God fearing man! He owns Majestic Motors, the Algonquin Hotel in Adobe Wells, Arizona Smelting and Proteus Steel. He's probably the richest man on this end of the state." Pride glowed in her voice. "He's also one of the leaders in St. Martin-in-the-Fields Catholic Church. That's where I attend," she confided, smugly.

"Do tell?" I said. I would have thought she would be somewhat less than the churchy type. "I would just love to see the inside of that place. I work for Colorado Homes, you know, the magazine? And I would like to do a feature on the house, I mean, since we are here." I felt David's eyes roll.

"Well, let me see." She tapped the counter with the long, red nail of her index finger. "I could call one of the deaconesses, Mary Meade. She's good friends with Mrs. Goddard. And I know she would ask. Mrs. G. would be happy to show you around, I'm sure."

Mrs. G?

"Well, thanks, Wilma!" I said.

"Hang on." She glided to the phone on the wall behind the

counter, picked it up, punched the numbers and murmured into the mouthpiece.

"Colorado Homes?" David whispered into my left ear through clenched teeth. "Suppose the woman calls and asks if you work there?"

I whispered in his left ear, "It's Saturday, and if she does call, they won't be open until Monday. Besides, a girl I went to college with is a feature editor, and I can get her to cover for me. Stop worrying, will ya?"

Wilma came slinking back. "Mary said she would call me back after she talks to Mrs. G., but she had to run out and do some errands, so it could be a while. Tell me where you're staying and I'll have her call you."

"Sure. We'll be in Adobe Wells at the Red Apple."

"Oh, yes. I know the place. Let me get your pie and you can be on your way."

I dug around in my purse, found on old receipt, wrote the Red Apple number on the back and traded it for our pie. "Thanks, Wilma. We'll see you later!"

"Be seeing you," she murmured.

The drive was made in total silence until we crunched over the gravel drive of the Red Apple. David wouldn't look at me, much less speak to me, and I had a feeling I might have pushed his buttons one too many times. Unfortunately, he knew my goal and I wasn't about to change my operating gears at this point. Finding the killer or killers of the Carters, especially Frank, had become a mission.

We drove around the city, looking at the sights in silence. Finally, we found The Red Apple Inn, which was as picturesque as the web site had promised, reached by crossing a short bridge, which spanned a trickling stream. It gurgled and bounced over pebbles and boulders, happily taking advantage of the spring run-off. David pulled the car into the driveway and parked under an apple tree, no fruit in evidence but blooming with tiny white blossoms. He got out and came around to my side, opening my door then going to the trunk and getting our bags. We wordlessly walked to the door. The house was much more charming and much larger than it had appeared on the website, the roof edged in curlicue latticework, shutters trimmed in red and a brilliant, red door. On the door was a wreath made of twisted branches, studded with tiny plastic apples, and at the center on a small, hand-painted plaque were the words: The Red Apple Inn. David rang the bell. Within moments, a boy of about fifteen opened the door.

"Hi!" he said, his smile engaging. He was tall, blond and bursting with the health of a teen. "You must be Ms. Carter."

"Yup," I said.

"I'm Jason Grainger. Mom and Dad aren't here right now, but they told me to expect you. Come in." He stepped back and let us in the door.

Jason led us into a small sitting room, indistinguishable from any other small living room in any other ivy covered cottage, with the exception of the cash register, computer, and rack of brochures sitting on an antique desk in the furthest corner.

"Ok, Ms. Carter. Could I get you both to sign the register?" He brandished a pen with a silk rose fastened to the end, which I took and wrote my name and address. I passed the rose to David and proceeded to dig my wallet out of my purse. Just as I got my credit card out and proceeded to pass it to Jason, David snatched it out of my fingertips.

"I'll get it. You spend money like you had bundles of it," he growled.

"Suit 'cher self. I'm a poor little mama." I smiled brightly at him and he grimaced balefully.

"Ha, ha." His tone was mirthless and obviously he was in bad humor. When Jason passed the card back to him, he smiled, said thanks and tucked it back into the mouth of his wallet.

"Ok. I'll show you your rooms." He led the way, David carrying our bags, and me trailing behind. At the top of the stairs, he opened the first door to the right and motioned for us to go inside. Alice must have made her bed then ran out back to try to find the rabbit hole and would be in after her wonderland adventure. I was standing in her room. The bed was a canopied affair, covered with pillows edged with spun candy lace, a feature that outlined the white sheer curtains at the windows. A lace-topped hope chest was at the foot of the bed, and a braided rug in hues of pale pink, purple, blue and green was on the floor next to it. On every available surface was a Victorian doll – lying, sitting, standing – each wearing a pastel period dress and a large feather bedecked hat, each glass eye staring back at me. Pictures of halcyon fields, Victorian scenes, and more antique dolls in lacy frames decorated the walls completing a boudoir that would have made a six-year-old girl swoon with delight. I gagged and felt the need to hold back my lunch. This room was just too sweet.

I announced, "David, I will stay in here."

Without a word he dropped my bag on the chest. "Lead on, MacDuff," he said to Jason, and with a shrug, Jason took him out the door and across the hall. I peeked around the doorframe and ground my teeth when I saw David's room. It held a plain, sleigh bed tastefully adorned with what appeared to be a handmade quilt, a plain cherry hope chest at the foot, and curtains similar to mine, only without the candy. He turned and shot me a rather smug smile.

"I hope your rooms are comfortable." Jason walked back out into the hall and pointed. "The bathroom is the last door on the left and your towels and other toilet articles are in the hope chests. Call me if you need anything." With that, he smiled sheepishly and went downstairs. David motioned me in.

"I'll be comfortable if I keep my eyes shut. That room is so sweet, my teeth hurt," I exclaimed.

"Ah, now, and I thought it was rather, how you say, charming," David purred in a pitiful French accent.

"If it's so charming, you sleep in there!" I hissed.

"Nope." He threw himself down on the quilt. "This one'll suit me just fine, ma'am. In fact, close the door on your way out. I think I'll take a short nap." He closed his eyes.

I growled. "Ok. After we visit the Goddard's, we'll go home. Deal?"

"No reneging?"

"No reneging."

"Alright. Come over here and sit beside me." I went to the bed and plopped down. "I was just a little shocked to see that name on the mailbox," he admitted as he propped himself upon his elbows. "It was looking as if all this was just an exercise in futility, but, you know, I'm kinda interested in meeting whoever is in that house myself. Haven't seen a church going, upstanding citizen drug dealer in my life, even in my profession, and my curiosity is piqued."

"So...why don't we go introduce ourselves?"

"Not tonight, okay hon? Let's just hunker down and wait 'til the waitress/hooker...what was her name again?"

"Wilma."

"Yeah, Wilma. Let's wait until Wilma breaks the ice for us. Please?"

His eyes were pleading. I decided to concede. "Ok. I can wait until tomorrow. Want to go sightseeing?"

"I'd like to do something else." His smile was shy and sly at the same time.

"Jason's downstairs! Besides," I lowered my head and murmured, "I'm not sure I'm ready."

He sat up and hugged me. "I understand, sweetheart. I'll never push you, and I'm content to wait until it is perfect for both of us. When you're ready, I'll meet you in that dear little room across the hall."

"If we do anything remotely romantic in that 'dear, little

room' I might erp on you."

"I'll take my chances." He smiled, gently kissed my cheek and swung his feet to the floor. "Let's go sightseeing."

Adobe Wells is a Native American inspired town. In years past, its main industry was a steel mill and a mental hospital, but the hospital has closed, and the steel mill has competition in the form of a world-famous sex change, reassignment clinic. Although the clinic is discreet and the patients should have no fear of discovery, it is common knowledge that cures for mental illness is no longer the stock and trade of Adobe Wells. The mental patients have been shipped to other institutions if their illnesses are severe, or dumped on the city streets of Denver if judged functioning. It is not unusual to see shoddily dressed street people digging in the big, green trash bins on the 16th Street Mall. Most previous patients are identifiable not by their thrift store clothing but by their hollow-eyed stares. Some rave to themselves in their own mental seclusion, unaware of passersby, and most mornings find the Denver police rousting many from sleep where they had bedded down on the pristine lawns fronting the Civic Center, or the rolling green hills in front of the gold topped dome of the capitol building. The cops drive their squad cars onto the lawn, and then use their nightsticks to rap the lost souls to their feet. On cue, the street people slowly stand, roll the kinks out of their joints, and then shuffle off zombie-like in search of a dumpster breakfast. I always feel so sad to see them.

We angle parked our car on the main street, Conejos Avenue, got out and began to walk. The breeze that swooped down out of the Rocky Mountains was sweet and clean, and made me realize how smoggy the Denver metro really had become. Souvenir and tee shirt shops snuggled shoulder to shoulder with Mexican restaurants and Native American art galleries, all seeming to serve the needs of the variety of citizens on the street. We paused in front of a jewelry store, its window decorated with the gaudy and the beautiful. Some of the squash blossom necklaces were so large, a neck the size of a football lineman would be needed to carry the weight. In contrast, the displays of delicate, filigreed rings were breathtakingly beautiful.

"Want to look?" David asked me.

"Of course! I'm a sucker for a pretty ring."

A chime sounded when we entered, and the proprietor, a lovely young Latina came from the back and smiled as we approached the counter.

"You have some nice pieces in the window." David said.

"We're rather proud of most of them, although my choice has never been squash blossom," she said with a smile.

"I'm with you on that one," I laughed. "Could I see the rings in this tray?" I pointed to the velvet box beneath the glass.

"Sure." She unlocked the case and placed the tray on the counter.

I saw the one I wanted. It had an oval pale, purple cabochon of sugelite in the center, surrounded by a beaded edge. On either side were trilliant cuts of what had to be spiny oyster, the pinky orange a lovely contrast to the muted purple. It was very delicate and the setting was, of course, sterling silver. I lifted it from the tray and placed it on my right index finger. It was too big so I moved it left to my middle finger. It fit perfectly. Twisting it around, I looked at the tag for the price.

"How much?" David asked.

"Oh, it's only $48.00. I'll take it."

Before I could get my wallet out, David had presented the platinum Amex card.

"No," I said firmly. "You've paid for too much already."

He said, very gently, "No strings, ok?"

I looked up at him. He really is such a nice guy. "Ok."

She took his card, ran it through the machine then handed

it back. When the receipt printed, she handed him a pen and he signed, folding his copy and placing it in his wallet with his credit card.

"Thank you," the three of us said in unison, and we were back out on the street.

"Thank you, David." I placed my arms around his shoulders and on tip toes, kissed him firmly on the mouth. He tasted of cinnamon, a lingering sweetness from his lunch. He hugged me tightly and said, "Nia, I do love you."

"I love you, too," I whispered.

He took my hand and we started walking.

"It's funny, but I think I fell for you the first day I met you. Listen, do you believe in fate?" he asked. "Because I have never felt the way I feel for you. I've never told any other woman that I loved her, even when I was a teenager and had childish fantasies about love."

"Well, yes I do believe in fate or karma or whatever, and I always try to stick with my first impression. I'm usually right. I think I fell for you right off the bat, too."

He lifted my hand and kissed the fingertips. We walked in silence, looking in the storefronts. The sun was sliding behind the mountains, and I looked at my watch.

"Why don't we go back to that wonderful Mexican restaurant we just passed?"

"You know, I was thinking the same thing. I can't believe it, but lunch has worn off."

It was after I'd polished off my chimichanga, delicately seasoned with cilantro that my cell phone rang.

"Hi there. This is Nia," I answered.

"Nia Carter?" an obviously older voice of a woman asked.

"You've reached her."

"Well, my name is Mary Meade. Wilma asked me to call."

"Oh, yes, Mrs. Goddard's friend. I wanted to come in, take a few pictures of her house and do an article for Colorado Homes."

"So Wilma told me. I'm afraid Mrs. Goddard is out until tomorrow evening, but I spoke to the housekeeper, Mildred Reed, and she said that she would show you the house if you came by tomorrow morning about 9:00." Her voice held the same brand of pride in the Goddard's that Wilma's had.

"Hey, that would be great! Tell her we'll be by at 9:00 a.m. sharp, and thank you very much."

I closed the cell and looked up into David's face. He held his empty fork in mid-air and began to swing it in my direction.

"Well? You got the invite?"

"Tomorrow morning at 9:00," I chirped. "Great food, huh?"

"Fantastic." And he rolled his eyes heavenward and dug down into his food without another word.

CHAPTER 22

I had to bang on David's door to get him up at 7:00. He called out that he'd be ready in fifteen minutes. Men are so lucky that they don't have the morning rituals that women do. They can shower, shave, dress, and be out the door in fifteen minutes, while it takes us at least a half hour to be presentable. I wanted to look as professional as possible to the housekeeper, so that she would let me see all the nooks and crannies of the house, even the ones she didn't realize that she was going to let me see. This particular morning, it was going to take me at least forty-five minutes to look good.

I'd packed my Wonder Suit, a suit that I'd purchased while wondering if there could possibly be an occasion that I would not be able to wear it and look the part of the total professional. It's black, a silk skirt and jacket, knee length, which I always paired with sheer black hose and mid height heels. I always felt as though I was about to address the courtroom with my final speech on why my client was innocent when I wore it. It might not be suitable for a day at the beach, but for a day when I wanted to look good – this suit was the bomb.

My curiosity about Goddard and his relationship to Frank grew with every passing moment, and I was glad when David finally knocked. He had kissed me goodnight at my door when we returned to the inn, without a word about coming in for a while. I had a pea sized pebble of gladness that he had not come in, and a boulder of regret that I'd not invited him.

"Ready?" he said.

"Lead on, MacDuff!"

He shook his head, kissed the top of my head and took my hand. I had to giggle because he seemed so serious, although at this stage of the game, I sensed that he truly wasn't, after I saw the twinkle in his grey eyes. I knew it was the attorney in him. As we went down the stairs, we met one half of our team of hosts, Mrs. Grainger. We introduced ourselves. To the question about our rooms, we reported that they were wonderful, said goodbye, see you later and moved out the front door.

"Wonderful?" David was looking at me quizzically.

"Hey, I couldn't tell her I felt as though I was sleeping in a spun candy snowdrift, could I?"

Again, he shook his head. "You're a piece of work."

"Yup, and you love me!"

That brought a smile.

The drive over to the Goddard's was beautiful. I looked on the map and had David drive over Highway 47, which takes a direct route through the Garden of the Gods and also past my favorite house. Actually, the house is not what I was in love with. It was the landscaping; the decorations; the sculpture. I'd stumbled upon the house one summer afternoon while performing sightseeing duties for my aunt and uncle, in for a wedding, trying to find my way to Seven Falls, a place for tourist gawking and wallet diving. They loved that sort of stuff, and since I loved them, whether corny or calamitous, I took them to see the sights that were descended upon by the most "Looky Loos." They still had difficulty realizing that the number of bodies surrounding an object was not in direct proportion to the true value of the sight.

So, as we were on our way to Seven Falls, I'd taken a wrong turn, meandered down a two-lane road and ran smack dab into Wonderland. A modest home was set back on the property, barely noticed because of the "toys." Huge shiny, steel birds, two stories high, flew over the landscape, their metal wings glinting in the sunlight. An enormous mobile, the likes of which Alexander Calder had never dreamed, soared, twinkled and twisted in dancing partnership with the other sculpture. There were approximately twelve, two-story creations, all made of a brilliant, sun-catching metal, probably stainless steel. All were wind powered, and so precisely weighted that the slightest breeze set them in motion.

Besides the birds, many other members of the animal kingdom were represented, including an animated giraffe and a flying squirrel. The main piece, what else, a windmill, sat in the spot of honor, dead center of the property, holding minion over the other members of this extraordinary company. The appendages were so bright, they caught the light, threw it back, created warmth, and could not be looked at without sunglasses. Aunt Gladys and Uncle Robert were struck dumb from the sheer scope and genuine beauty, and even I gawked like a "Looky Loo." They took enough pictures to tile their Pittsburg walls, and after reading all of the literature on the project, we moved on to Seven Falls, which they both admitted was a major disappointment.

The awe that I'd experienced when first seeing the sculptures was mirrored in David's eyes. His lower jaw actually dropped, and he looked like a kid who had just seen a real dinosaur.

"Wow," was all he murmured as we circled the fence; the only sound the insect-like clicks of his camera. He took enough pictures to paper his big, lawyerly office. When we were on the road again, he asked me what I was going to do when we reached the Goddard's.

"Don't start worrying yet. I have no plans to storm the battlements, or whatever they're called."

"All I'm asking is that you don't get in there and clown so much that she's forced to throw you out," he said.

"Clown? Well, I'll be. Clown?!? Hoo, doggies! Don't worry. I won't embarrass you." It was my turn to do the eye roll. All he could do was smile. And, just about then, the house came in to view.

David drove up the wide expanse of driveway until he was opposite the call box. Massive iron gates barred the way. David gave my name to the disembodied voice on the intercom, then moments later, the gates noiselessly swung inward. David crept up the drive. On both sides of the meticulously groomed lawn, were sculptures; pieces of rather corny examples of sculpture, poor imitations of Rubenesque figures. The front door could and may have done duty at Camelot; it was that big and it looked that medieval. It fit the rest of the accouterments of the house. I stepped out of the car towing my purse behind me when I felt David lightly tug at the strap.

"Ok. Here's how we do this. I'll go along toting the camera..."

"No! You stay here!" I spit.

"Nope. You go – I go. I don't go – you getting this? You need a keeper and I'm taking the job." He was reaching into the backseat, fishing around for his camera.

I moaned and he shot me a look. "Ok," I relented. "I go – you go."

He shook his head in affirmation. He found the Nikon, came around and helped me out of the car.

"Can I at least do the talking and act like the boss?"

"I'm yours to command."

The steps up to the house s-curved, the door twenty paces

from the flat of the sidewalk. I rang the bell.

And nearly fainted.

The door opened and I came face to face with Suzy Mae Jackson, Gerber's mother.

CHAPTER 23

I was speechless.

"Good morning." She had Mrs. Jackson's voice. David poked me in the back.

"Uh, good morning. Mrs. Goddard?" I asked, inanely. "I'd been told Mrs. Goddard wasn't going to be in today?"

"No, no, she is out. I'm the housekeeper, Mildred Reed. You must be Ms. Carter."

"Yes!" I said a bit too brightly. "I came to see this wonderful house!"

"Do come in."

"Thank you, Mrs. Reed." I introduced David. "This is my photographer, Francesco Scavullo."

She nodded and smiled at "Francesco," didn't bat an eyelash at his name, then proceeded into the tour.

We were led into a foyer bigger than my living room and dining room combined. To our left was an all-white room, presumably the sitting room which could hardly have been used for sitting. The only touches of color came from the pale mauve sheers at the window and a vase of what looked like pink plumeria. David dutifully snapped shots from intriguing angles, moving more like what was seen on TV as a fashion photographer than one hired to shoot interiors. We moved on to the movie theatre, ten seats strong with a screen the size of four big screen televisions. The décor was overstuffed leather chairs, some covered in a mini zebra print, teak tables with, sadly, Formica tops, lending a somewhat warring atmosphere of chic meets trailer trash to what could have been a fabulous room.

What was of interest was the photo gallery centered between two floor-to-ceiling windows. There were studio and candid shots of what must have been the Goddards – shots of Mr. playing golf, Mr. sitting behind a desk, Mr. relaxing by a pool, Mr. shaking hands with the governor, the mayor of Denver, POTUS. All of the candid photos were of him. I then focused on the largest, most imposing photograph of the lot. Easily 2'x3' in size, it was a beautiful study of two beautiful people.

"Is this Mrs. Goddard?" I asked Mrs. Reed.

"Yes." She fidgeted a little then said, "Come and I'll show you the rest of the house."

I hesitated and studied the photo. Mrs. Goddard was a striking woman; long, thick hair the color of a sable coat. Her eyes were a beautiful, bluish green and her age was indeterminate, but she was a good deal younger than her husband. She wore a pale, aqua, obviously silk and obviously expensive dress, accented by a swath of matching silk scarf tied around her neck and draped to one side, secured by a diamond brooch (big diamond). Diamond earrings glittered at either side of her face.

Goddard was an imposing and distinguished man, and, in a word, handsome. He really looked familiar although I couldn't place where I knew him. Few wrinkles creased his eyes, brow or neck, and he seemed to have all of his own hair, a thick bush of silver with a compliment of darker strands. The photo showed him standing beside his wife, hand resting on her shoulder. His suit was well cut, impeccable, his tie a subtle geometric creation that supplemented the color of his bottle tanned face. They were the epitome of prosperous white folks, secure in their wealth and their position in the world.

Looking at the photos was interrupted when Mrs. Reed took my arm and forcibly steered me away from the pictures. She smiled thinly and said, "Let's continue."

"Is Mr. Goddard in town?"

"Yes," she answered abruptly. "He went down to his office."

Hmmm...

The remainder of the house was pretty much standard upscale domain – bedrooms the size of three sizable ones combined, with closets equal to a normal bedroom; bathrooms of the floor space found in a two-car garage; and a kitchen so spacious, a catering company could operate cheerfully and profitably. Though beautiful, the entire house had a thin veneer of questionable taste, apparent in a few corny touches, such as an electric brass candle in the shape of the Washington Monument. In a less auspicious setting, it might have been kitschy. Here, it was strongly out of place.

I didn't see any hint of anything that might connect anyone in the Goddard household to Frank or drugs; in fact, Mrs. Reed was as kind as her sister, and I needed to find out if she truly was her sister. We were in the family room, a bright and open, game laden environment – PS2 and GameCube games enough to send Alex into cardiac arrest – which seemed to be as good a spot as any to question the housekeeper.

I started cheerily, "Mrs. Reed, you look so familiar. So, do you have a sister in Denver?"

She looked as though I'd slapped her. "Sister? Well, I have a few relatives in Denver," she mumbled.

"Does she attend New Light Baptist Church?" I continued.

"Why do you ask?" she blurted.

"Well, I attend New Light and I'd swear Suzy Mae Jackson was your sister. She looks just like you!" I was smiling and looking as innocent as I could muster. David shot me a warning look.

"No!" she nearly shouted. "Do you have enough pictures, because I have work to do." Her demeanor had totally changed, and I could tell that the answer she was wanting from me was yes.

"Well, yes, I guess so. Are there any other rooms to see?"

"No." End of conversation.

David cleared his throat to alert me of the big man I hadn't noticed that had come into the room. He had slipped in when she had shouted, I guess.

"Do you need me, Mrs. Reed?" His voice was rather indeterminate, slightly high and a small step above a whisper, which did not fit his body. He was taller than David, wide bodied, with a face that was as incongruous as his bulk; handsome, delicate features, pale blond hair that was short and well groomed, and a nicely trimmed beard. He stood as a recruit might, hands behind his back, feet apart.

"No, I don't need you. Ms. Carter and Mr. School were just leaving. Would you escort them out?" With a nod of her head she turned and fairly ran into the kitchen.

David looked at me. I looked at him. We followed the man to the door. He opened it, stood back and both of us meekly walked out, feeling the definite breeze of the closing door as we left. When we got into the car we sat in silence.

"You had to ask, right?" David said as he started the engine.

"Drive, Mr. School."

CHAPTER 24

"What say we drop by Proteus Steel?" I asked David after we had cleared the driveway.

"Lord, have mercy Jesus!" he murmured. "This woman is crazy! Why, Nia, why pray tell? It's Saturday!"

"Mrs. Reed said he was at his office. I want to see this guy face to face."

David sighed. He scratched his head. He bit his lip. Finally, he said, "What's the address?"

Consulting my notes, "3942 E. Manitou, and thank you sweetie!" And I kissed his cheek.

When we arrived in the parking lot of Proteus, I touched David's arm and asked him to hold on for a bit. I decided to call Proteus to be sure Mr. Goddard was in.

"Proteus Steel," a cheery female voice answered. "How may I direct your call?"

"May I have Mr. Goddard's office, please."

"Just one moment..."

The line clicked, rang once and another voice answered,

"Mr. Goddard's office. This is Lorraine."

"Hi. I was just wondering if Mr. Goddard was in. I'm doing a spread for Young Colorado Republicans and Mr. Goddard will be prominently featured in our magazine this month. I wanted to ask him just a few questions."

David's eyes didn't roll this time. They bucked and he uttered, "Wha' the?"

Shushing him, I listened when she said, "Young Colorado Republicans? Why I'm not familiar with that magazine."

"Well, it's not actually a magazine. We publish for all of the Denver high schools, and Mr. Goddard seems like an upstanding Republican to have as a role model for us kids. I won't take but a few minutes of his time. Please?" My little girl, cheerleader voice came in handy.

"Well, he just stopped in for a few minutes and he has a tee time at the Broadmoor in forty-five minutes. If you can be here in about ten minutes, I think he could give you a bit."

"I'll be there in five, and thanks!"

I stared straight ahead, giggling to myself, then finally turned and looked at David. He was not giggling. He wasn't even smiling.

"Well, I had to get in!" I squealed. "Stop looking at me like that!" His face had slipped down from dour, and he looked like a father who had just caught his daughter smoking pot. Shock and anger held equal parts in his face. I ruffled my hair and took off my jacket.

"I'll be right back!" I said and then hopped out of the car before he could grab me. "Stop worrying, will ya?"

He turned to open his door. "Stay!" I ordered.

"Fine. But if you're not back in ten minutes, I'm coming in! Swinging!" He finished and slumped back, staring straight ahead.

Walking purposefully to the door, I pulled my pen and the pad I used to jot notes out of my purse. At the front desk, I got directions to Goddard's office. Riding to the 10th floor, I got off and turned left as the receptionist had instructed, and in front of me at the end of the hall, was a double oak door, one side open. I knocked and peeked in.

"Are you Nia Carter?" Lorraine asked. "My, that was quick!"

"Well, yes, I was just down the street." I lied.

"Well, go on in. He's waiting."

The room was huge, oval and impressive. One wall was covered in photos, much like his home, showing him with even more celebrities. His desk was the size of a king bed, dark wood with grey metal at the corners, probably Proteus steel. He stood in front of it, staring down at me. I still had a creepy feeling that I knew him, more, now that I had seen him in person.

The pictures didn't do him justice. Goddard was a big man, taller than David, and although old enough to be David's father, he looked nearly as fit. He was dressed in a flattering outfit of pale, blue polo shirt and khaki trousers. His unlined, what I determined had to be Botoxed face was topped with thick hair the color of fine platinum, combed back and expertly cut. He was very handsome, and his most striking features were his eyes – deep blue, the color of tanzanite, crisp, cold, and assessing. I hoped he didn't realize that I was not a high school girl, and with a thrill of fear, I hoped he didn't relate me to Frank.

"Mr. Goddard?" I stuck my hand out and smiled my most brilliant smile. He took my hand but didn't say hello right away. He stared.

"Hello, Ms. Carter," he drawled finally. His voice was like heavy cream, soft and rich. "Please have a seat."

Still holding my hand, he led me to a large round table, situated in front of a floor to ceiling window that looked out over the city. I could see David's car in the parking lot.

"So, what can I tell you?" He had leaned back in his chair and continued to look at me. "You're very pretty, and you look very mature to be in high school." He had steepled his hands and tapped his bottom lip thoughtfully.

"Well, I'm eighteen. I graduated this year from Grandview, in Centennial, Colorado, but I'd promised to finish this article for our little magazine. I've always looked a bit older than my years." I hoisted my pen and pad then tried to slump like a teen would.

"Hmm, Grandview. I'm not familiar with it. Well," he said, and put both hands on the table palms down. "Ask away."

I asked him how long he had been in Adobe Wells. "I've lived in the area since the seventies. The dark ages, to someone as young as you are." His smile was lascivious. I giggled nervously.

"What brought you here?"

"My aunt was ill and when I got out of the service, I came to help her run her company. When she died, I became the owner and built it up to what it is today." He was so smug.

"Did you ever live in Florida?"

His eyes took on a suspicious look. "No. I came straight to Adobe Wells after I got out of the service. Look, Ms. Carter," he said abruptly, rising from his chair and glancing at his watch. "I have a tee time in less than half an hour and I need to get to the Broadmoor. If you look on the Internet, there are many good articles about me. Just put in Ronald Goddard and you'll be sure to find them."

He had come around the table and put his arm around my shoulder, guiding me to the door. He gripped my upper arm tightly in his fingers. He had the overpowering presence of a bear, a large, fleshy, carnivore; his expensive scent pulsed in my nostrils as he held me closer than he should have. I pulled away and turned to face him, taking his hand and shaking it.

"Thank you for seeing me. I appreciate it, and I'll get the information as soon as I get back." I ran out of the door before he could say another word. I said goodbye to Lorraine and ran down the hall to the elevators. Just before I got into the elevator car, I looked back. He was standing in the door, smiling. He gave a slight salute. I waved back.

He looked just plain evil.

CHAPTER 25

The drive back to Denver Sunday afternoon was uneventful, although David felt the need to poke me when I least expected it to get me to smile even a little. He smiled all the way home. I managed to break his humor when I told him about the visit with Goddard. He was quiet for a minute, and then he said, "I hope you're done now."

I nodded. I really hadn't learned a lot from him nor from the house tour, but Mrs. Reed's reaction to my question about her sister made me wonder what she was hiding. In my opinion, and I think the opinion of most of the congregation, was that Mrs. Jackson was a fine woman and not a sister to be ashamed of. A long-standing member of the church, she had always treated me as though I was still in elementary school, probably because I was so small, and when I'd married, she'd given Frank and I our most expensive gifts: two Waterford crystal candleholders. The items were on my registry as afterthoughts, and I was fairly certain that I would not truly receive them. She said it was because I was the dearest child she knew even though it saddened her that I hadn't married her Isaac.

It was about three p.m. when we drove up my driveway. When we got to the door, David said, "I have a brief that I need to work on for a bit, but, want to go to dinner later?"

"My choice?"

"Your choice."

"Ok. Since Alex isn't here and I can dress up a tad, how about the Cliff House?" I said.

"If that is where you want to go, then that is where we dine. Pick you up at 6:30."

He kissed me gently, sweetly, and lovingly. "See you."

I went in, tossed my gear beside my desk and while there, checked messages. None, so I assumed no one had died while we had been gone, which was comforting. I decided to do the things I rarely got to do while my son was at home: take a long shower, have a beer, watch the NCIS episode I'd taped, then take a short nap with my Patterson in tow. I'd been lying there reading for about an hour, when the phone rang. It was Laurinda. She had just returned from dropping her dad's ashes off at Ft. Logan and was subdued.

"You ok?" I asked her.

"Yup. I'm hangin'. Mr. Goddard took care of everything."

"Mr. Goddard?" I whispered.

"Yeah, Sonny's boss. Why?"

I thought for a moment then decided to ask her. "Did Sonny work at a big old house a few miles from the zoo in Adobe Wells?"

"Yeah." She was whispering now. "How did you know?"

"I was just at that house today. Big, pink, ultra-modern pile."

"Yeah, that sounds right. He does live in Adobe Wells and how many big, pink, ultra-modern piles can there be in a town that small?" She confirmed what I knew had to be true.

I continued, "Housekeeper's name is Reed and I could

swear she was Suzy Mae's twin sister. Looks just like her. You remember Suzy Mae Jackson, Gerber's mother, from New Light?"

"Oh, yeah. I remember her from when we were kids. Nice lady." Laurinda was thoughtful. "What has she got to do with Sonny?"

"Where exactly did Sonny die?"

"From what they tell me, Mr. G. found him in the shed in the backyard."

"What kind of shed was it again? Tool shed? Garden shed?"

"I guess so. Something like that. What's going on, Nia?" I could hear fear creeping into her voice.

"I really don't know yet, but I'll be finding out."

We talked a bit more, then she rang off. I lay there on the bed then jumped up and ran to the computer. This time, I Googled and first went to the Adobe Wells Chronicle archives. I found the article about Sonny's death. It stated that he had been intoxicated and fallen on a pitchfork in the shed in back of Goddard's house (how do you fall on a pitchfork?). Mr. Ronald Goddard had found his body. A short article, it didn't seem to question the death at all, just take it for granted that the man had fallen, gotten pierced and died, all due to being drunk.

I then looked up Goddard and Adobe Wells. An excess of twenty articles popped up and I chose the one with a biography. A click on the hyperlink whisked to a picture of a man with an article beneath it. There was the photo I'd seen at their house. And the man I'd met that afternoon. I began to read the copy:

"Ronald James Goddard was born in Denver, Colorado on June 3, 1946, the only child of Michael and Jane Goddard. He attended Milton Elementary School, Carlyle Middle School, and was preparing to attend high school when his parents were killed in a car accident. He moved to Adobe Wells,

Colorado to live with his aunt, Judith Goddard. There, he took a job at a restaurant, washing dishes and waiting tables, while still continuing his studies at Mendenhall High School. Mr. Goddard was devoted to his church, and was active in sports, primarily basketball and football. When the call came for recruits to serve our country, he left school and enlisted in the U.S. Marines, completing his basic training and accompanied his platoon to Vietnam. Though wounded, he was the lone survivor of the massacre at Đồng Xoài, Vietnam. Mr. Goddard lived in a village outside of Saigon, trying to find U. S. troops in the area for a year while working alongside the villagers.

Finally, he was reunited with an Army troop in Saigon and returned home to Adobe Wells to help his Aunt Judith run her company, Proteus Steel. There, he met and married the former Edith Martin. He worked hard and built Proteus Steel into the largest and most profitable enterprise in southern Colorado. He became president of the company when his aunt died in 1983. He also owns a number of other businesses, including a car dealership and a hotel.

Tragedy struck Mr. Goddard in 1993 when Edith died from a fall. He married the former Miranda Rein in 1996. Mr. Goddard ran for city councilman and won with ease, receiving more votes than the other candidates combined. He then ran unopposed and became mayor of the city in 1994, leaving his political career in 1999. St-Martin-in-the-Fields Church is pleased to have Mr. Goddard as a member, which is where, in 1998 he began planning to build CenterPoint, a family oriented, religious center located in Adobe Wells. CenterPoint has helped to instill a sense of family and wholesomeness in the community and is nationally known for the work done to bring religion back into the mainstream.

After a brief hiatus from the political arena, he has been tapped by the President of the United States to serve on the Youth Council. The outlook is bright for this new venture and he is primed to lend his expertise to the benefit of America's young citizens and to the remainder of the world. We wish Ronald Goddard the very best in his endeavors."

I leaned back in my chair and thought about Mr. Ronald Goddard. Here was a man who, ostensibly, was a pillar of the community, a war hero and beloved by all who met him. I looked at the photo again. His face looked like one that had never had a cut from a razor, much less from shrapnel. I looked closely at his hands. Although there were a few liver spots, they too, were not scarred in any way. He bore not a trace of a scar from his war injuries. I pulled up as many pictures of Goddard as I could find, and those taken in 1974, those taken in 1987, and those from all years before and after up to the present were of a man with a complexion as clear as could be, considering his age. No scars. Dad had been in Vietnam for a very short time, and had been hit in the face with shrapnel from a bomb. His cheek had a scar that had turned into a keloid the size of my little finger, and his right leg bore a three-inch long scar, both still plainly visible. Maybe Goddard had plastic surgery, or maybe he was never wounded in the first place.

God, this was confusing!

With a sigh, I shut down the computer and went back to my room to get ready for my date. It was nearly five, and for the remainder of the day, Mr. Goddard could wait, but David couldn't. Nearly skipping to the bathroom, I showered, got out and slathered moisturizer on my face, picked my hair out, slicked on mascara, brushed my teeth, then went back to my bedroom. Panties and bra were fished out of the dresser and looking in the closet, I selected the evening's outfit; my one and only expensive dress – a figure enhancing, deep green peau de soie Carol Little, which I slid into. My jewelry box held mostly costume stuff, but it also guarded my one and only expensive set of jewelry – earrings and a strand of perfectly matched cream-colored pearls. I slipped the earrings into my ears, locked the necklace into place, then looked into my lingerie drawer, found and pulled on black, opaque pantyhose. My feet slid into a pair of two-inch, black, Evins heels. These items were B.M. purchases – Before Marriage. I bought them just before marrying Frank and still wore them since classics never went out of style. Standing back from the cheval, I had to admit it. I looked good!

Then I turned for a booty shot and looked down at the hose. A run the width of my little finger snaked all the way up the back of my right leg. Groaning, I tumbled through the drawer to no avail. I didn't have another pair of black hose. I had to have them, so I took the runners off, put on a pair of sandals and got my car keys.

I got to Marshall's within ten minutes and nearly ran back to the hosiery department. Thumbing through, I could not seem to find my size and looked around frantically for a salesgirl. Although he ducked his head and quickly turned away, I looked into the face of the man from Goddard's. He started walking away and I followed. He glanced back over his shoulder and realized that I'd recognized him, causing him to step up the pace and nearly run from the store with me in pursuit. He ran out the door and around the corner just as I reached the cash register. The cashier looked at me quizzically.

"Thought that guy was a friend of my dad's, but I guess not," I told her with a shrug.

I went back to the house. So, he was following me. The thought gave me a little shiver. All I could figure was that he'd followed us back from Goddard's home or office and now he must know where I lived. I beckoned to a salesgirl and she helped me find the right color and size and I walked to the cashier. She looked at me strangely, took my money, and said, "Thank you and have a nice day."

I didn't see the big man when I went out of the store, but I was sure he lurked somewhere in the parking lot. Once in the car, I swiveled my head nearly Linda Blair style searching for a glimpse of him, to no avail. He was gone. Turning the key, I started the car and drove back home, one eye locked on the rear view. No one was following.

At my house, I went in through the garage, making certain the door was down before I got out. Inside, I set the alarm then went from room to room and checked each window to be sure they were securely locked. Nothing was open, but I felt ill at ease and jumpy. I had to get ready to meet David since it was now nearly 6:20. The hose were pulled on with care, and though I looked to make sure no runs appeared, my assessment of my outfit was now perfunctory.

At 6:27, the doorbell rang. I peered through the peephole and saw David standing tall and handsome under the porch light, and I unlocked and opened the door with relief. His admiring glance told me the dress was just the outfit.

"The Cliff House awaits," he announced.

The Cliff House sits on a promontory on the outskirts of downtown. Long known for its superb food, service, and romantic atmosphere enhanced by the view of the mountains, it is one of the outstanding restaurants in the metro area. I'd not been there since my senior prom. We wound up the lighted hill in anticipation of a stellar evening. The waiter checked our reservations then led us to a table with a view of the Rockies, their beauty enhanced by the sun setting in watercolor swashes of dusky pink, violet, and pale blue. David smiled and held my hand. I hadn't told him about the man during our drive up to the restaurant, and decided not to. I could take care of myself, and since David was absolutely a worrier, I didn't want to burden him with unnecessary thoughts of the guy. When we were seated, the waiter came over with a wine list that David perused then we made our order.

The menu, in addition to food that is good for you, described marvelously sumptuous dishes from the four essential food groups: fatty, salty, sweet and sour. I did not know where to begin, but finally settled on, Peaky Toe Crab

Spring Rolls (Peaky Toe?) as my appetizer, a field greens salad, and an entrée of pecan crusted beef tenderloin with puree of butternut squash and caramelized shallots, haricot verts (I hadn't a clue of what a "haricot vert" was, but it sounded good) and sun-dried cherry port sauce. I then looked at the dessert menu that had my favorite chocolate suicide desserts – Chocolate, Chocolate Truffles Cake, and the ubiquitous hot fudge sundae. I chose Chocolate, Chocolate Truffles Cake. David liked the sound of my meal so much; he ordered the same, down to the cake. The waiter brought the bottle of wine for David's approval, uncorked it and poured a glass for each of us. I sipped and felt more at ease.

We didn't talk about Frank or death or our jobs, just his family, which brought sneers, and mine, which brought laughs. I ate like a little, brown pig. Dad would have said I was a shoat, moving on to the trough. As I was relishing the next to the last bite of my cake, washing it down with my second glass of wine, his cell phone rang. It was a client who had gotten his name and number from another inmate while residing in the county lockup.

"He says he needs a good lawyer – right now – to help him prepare for his arraignment tomorrow." He told me after he closed the phone.

"Then you need to go. No problem."

"You sure?" he asked.

"Sure. I'll catch a cab."

"Ok, sweetie. I love you." He had said it! He gave me a wad of cash, called our waiter over and paid for the dinner with the ever-present Amex, then kissed me and left. I sighed and managed to get the last piece of cake into my face.

At the front desk, I asked the hostess to call me a cab, and since it was such a nice night, and I needed to let my food move about, I decided to walk out and wait on the patio. Indirect lighting illuminated the garden and walkway, so I strolled around towards the back.

How he came upon me so silently, I will never know. Cats could take sneaky lessons from this guy. I felt the flat, circular pressure of what I knew had to be a gun in the lower left of my back, and in a panic, I wished that I'd left that last glass of wine in the bottle.

"Let's go, an' it'd be better if you didn't struggle or scream or anything." He whispered in his falsetto voice.

I'm no dummy. I knew what the "or anything" was: don't ask to play canasta. Clutching my purse, I went the way he gently persuaded, around the side of the Cliff House. There in the back, the unlit back I might add, was a big, old car. It had to be a '39, a '48 or a '52 Ford, Cadillac, Chevy, whatever. Old but even in my panic, I could see that it was beautiful. It was pale yellow, and I felt as though I had seen it somewhere before; definitely hump-backed in the way a '39, a '48 or a '52 Ford, Cadillac, Chevy, whatever might be. I knew it wasn't a Porsche or Lamborghini because the next thing he did was shove me not so gently into the yawning mouth of the open trunk. Those foreign jobbies don't have large trunks and I could have entertained Alex's soccer team in this one.

"Ok. Not a peep!" he said.

"I got it, I got it!" I whispered back. "Is laughing an option?"

"See how easy it is to laugh when I drop you off!" he whispered.

Man! This guy had the sense of humor of a spud. I settled down in my temporary home, worried that I would ruin my dress or run my new hose, banging my head on something very unsoft. It had to be a baby car that this mommy vehicle was giving birth to. I felt around for the baby's toy and was bountifully rewarded with a long, metal, very solid bar. It was a jack part, about two feet long and ribbed, which was a bonus, because I could grip it better. The heft of the bar sobered me up and I brandished it, waiting for the moment when it could get up close and intimate with the head, or any other part of my driver's body.

There was enough room to sit up, sort of, a little angled but not too uncomfortable. I kept thinking about Alex; what would happen to him if something happened to me? My son deserved better than to lose both of his parents in less than a month. No matter what, I was going to stay alive for my son.

We started off and pretty soon I got into the rhythm of the stoplights. He drove very fast. Racing the engine, he'd slam on his brakes when the light turned red. On each green he seemed to speed up, afraid red would wink before he got through. My head flipped forward then back, bumping the crown on the ceiling until I got the hang of the lights. I could hear when he got to the bridge over I-25. We had to be traveling south on Monmouth. When the light changed, we charged forward, immediately halted by the second light on the bridge. He started to drive more sedately, probably being cautious so that suspicious police would not stop and detain him. I had hoped he would make a mistake so I could start peeping.

He turned right after about two minutes. Judging from the time span, we had to be on Decatur. The next turn was a left at the base of what felt like a shallow valley that I knew had to be the DTC Parkway. Now we drove without interruption for probably three miles. When we crossed beneath I-25, I could hear the noise of elevated cars. We were almost to Arapahoe Road. On Arapahoe he stopped for the light, turned neither right nor left but instead continued down DTC. We veered left, then right, climbed the slight hill and stopped at another stoplight. This had to be Dry Creek. Down another shallow valley, up a little hill then flat for a while, then abruptly he turned right.

At first, I couldn't decide if we had made it to County Line or he had turned into one of the complexes but eventually, the road told me. Swoop down in a deep valley, soar up the high hill, and then immediately repeat. Swoop down, soar up. County Line! No street can make your car soar like County Line.

I remembered when I was a junior in high school, my "wild phase" my mother said. My boyfriend was my first and only rebellion, Lotter's Bad Boy, Jesse. Jesse Lotter had a Harley, and they have always been awesome. Suzukis couldn't hold a candle and Hondas possessed a totally different reputation than they wear now. The label "piece of shit" fit then as well as "solid" fits now. The only bike to come close was a Ducati. Now there was a bike. Jesse's buddy, Lucas, drove one, and we would race him and his girlfriend up and down those hills every Saturday night. Ah, memories, memories.

The blow my head received when we turned left brought me out of my reverie. The road noises were louder so we had to have reached Piccadilly Road. Piccadilly is dirt, and I could hear the gravel pinging off the wheel wells. That's when the real journey began. We must have gone ten, dusty, choking miles before he slowly braked and came to a complete halt. My eyes were stinging and my throat was sore from the dust I'd eaten but I had my weapon ready, poised between my knees, hopeful that he would assume I was a bit woozy, and not prepared for my attack. The key clicked in the lock and slowly the antique lid came open. With both hands gripping the knobby end of the jack, I came up with all my strength.

Bull's eye!

I caught him square beneath his chin, causing his head to follow my upward mobility. He went down like a felled tree. I climbed out of the trunk, shut the lid and stood over his motionless body. Leaning down, I put my head to his chest. Yep, it was still beating. I flicked the light of my penlight on his face. Yep, just as I thought. It was the guy from the Goddard house.

"Tim-ber!" I murmured.

Quickly scrounging around on the ground, my fingers located the keys where he had dropped them. It was murky dark, an iridescent sliver of a moon providing little illumination.

I climbed into the front seat of my wonderful new, old car, and locked both doors. Sticking the key in the ignition, I marveled at the contented hum of its engine. It was a convertible, and the top was up and locked. What a piece of work! Glancing over my shoulder at his still motionless form, with a shrug, I drove away.

CHAPTER 26

I drove about five miles north in the direction of Denver but had to pull off of the highway because I was shaking so badly, the police might have pulled me over thinking I was a drunk driver. I sat at the base of the off ramp then turned into a hotel parking lot. The tremors did not abate. That guy was going to kill me! After my initial fears for him, I had tamped down thoughts of Alex, not allowing them to creep into my mind while I was in the trunk, but now, I started to blubber in sheer terror with the thought of my son growing up without me. The impact of the reality was like a blow to the stomach. He had his grandparents, but I am his mother and I had vowed to be with him for the rest of his life no matter what. Sitting and shaking as though I had a chill, I felt along the dashboard found and turned the dial on the ancient radio, expecting to hear maybe Louis Armstrong since the car was so old. Instead, the speakers emitted the dulcet tones of Kiri Te Kanawa. At first, she calmed me then a slow eruption began. It started lightly then rumbled to my chest, scorching through my body then up to my mouth.

"Shit! Shit! Shit!" I screamed. "What the hell?"

I was not about to lie down and allow some unknown bastard to take or threaten my life! It was time to really get down to business. My first inclination was to drive straight to University Station to talk to Uncle Harold or one of the other officers, but by the time I reached I-25 and Yale I'd re-evaluated that idea. Uncle Harold would put me in lockdown, 24/7 guard and all that. Although I was still shaky, I decided to go home, change and go back to Adobe Wells.

By 9:30, I had a bag packed, and had changed into my black tennies, black tee shirt, and black jeans. The black hose was ruined, but the dress could be cleaned and used for another outing. I was about ready to go. I'd packed toiletries, a couple of days' worth of clothes, (didn't know for sure how long I would be gone) my laptop, and an extra power backup for my iPhone. Since I'd done a few sneak in - sneak out jobs in my time, I also included a can of WD 40, five large, plastic zip close bags in case I found something I needed as evidence, twist ties, and some rubber bands.

One more item. I rummaged around on the top shelf of my closet and pulled down the strong box I'd purchased precisely for the purpose and removed my gun. The gun was a gift from my brother Adam when I'd been accepted at the academy, a Glock 21 Gen4, sleek and matte black. I'd bought the strongbox, placed the gun in it, and put it up there as soon as I'd moved into the house. Alex had no clue of its existence and since the box had a combination and a padlock on it for safe keeping, I had little fear that he would be able to do anything mischievous with it. My gun had become just a memory from my police days, an item I hadn't thought about or felt the need to look at for some time, but given the circumstances, it was a necessary precaution, and I was not about to get taken down again. The bullets were in another smaller, locked strongbox also on the top shelf of the bookcases.

Returning to my bedroom, I loaded the gun, clicked the safety and placed it in the bag. It's a little more than eight inches long and fitted snuggly in my purse. Checking to make sure every door and window was locked, I set the alarm, picked up my gear and went out to the front of the house to my car. I'd pulled it out of the garage and replaced it with my new/old, what turned out to be a Chevy, making certain that the garage door was securely locked. I didn't think it would be wise to leave the hump backed wonder in front of my house.

By the time I passed Dry Creek, I'd sorted out a few of the ideas I had swimming in my head. I was going to interview a few of the Adobe Wells residents, to see just how fabulous 'ol Ronny Goddard really was. What had been nagging at me had to be nailed down. What did Goddard have to do with Frank? Was he the supplier or the salesman? How did Sonny die from a fall on a pitchfork to the chest at a fabulous home without a trace of hay for miles around? Did Isaac kill Frank? Did Myrlie and John really die from carbon monoxide poisoning? And... why was the Goddard "butler" (I called him Chevy, in homage to the car) attempting to abduct me? My theory was that either Ronald Goddard or someone in his house was not on the up and up, and, remembering his look when I was leaving his office, that someone could very well be Goddard himself.

I got my cell phone and left a message on David's office phone, sure that he would get it Monday morning, shout epithets at the top of his lungs at me, then worry for the remainder of the day. I had no intention of going back to the Red Apple, but instead decided to try a chain, a Best Western or Holiday Inn. I drove to Adobe much faster than David had, keeping an eye on the rearview for highway patrol cars. There was a Best Western on East Manitou Boulevard, which was centrally located, and would suit my needs. I arrived at the hotel, checked in, went straight to my room, unpacked all the stuff I needed for my night reconnaissance, and put it in the small backpack I'd brought for the purpose. It was only about

11:00, but I was pumped and still had enough heat in my gut to fuel me. I drove to Goddard's.

There were few lights on in the house, so I bypassed the big front gate and went to the back. Parking down the street nearly two blocks away, I jogged back up the hill to the house. The little shed where Sonny must have died stood hunched in a small grove of aspen and pines about fifty yards from the main house. There was a driveway, probably for service vehicles, that wound its way up the hill to the shed. In front of me was a gate used to wheel out the trash and wonder of wonders, when I pushed it, it opened with a gentle squeak. I quickly I reached into my bag, retrieved the can of WD 40, sprayed it on the hinges, then paused, listening to the night sounds. I was almost afraid to go in for fear that a Doberman or, God forbid, a large toothy Pit Bull, would come bounding over the grass intent on ripping intruders to shreds. I breathlessly counted to fifty, then pushed open the gate and continued up the drive.

I got to the shed and hunkered down, scouting the grounds, then looking up at the door. The mouth of the small structure was not secured, merely held closed by a hasp, no lock. I spritzed a bit of WD on both sides of the hinges, then the hasp. The hasp pulled up soundlessly. Grasping the right door, it opened without a squeak. By the beam of my penlight, I could see that the shed was as purported, used for gardening. Small garden spades, a hoe, a few shovels of varying sizes, and other gardening paraphernalia decorated the walls, and in the corner, bags of fertilizer and potting soil sat like dumpy old women.

The floor of the structure was dominated by a riding mower Dad would have sold Mom for; top of the line and clean as a whistle. All of the equipment fit the surroundings and nothing seemed to be out of place. I shined the beam beneath the tractor. There, on the cement floor, was a spot that had obviously been washed, probably to remove Sonny's blood.

The rest of the floor bore the normal detritus to be found in a shed in the form of dust, bits of grass, and leaves. Nothing seemed out of place and although I looked to try to find a spare peg that a pitchfork might have hung from, each hook held a utensil, and there were no empty hooks. I gently closed the door and replaced the hasp as it had been, carefully wiping the WD from the door and hinges.

Now, a decision needed to be made: did I stay under cover of the trees or make my way closer to the house? I decided to risk it. Down on my haunches, my stomach sliding along the dew-laden grass, I wiggled up the hill. I felt a sting on my left hand, looked down and saw a mosquito gorging himself on my blood. Slapping him hard, creating a dime sized smear on my hand, I crawled on. The castle was lighted in about three of its rooms, and the one I was looking in was what I remembered to be the living room. There were two people in the room, a man and a woman. I got my binoculars out and looked at the couple, and sure enough, there was Ronald Goddard. He was reading a magazine and seemed oblivious to the woman who sat on the sofa beside him. It was Mrs. Goddard, the former Miranda Rein, her hair and makeup perfect even at this hour. The huge windows were opened to let in the cool breeze, and let out the smoke from Goddard's cigarette, burning in an ashtray on a small table beside him. Mrs. G sat with her legs curled beneath her, staring at a television on the far wall.

I heard a car drive up and flattened myself to the ground. I couldn't see the front of the house, so I lay there and waited. The doorbell sounded from somewhere in the house. Who would be visiting at this hour? I rose slightly to look and moments later, in walked my Chevy buddy from earlier in the evening. The bottom of his face was an angry dark blue, almost black, his jaw hanging at a funky angle, and he looked as though he had run into a Southern Pacific barreling along full speed. His hair was seriously disheveled, and his rumpled clothes were still bearing the marks of the dirt from Piccadilly.

He must have called and gotten an Uber to get back down here so quickly. He haltingly spoke with Goddard, and I wished I could have been the proverbial fly on the wall. I could tell that whatever he was relating to Goddard was not taken well. Goddard's face flushed deep red from chin to hairline, and he shouted, "Get out!" Mrs. G. lifted her head.

I did a double take, not quite able to assimilate what was out of place. Finally, it hit me.

She had a slight, but definite, Adam's apple.

CHAPTER 27

Miranda Rein had not had an easy life. Born in a family of sharecroppers, she had started work in the soybean fields of North Dakota at a very young age and escaped the life of a farmer when she was seventeen. She was delicate, not hearty like her four brothers, considered the runt of the litter. She knew in the depths of her soul that she was not like her siblings; not meant to work from sunup to sundown, and the finer things in life were her destiny.

Armed with everything she owned in a duffle, including the precious makeup kit she had stolen from Sears, she hitchhiked across the country. In the beginning, she stopped for brief periods to work as a waitress in small, nondescript towns. She avoided any town smaller than her hometown of New Rockford, knowing that she could be herself, something she'd not been able to do at home. Her hair was dark brown, long and thick. She had beautiful eyes, which she accented with the tools in her kit. Her breasts, though small, were made large using inserts, and with padded, butt enhancing panties, her figure was made to appear curvy. When she started out in her profession, she found it easy to give a man pleasure with blow jobs, and it became her specialty, but the occasions did arise that she had to flee town in whatever mode of transportation was available, when the men realized after fondling her, that she was endowed with the same equipment they possessed.

Her goal in life was to find a man with money, who would pay for her sexual reassignment.

Mrs. Goddard looked like a model, seemed to have a great figure, but what woman has an Adam's apple? I took out the phone and made countless shots of her, the man Chevy, and Goddard. The camera was great, since it took fabulous pictures in situations such as this one with a limited light source. After the shout, the man hung his head then left the room. I clicked about ten more pictures then decided that I'd had enough. The camera was ferreted back into the duffle along with my other supplies and I slid back out. Once at the shed, I got up and hustled down the hill.

When I got back to the hotel, I downloaded my pictures to my laptop and started looking at all of them, blowing up those of Mrs. Goddard's face and neck. Yep, it was definitely not just a lump in her throat and proclaimed to all who were paying attention that she was a man. Something was wrong here. My guess was that she had been a patient at the sex reassignment clinic in Adobe Wells. How to find out. Okay, okay, I was a trained investigator. I could figure this out.

I'd thought I'd remembered everything, but I realized my portfolio was sitting on my desk at home in my office, so I had to make notes on the hotel supplied pad. What was my next step to finding out all I could about Mrs. G. and how did Mr. G. come to be married to her? I mulled the problem over in my mind. I needed a fingerprint from the wife to find out if she was Miranda Rein Goddard, who in a former life had been

Malcolm, Marcell or Mahmoud Rein. But I didn't have a kit to take fingerprints with. I mulled it over and then with a start, remembered that Barnes and Noble sold kiddy ones, used by parents to fingerprint and safeguard their children. I'd used one for Alex when he was two. They could be used in a pinch, so I could pick one up in the morning.

What was I thinking? How could I get back into the house to even get a print when Goddard, Mrs. Reed and the cretin Chevy were lurking around? Best thing to do was to wait until she went out and get one from the handle of the car she drove. Hm...risky but do-able. Hopefully, Chevy would be too under the weather to take her. Either way, I was going to be there.

Okay, so I had a plan of action. By now, it was nearly three and I decided that I was too tired to mull anymore. I got into my 'jammies and climbed into bed.

I'd pulled the drapes when I'd gone to bed, so the warmth of sunlight hadn't wakened me. It was after eight, and I had a lot to do. The shower was a goody; very hot and with a hard burst of water, perfect for smacking the sleep from my eyes and the cramps from my body, earned while crawling in the Goddard yard. I dressed in shorts and a plain, white tee shirt, sandals and my dark green, New Belgium hat. I was on the case and ready to rock and roll!

First stop was Barnes and Noble for the fingerprint kit. I couldn't find one like the one I'd bought previously, but I did find a scientist kit based on the forensics used on the program *CSI*. It had fingerprint paraphernalia, so I bought it and left the store. Next, it seemed like a good idea to eat, since I'd not had a mouthful after the Cliff House, and I was hungry. A bagel and cream cheese, whipped strawberry, and a large coffee was what I craved; Einstein's called, and I listened, but I also needed my potassium, so I got a banana. My cell phone vibrated a couple of times, but when I saw David's name on caller id, I decided to let him leave his epithets on my voice mail. He'd be in better shape if he didn't know what I was doing until after the fact. I also had a feeling that I was going to miss work, so I called Jason.

"Hey, Jason!" My voice was overly jolly.

"Not coming in, are ya." Statement – not question.

"Ah...well, I'm working on a case. Hopefully, I'll be in late."

"You have vacation time, so go ahead and take it so you can work on your 'case.' Ellen told me about your in-laws, ex in-laws, and I know how intense your need to know is." Jason seemed genuine in his backward compliment.

"Thanks, Jason. Yeah, I have to find out what this is all about."

"Go ahead and take the time. Forget about using vacation. You need and deserve the time off. Talk to you later."

"Gee, thanks again. I really appreciate it, and I promise, I won't be gone long." I said.

"No prob. But please, be careful."

We said our goodbyes, and I was glad I had an understanding boss. Jason was the only one who knew I was competent.

I drove to Goddard's house and took up my position down the street. The vantage point was exceptional, as I could see part of the front yard and all of the back and the garage. As a bonus, the position allowed me to see anyone coming up the hill prior to their spotting me, just in case Chevy or Mrs. Reed happened by. My little Beetle was just nondescript enough to blend into the neighborhood.

The wait had been less than an hour when the garage door opened and out drove Mrs. G., convertible top down, scarf around her neck and head. Most importantly – by herself. I waited for her to get a block or so ahead of me then started up to follow. She drove slowly, observed all traffic rules and was easy to keep up with. We turned out of the residential area, hit Navajo Avenue, and I had a feeling she was headed for the mall.

Turned out that I was right. Her destination was the Solaris Mall on the east side of town. Solaris is a sprawling mall with all of the best stores. There's a Macy's, a Nordstrom, Eddie Bauer – all my favorite stores when I have chump change in my pocket. In addition, there is a Lord & Taylors, a Prada, and a Louis Vuitton. Perfect upscale stores for the wife of an executive to shop.

She drove directly to valet parking, and two young men smiled in unison at the customer they obviously knew. She climbed out of the car. She wore a short skirt, sandals and, I could see when she moved her scarf, a white sleeveless turtleneck. She pointed to a spot; one of the boys looked, nodded his head and got behind the wheel. He put the car in a space under the cement canopy to keep the sun off, raised the top, then got out, hit the automatic locks and walked back to his post. The metallic "beep" was audible, and I heard it as I pulled into a space to check out the surroundings. There wasn't a clue to how much time I had before she came swirling back out, but I felt that I needed to work fast. The fingerprint kit would pick up the valets as well as hers, but I could weed them out when I returned to my office. The two boys were not going to be too much of a problem since both of them were enjoying the fine day and the parade of fine young women in shorts and midriff baring tops. The smiles on their lips were pulling back far enough to show eyeteeth.

Her car was two aisles over, and in between were a number of minivans and SUV's, the bulbous bodies offering a screen to hide my exploits. Not a soul was in sight, so I got out of my car and slipped between the other vehicles, until I was at the driver's door. I plastered the tape on the handle, pulled it, stowed it away then did the same on in two places on the doorframe. Glancing up, I noted that the boys were still flirting and smiling, and I had to give thanks to the sunshine for bringing so many little cuties to the mall.

Job complete, I climbed into my car. My next stop was Majestic Motors. Turned out that Majestic sold Mercedes and Porsche. The bright, new vehicles winked in the afternoon sun, clean and ready to hit the asphalt. Impeccably suited salesmen (the official uniform appeared to be a burgundy blazer, sky blue pinstripe shirt and khaki slacks) were helping customers; quite a few considering it was a Monday afternoon. I walked up the stairs of the entry, shaded by a blue awning, and went into the store. To my left was a gorgeous silver CLS Mercedes. On the right was a fabulous silver SL 500 roadster, and holding center stage was a black Porsche like David's – a 911 Carrera 4S Cabriolet. I looked at the discrete sticker closely and realized that it couldn't be the same model as David's. The doggone car was $133,000, and I knew David was not stupid enough to pay that kind of money for a car. At least I hoped he wasn't. Looking around at Goddard's establishment, I thought: this guy really *was* rich.

To the right of the front door was a reception desk, guarding about ten glass-fronted offices. I walked up to the perky young woman behind the desk.

"Hi there," I said. "I have an appointment to see Mr. Goddard at 2:00." I glanced at my watch. It was 1:57 p.m.

"Hi!" she chirped. She was as cute as the proverbial button (were buttons really considered cute?), cheerleader-perky and as vacuous as a beauty queen. Dim light glowed behind her blue eyes and she looked puzzled, cocking her head, first left then right, looking totally like a baby sparrow stalking a bug.

"Mr. Goddard isn't in."

"Are you his AA?" I asked.

"Mmm-hmm. I work here at the front desk and for him when he needs me." She was so energetic she made me tired.

My turn to cock the head left then right. "Really? But I called this morning, and he said he would be in the dealership today. I wanted to talk to him about that silver Mercedes."

She stared up at me, her blue eyes anxious and sympathetic. "Oh? Well can one of the salesmen help you?"

"No, no. Mr. Goddard is a friend of my dad's, and he told me to come in anytime and he would help me personally. Does he have a cell?"

"Oh, Mr. Goddard would fire me if I gave anyone his cell number," she whispered.

"Ok." I sighed and looked around the room. "I'll hang out here a while and look at the cars. This is a beautiful dealership," I said.

"We're proud of it. Want to give me your name and I can call him?"

"Naw, don't bother. I can talk to him later. Thanks though."

I wandered outside and looked at the cars. I looked up and saw the service area and decided to go ask a few questions of the help. Peeking into the large bay doors, it looked like any other car repair center. Steel items and paraphernalia of all shapes and sizes hung from the walls and stuck out of metal, coffin-like toolboxes, ready to heal the waiting engines. I opened the side door. I was the only customer, and an attendant greeted me as I entered. I told him that I was from the Chronicle, doing an article on Mr. Goddard, and he reminded me of Wilma at the restaurant.

"Oh, Mr. Goddard is a great boss, best I've ever worked for." He was as gushy as Wilma had been. "He gives us the best insurance in the industry, and we have great vacations. He even lets us use his condo in Aspen in the winter, free of charge."

I could see that he was not going to say anything bad about the guy so I thanked him and headed out. No one had a rotten word about Mr. Ronald Goddard. I decided to go back to my hotel.

Traffic was light and I was back to my hotel inside of ten minutes. I entered all of my notes into the laptop then sat for a long time running what I knew and what I didn't know over in my mind. Finally, realizing that I was hungry, I changed and went downstairs and had a great dinner of grilled chicken and Caesar salad. I went back to my room, read a little Patterson then turned the light off at about nine and went to sleep.

Again, I slept late and didn't get on my way back to Denver until one in the afternoon. I gave myself a mental head slap, jumped up, showered, packed and checked out of the hotel. I stopped at another Einstein's, and I knew I should get out of Goddard's town as quickly as I could.

"Morning, morning." I chirped as I strolled to my office, duffle over my shoulder. I'd transferred my gun to the compartment with my spare tire, deciding that bringing it into the office would not be a good idea. I was sitting at my desk when the door opened, and Ellen strolled in.

"Morning?" she asked.

"Well, I've only missed it by an hour or so." I glanced at my watch. It was a bit after 2:00 in the afternoon. "I had a few things to finish before I came in, but I showed up. Proud of me?"

"Oh, yeah. Real proud."

"Hey, do me a favor. I need to process some prints, so would you get me a kit?"

"Sure. I was on my way out, but I'll get it for you. Whose prints did you get?"

"Not sure, but I'll know as soon as I run them, and if you're on your way out, don't worry about it. I'll get it myself."

"No problem. I'll be right back." She turned and left my office, returning within a few minutes with a processing kit. She smiled, shook her head and turned to the door.

"What?" I asked, palms in the air.

"Nothing. You are Nia Carter, a soul in need of serious observation, but I'll just wait to see if anything happens to you then jump in and save your sorry butt."

"I'm okay. I just have a bunch of things to do."

"Right," she said without enthusiasm. "I'll tell you see you tomorrow, 'cause I figure your head will be down the rest of this afternoon." She went out and closed the door behind her. The phone rang and I picked it up. It was Jason.

"Came in anyway, huh?" he asked.

"I need to process some prints. I'll be here a while, okay?"

"Like I told you, girl. Do what you need to do."

"You are a fabulous boss. Can I take you to lunch next week?" I asked.

"Your treat?"

"Would I ask you, then make you pay?"

"Yes."

"Next week, buddy. Save me a day." I heard him chuckling as I hung up.

I processed the prints and got them ready to take downstairs to the lab. Since we did so many fraud investigations, our lab was fairly well equipped – blood analysis, fingerprints, background checks – and other necessary equipment for tracking insurance fraud. I checked the prints against the database. The first set came up and identified the owner as Jared Congley, whose birth date was listed as 04/17/05. He was too young to be Goddard's wife.

I slipped in the second set and waited. Moments later, the screen came up with her driver's license. Mrs. Goddard was born on January 23, 1983. Hmm...quite a bit younger than her husband. Maybe I could find something if I cast my net a bit further. I decided to do a nationwide search, which would take a bit of time, so I input the data then strolled out in the hall to the vending machines and bought a soda. A couple of folks I knew from the car insurance division stood there, loitering in the hall, so we struck up a conversation about new cars. They knew I had lost my car to bad driving and gave me pointers about what I needed in my next vehicle. Ten minutes passed, filled with helpful information, then I excused myself and went back to the room.

By the time I got back, the screen had gone dark. I jimmied the mouse and was gratified to see the screen come up with the happy words 'MATCH FOUND." Hoo, baby! I looked at what had been hatched and felt gratified. Lucky for me, she had been picked up on a pandering charge in New Mexico, so her prints were in the nationwide database. The birth date matched.

Although I'd been incorrect in assuming her former name had been something like Mahmoud Rein or something else with an "M," I was not too far off the mark. The name had been Michael Rein. Well, maybe a little off the mark. Maybe she'd had monogrammed towels and hated to waste them. I clicked on the icon for the picture, and there, in living color, dull brown hair, a patchy growth of beard on his cheeks and chin, sullen expression and minus the diamonds, was Mrs. Miranda Rein Goddard with Adam's apple intact. There was no mistake. This was the wife, and as I absentmindedly scratched the bug bite on my hand, I decided this was probably the reason Frank had been killed. A pillar of society would be hard pressed to explain why he had a wife that had formerly been a man.

So, identity had been established. But where did Gerber fit in all of this? And why were the Carters killed? Back to my office. At my desk I listed out my cast of characters:

- Darlene – deceased
- Frank – deceased
- Mr. and Mrs. John Carter – deceased
- Sonny Hickman - deceased
- Ronald Goddard – drug lord and the rich employer of Chevy and Mrs. Reed?
- Miranda Goddard – wife of Ronald Goddard and transgendered
- Mrs. Mildred Reed – housekeeper and twin sister of Suzy Mae Jackson
- Chevy – Goddard henchman
- Suzy Mae Jackson – Isaac's mother?
- Isaac Jackson – DEA agent, drug lord and murderer?

When I read what I'd written, a prickling began on my

mosquito bitten hand. It rose up my arm. It advanced to my shoulder then scooted throughout my body. I got up and started to scratch and pace. I started to jig! I whooped!

I HAD IT!

Or so I thought.

CHAPTER 28

When I'd calmed a bit, I thought about what I knew and realized I still had a few loose ends. I still needed to find out more about what Goddard's place was in all of this. I had no fingerprints for him, and nothing with which to trace him.

And then it came to me. Goddard had told me how.

I hurriedly collected my stuff, turned off my computer, then closed and locked my door. The office was fairly empty, so I bade the stragglers goodbye and headed home.

I drove back home, checked to be sure no one had tampered with my house during my absence, took a shower and hit the sack. Early next morning, my destination was the Denver Federal Center. The Denver Federal Center is a big, old, red brick building that has looked the same inside and out as long as I can remember. It is the repository for a wealth of information, and I was sure what I was seeking would be there. I signed in at the desk, was given directions to the room that I needed, and brusquely sent on my way. The room looked like an ordinary library, overstuffed and a bit dusty, and I wasn't surprised they had microfilm machines that were very old. I sat down to the green screen of the computer, also rather antiquated, and typed in the name. Writing the source file on the slip of paper, I navigated the aisles till I found the can I needed. It slipped into the old microfilm machine like a well-worn puzzle piece, and after spinning the wheel a few times, I found the document I needed: Ronald Goddard's military discharge papers.

I made copies of all of the pages then retrieved them from the printer. A corner table was vacant. Heck, most of the tables were vacant so I sat down beneath the diminished lighting, and began to read. The first page was the official discharge stating the gratitude of the nation and so on and so forth. Pretty standard but he had indeed been in Vietnam. The next was Ronald Goddard's military record. He'd earned a sharpshooter's medal and a couple of other nondescript awards. No Purple Heart. No mention of wounds. Next was a page of his vitals and here is where I stopped.

It said Ronald Goddard had been born in Ruskin, Kansas. His webpage had said he was born in Denver. He hadn't been wounded, and he had been born somewhere else.

Maybe Ronald Goddard was not Ronald Goddard.

I folded the discharge papers and put them in my duffle. I needed to go to Kansas.

CHAPTER 29

Kansas is a place that had never held my interest and the idea of going was a bit distasteful. As I'd once heard a comedian say, if the entire state of Kansas was blown up, the rest of the U.S. would never know it and would never miss it. Nonetheless, I logged in and signed up for a buddy pass. Khari could kick my butt later for using so many of his passes, but right now that was a secondary concern. I listed myself on the next flight from DIA to Wichita Municipal Airport and a return flight leaving about six hours later to come back to Denver. The flight left at 11:00 a.m., so I hightailed it out of downtown and arrived at DIA by 9:30.

While waiting for my name to be called for standby, I looked at the map. Ruskin was about a hundred miles from Wichita, so I was going to need a car. Renting should be easy, and I could see no need to call ahead. How many businesspeople went to Ruskin, Kansas and required a rental?

My name was the first one called, since I was the only one waiting as a standby, so I was able to get a first-class seat. I stowed my duffle in the overhead, sat down in my seat, and nodded to the only other passenger in first class. We took off and by the time we must have reached altitude, I was asleep.

The flight only took about an hour and a half, and when the flight attendant gently shook my shoulder, we were on the ground. The rental agency was easy to find, and after getting a mid-sized, blue Ford I got a map and directions from the information booth and was on my way to Ruskin.

Kansas truly, seriously, is flat and truly, seriously, is boring. All dirt and few trees, I had trouble remembering when I'd last driven such a lackluster stretch of highway. I was in Ruskin within no time, owing to the lack of traffic once I'd gotten out of Wichita. My plan was to check public county records for the Goddard family, then get out of town. Everything I needed to know would probably be in those files. The little town made me think of the Andy Hardy films I watched on TCM; it was sleepy, nondescript and actually, would not have been a bad place to grow up. The library was the first official building I spied when I drove up, and I decided to stop first and look at yearbooks. Worth a shot.

It was a brick building of fairly modern design. When I got inside, I found that it was small but surprisingly airy with computers and everything. Technology had definitely come to the heartland. I asked the first librarian I met if they had yearbooks on file for the high schools.

"Why, of course! There's only one: Ruskin High School." She was also a bit of a surprise. Young and African American. So Black folks lived in the little town, too.

She led me to the bookcase holding what would be considered a meager total of books if they were compared to the ones from a Denver school.

"How far back do they go?" I asked.

"Well, let's see." She started tapping her jaw with her index finger then said, "I think Ruskin High School was opened sometime around the turn of the century, last century," she added with a smile," and they started yearbooks around ten years later. What years would you be needing?"

"Oh, I think from around '80 to about '90." I answered.

She went to the stacks and ran her finger along the bindings, finally selecting five books.

"This should start you off, and if you need any prior or subsequent years, just look here." She showed me where she had removed the volumes.

"Copier's over there," she pointed to a nice copying machine, "in case you need a copy of a picture. These cannot be removed from the library."

"Thanks," I said. "You've been very helpful."

"Fine, then call me if you need anything else." She smiled and went back to her filing.

Carrying my load to a table in the corner, I began to look for Ronald Goddard. I thumbed through countless pages and found interest in the old photos of the class king, football and baseball, and thespian clubs. The pictures had faded over the years but were still in good shape and gave a good account of small-town life. All of the kids looked wholesome, not a Mohawk or mullet in the bunch, and I laughed to myself for even considering the idea.

Sure enough, in '63, I hit gold. Here was his senior class picture. Although he bore a strong resemblance to the Ronald Goddard I'd seen, albeit, about fifty years younger, the one I'd met was not the one in this photo. This kid had a stronger, more prominent jaw, beautiful teeth and very square, unsloping shoulders. His hair was thin and brown; his adolescent cheeks devoid of beard and marked by a score of pimples wanting concealment by Clearasil. Rather good looking, nonetheless, but not as handsome as he would have grown up to be. And, at this point, I was certain he had not progressed far past this photo.

This Ronald Goddard was dead.

CHAPTER 30

I took the yearbook to the copier and placed it on the screen, noting that a dime was not needed for a copy. I copied that picture and one I'd found in the sports section - a real gipperish, knee up, left hand out, right hand clutching the football, pose – that showed his smiling, teenage face. I put all of the yearbooks back on the shelf, and when I passed the librarian, I asked her if I owed for the copies.

"Ten cents each," she said and held out her hand. I guess capitalism did extend to Kansas.

Handing her the change, I asked, "Where is the Hall of Records? I need to get a copy of a birth certificate."

"Just keep heading north on Ruskin Avenue and you'll see it on the right side of the street. Big, gray stone building."

I told her thanks and went to my car. I looked down the street and saw the building. It was less than a block away, so, putting my copies in the car, I walked to the hall of records. Once inside, I asked directions and found a copy of Ronald Goddard's birth certificate with relative ease. The birth certificate had the address young Ronald had gone home to, and his parent's names were Hannah and Joshua, not Michael and Jane. The phony Goddard had obviously not done his homework. I looked in the death records and found that Hannah had died in 1968, Joshua in 1969. I copied the birth certificate and the death certificates. These copies also cost a dime each, and I paid the clerk and got a receipt – for thirty cents! Cracked me up.

Since my flight back to Denver was about four hours away, I decided to see the sights of Ruskin and visit Ronald's home. 134 Pine was easily found when I asked the clerk for directions. Two blocks over, one block down and I'd find a white, clapboard home. I went back to my car and drove the distance. The present owners were a family by the name of Jenkins. The house again made me think of Andy Hardy, even had a big tree in the front yard, and I decided that Ronald had probably lived a reasonably pleasant life, even though he had lost his parents at such a young age.

I left the house and drove back to the main street, found a Denny's, went in and ordered the big breakfast, minus eggs, and enjoyed every morsel. Nothing else to see, nothing else to do, I drove back to the airport, dropped the car off, went to the gate, checked in and waited for my flight.

I was back in Denver by 6:00 p.m.

CHAPTER 31

When I got home, I put the car in the garage then walked the perimeter to be sure all was secure, and I almost missed it. Beneath Alex's bedroom window, my rose bushes were crushed. There in the dirt was a large, man's footprint. I shuddered a bit, then went back and got my gun out of the trunk. After turning off the alarm, I cautiously entered the house, carefully searching each room and anywhere that could serve as a hidey-hole. Satisfied that the intruder had not gotten in, I set the alarm, put away my stuff then sat at the desk and looked over the copies I'd made in Ruskin. I opened my laptop and went back to the Goddard site. The young, true Goddard really didn't look like the old, phony Goddard, but as I'd thought, the resemblance was slight. They were the approximately the same age, similar build and could have been taken for brothers. Since he obviously was a phony, what was his real name? I needed to check the Denver records, and hopefully, since it said that he had been born there, I might get lucky and find a birth certificate. I'd have to wait until the next day to go the City and County and check for a birth certificate for the phony.

My other destination for the next day was in town – my cousin Chuck's house.

Chuck is a guy who saves nearly everything. He can, given a reasonable amount of time, lay his hands on most toys that he had as a child or the football he won with in middle school. His blue minivan was out on the street when I drove up, so I sighed with relief for one hurdle crossed. When I rang the bell, he came within a minute, calling out, "Hold on!" as he made his way to the door.

"Cuz!" he shouted when he saw me. He bundled me up in his arms and lifted me right off of my feet.

"Chuck-ie!" I squeaked. "How ya doin'?"

"I'm fine! Fine! What brings you into my neck of the woods?" he asked when I'd regained my footing. He closed the door.

"I need your help."

"Always here to give it, cuz."

His enthusiasm is wonderful, and he truly is ready to help out whenever anyone requests something of him. His bald head was shining in the overhead lights as brightly as his even, white teeth.

"C'mon in."

I followed him into his living room, which was strewn with papers, books and other paraphernalia. Neatness was not his strong suit, but he more than made up for it with his fabulous brain. Chuck is a freelance computer geek: doing searches for an odd assortment of clients using the Internet, writing customized programs for anyone who can afford him, tracking the bugs in others' programs, and in addition, taking care of my uncle and aunt in a finer fashion than they could ever afford on their retirement pay. Most of the money he earned, and it was a sizeable sum, was given to them and the charities he loved. Chuck lives a life of self-imposed poverty with occasional backslides into collecting Hot Wheels. Their little chrome grills grinned from every available shelf and were the only dust free items in his house. He kept nearly everything, but Hot Wheels were his passion.

After hustling into the kitchen to pour me a cup of Earl Gray tea, the only beverage he drank, he settled down and asked me, "What can I do for you, cuz?"

"Do you have your yearbooks from Gilbert High?" I knew the answer.

"Course I do. What years?"

"Which year?"

"Yeah. I need to know, 'cause I have all of our yearbooks – mine, Danny's, Bobby's and Pooh's." Pooh is my cousin Christine and his younger sister.

"Ah...I think yours and Bobby's should do it. I'm looking for a person who attended Gilbert in the late eighties or early nineties, say about '87 to '93."

"Um...that'd be me. Hang on." He cleared a space on the table and put his teacup down, disappearing into the hallway leading to the basement. I got up and looked at his Hot Wheels and was not even a third through them when I heard him clomping up the stairs.

"Here ya go. Who you looking for?"

"Isaac Jackson."

"Ah, girl. You shoulda told me. Isaac graduated in '92." I should have remembered that Chuck's mind held details like a fat woman's body held calories. He could remember almost anything.

"I got 'em here." He thumbed through. "Here he is."

He smoothed the page and showed me Isaac's picture. It was a younger version, but it was Isaac.

"Where's your computer?" I asked Chuck.

"Got one over here." He removed a newspaper tent from the desk in the corner to reveal a nice HP.

"Internet access?"

"You kidding?" He harrumphed and hit the little Google symbol with the finger of the mouse. Instantly, his web page sprung up, his beaming face dead center.

"Nice pic." I said as I navigated from it to Ron Goddard's site. Holding the yearbook picture of Isaac beside the picture of Goddard, I asked Chuck, "See a resemblance?"

"Yeah..." He breathed slowly. "They look like father and son."

"They *are* father and son."

"Nia, what the..."

"No questions for now. Please print that for me. I have work to do."

CHAPTER 32

So I had all of my parts, save one, but I knew the greater portion of what I needed to know.

After I left Chuck's, I was faced with the problem of where I would be laying my weary head. Even with the sophisticated alarm system, I was a little nervous, since third time was charm. My house may have been compromised, and I was a little scared to go home. One of my siblings'? Didn't want to drag them into this yet. David's? He probably wouldn't let me in. Okay, so where to go? Driving down Broadway, I took a right and as if by instinct, made my way to I-25, then to 36. Mom and Dad's. I had a key to their house, and I knew that I'd be secure there, and I had to face it: I had no other options.

I arrived at their house, went in and shut off the burglar alarm. I turned on the light in the living room and kitchen then took my gear to the spare bedroom I had always claimed as my own down the hall. Minutes later, the doorbell rang. Looking out through the peephole, I saw the fisheye distorted face of their next-door neighbor, Robert Lee. Uncle Robert lived on the other side of the hill and in a valley nearly a mile away, and I could only ascertain that he'd seen me drive by on the way to my parent's house.

"Hi Nia!" he said, when I opened the door.

"Hi, Uncle Robert. What brings you here?" I gave him a peck on the cheek.

His long face had broken into a smile when he saw me. Uncle Robert was not a relative, but he had been like an uncle to us since we were kids. He had met Dad more than forty years prior in Caboose Hobbies, a model train store on Broadway. Both of them were model train fanatics, and their friendship had grown from the shared hobby. Uncle Robert had helped Dad find property, and Dad bought the ten acres, planning for his retirement. A fellow Rotarian and widower for many years, Uncle Robert was also Dad's fishing buddy, the two of them driving down to Ogallala, Nebraska with my brothers and brother-in-law in tow, to drop their poles in their favorite lake. Mom, T'ene and I loved those long weekends, which we spent doing girlie things. He had worked tirelessly along with all of us to build my parent's dream retirement home.

"I thought I'd come over when I saw your car. You didn't need to come up, you know. I'll feed the dogs." He said when he came into the hallway.

"Oh, that's ok. I thought I'd stay the night. I was up here visiting some friends, and I didn't feel like driving all the way home." I lied.

"Well, alright. I'll be around if you need me, sweetie. I'll be going now." He pecked me on the cheek and waved as he walked to his car.

Closing the door, I went to rummage in Mom's fridge. Since she hadn't been too sure when they would return, it was pretty bare. But Mom was the queen of the freezer, and I knew there would be a cache fit for a Mormon in there. I was not disappointed. Little pizzas and hamburgers rubbed icy shoulders with steaks and ribs. I was famished and knew the pizzas wouldn't do, so I pulled out a nice rib eye and went back to the kitchen. Yup, plenty of steak sauce, but I'd have to make do with fat frozen cottage fries instead of a baked potato, and no lettuce, so no salad.

I thawed and put my steak on her Jenn-Air, then dropped a handful of fries in the deep fryer. When it was all ready, I grabbed a soda from the fridge, a real treat, plated my food, and settled in the family room in front of the TV. I really don't have a clue of what I watched. I was keyed up but very tired, so after I'd eaten every morsel, I set the alarm, took a shower and went to my bedroom. On the floor beside my bed, between the bed frame and the table, I placed my Glock. With it in easy reach, I felt safe and drifted into a light slumber.

CHAPTER 33

I think it was the little chuffing noise that the dogs made that caused me to wake up. It was slight, not really a bark, but more of a cut off outburst of air from one of the shepherds. I glanced at my bedside clock, 3:45, so I got up, pulled back my shade slightly and looked in the direction of their dog run. A moonless night prevented me from seeing more than ten feet from my window and I couldn't see either dog. I got back into bed and lay there for a few beats then I realized what the problem was.

It was dark.

Dad had installed motion lights on every corner of the house's perimeter, yet it was dark. Someone had taken out each of the lights. This also meant the alarm may have been compromised.

My hand automatically reached down for the gun. I'd decided that, if I got up and roamed the house in search of the reason the lights were off and maybe the alarm as well, I would be at a disadvantage. I'd let the evil come to me.

I heard the slight creak of a floorboard. The alarm had been compromised because the intruder was definitely in the house. I released the safety on my gun and placed my hand under the pillow to the right of my head, pointing at the door.

I didn't have long to wait. Though his footfalls were exceedingly light, I felt more than heard his slow progress down the hall. He must have looked first in my parent's room, then Alex's, and finally, I felt him standing outside of my door.

The door soundlessly moved open, and I remained still. The inrush of coolness from the hall made me aware that he was in the room; his slight movement to look down on me stirred the air, announcing his closeness. I'd adjusted my pose. In the opaque light, I saw his bulk flow in, his darkness a tone-on-tone contrast to the darkness of the room. He stood above me, seemingly trying to see in the dark. My eyes were now accustomed, and I could see him slowly raise his right arm. But I was ready, my gun in my hand lying in wait beneath the pillow, pointed like an unwavering, exceedingly accurate cobra, his head the target of my strike.

I fired.

I fired again.

I felt the warm rain of his blood as it sprayed me in a gruesome shower. His automatic shot the bed, missing my right heel by mere inches. He went down. Quickly, I turned on the bedside light, all the while pointing my gun at him. The glaring light startled me momentarily, and when I looked down, I saw him moving his right hand up for another shot. I did not shake nor waver, but firmly kept my finger on the trigger. I looked him dead in the eye.

"Do it fucker and die," I whispered.

Chevy shoved the gun away as though it had been the one who had shot him then lowered his hand. I'd sort of missed my objective, his head, but the bullet had caught him low in the bicep, traveled up and taken off most of his left ear, grinding a path up his skull, although it didn't seem to have penetrated it. My second bullet had hit him in the left of his chest, and from the bloody rime on his lips, I could tell his lung had been punctured. The fight had gone out of him. I climbed out of the bed, then circled and stood facing him. His eyes never left mine. Keeping him in my sights, I bent down and picked up his gun.

"You'll live, and your boss will pay dearly. He's also going to pay to fix my parents' house!"

CHAPTER 34

Considering that Mom and Dad's is a good distance from the Evergreen city limits, the police got there in record time. I think it had to do with the fact that I told them I had a man bleeding, maybe dying on the new, mauve carpet in one of my mother's bedrooms.

"Police!" they called when they arrived. The front door was standing open, and I called out, "Back here. I'm in the room with the light on!"

They came in, guns drawn, turning on lights as they moved, and found me sitting on the bloody bed, my eyes firmly fixed on Chevy's.

"Put down your gun, ma'am." A tall drink of water in a navy uniform said.

"Sure, as long as you keep yours trained on him." I said, as I handed it to him. First my gun, then Chevy's, both butts first. "Careful of the Glock. It was a gift so it's precious to me."

"Have you been shot?" he said, clutching my elbow and lifting me from the bed.

"Nope, but he has." I pointed to Chevy who was harshly rasping with the effort of staying on this side of the shade. He was badly wounded, as one of the paramedics stated after examining him. I allowed Tree Top, Officer John Golden, to lead me to the bathroom. Another officer stood a few feet away from Chevy, his gun pointing directly at him.

Once inside the bathroom, I stared at the blood-soaked apparition in the mirror. My hair looked as though it was plastered with garnet colored styling gel, which dripped in thick clots down the bangs it had created. My tee shirt was splattered from about the waist up and short rivulets had made their way down the remainder of the garment.

"Could I take a shower before we go down to the station? I really need to get a bit more presentable."

"Of course. If you need anything out of your bedroom, you can go back in and get it," he said.

"No!" I shouted. "I really don't think I could hold the remainder of my dinner if I had to go back in there and look at that."

"Ahh...I understand."

We stopped talking as the gurney holding Chevy was rolled past the door. He had an oxygen mask secured around his face, but his eyes were visible above it.

He telegraphed, "You win."

I telegraphed, "I know."

I gave Officer Golden directions of what to get out of my duffle: a clean tee shirt, sweat shorts, panties and bra and my sandals. He blushed a bit but went to retrieve the items. I stood in the same spot until he returned then asked him to wait, that I wouldn't be long.

CHAPTER 35

David opened the door, grunted, turned and walked back into the living room. He really didn't acknowledge that I had come in.

"I have it figured out." I said after I closed the door. David had sat down on his sofa, crossed his arms and sat looking at me with anger twinkling in his eyes. They now looked like stormy seas.

"Just listen to me." I pleaded.

He stonily sat there so I started telling my story. It had been mid-afternoon when the police let me leave. Chevy was listed in serious but stable condition, his prognosis good, and lucky or unlucky for him, he was alone in a rather luxurious lockdown room, complete with a nice bathroom in Evergreen General Hospital. He was receiving excellent care, and he absolutely refused to answer any questions.

The police had contacted Uncle Harold and he'd driven up to get the whole story from this little mare's mouth. It was a bit difficult for him to keep his composure while listening to me, a situation further exacerbated because Evergreen doesn't allow smoking in official buildings. His Pall Mall box received many a loving stroke while he listened to me.

He grumbled and complained, and hid his enthusiasm, but he was unable to hide his respect.

"I'm going to check all of this out, but it looks to me like you've done some pretty good detective work, little missy. All this to find out who killed a guy you didn't care about."

"I owed it to my son." I said with a shrug. I guess that really was the truth of it.

I'd driven to David's as soon as all of the paperwork was completed in Evergreen, related the events of the previous days, including the surveillance on the Goddard house, following Mrs. Goddard, the military records, the sojourn to Kansas – everything. I showed him the copies Officer Golden had allowed me to make of my list, the pictures, the military record and the yearbook pictures next to a picture I'd printed of Goddard. He reluctantly was showing interest and by the time it had all been laid out, he seemed as excited as I was.

He leaned back in his chair. "I'm still mad at you, but I gotta hand it to you. You really are a bulldog. Tenacious!"

So, Uncle Harold went to work. He used the influence he had amassed in all of his years as a cop. The following day, he went to Adobe Wells and first poked around about Goddard. When it all shook down, the story was extraordinary and made the next week's fascinating ones.

Frank was killed because he knew one thing – not that Miranda had been a man, but that Isaac's mother was Mildred Reed. Uncle Harold started with the Goddard household and Mildred Reed told the story with very little prodding. She had given birth to Isaac after being raped by Mr. Goddard and had been forced to give the child to Suzy Mae and Fenton, and they had raised the boy as their own. Mildred also knew that Goddard had taken someone else's identity and killed a prostitute in Vietnam, because soon after Isaac had been born,

Goddard had told her. He used the information as a threat, letting her know that she was dead if she ever told anyone about Isaac's birth. Drugs were never a part of the picture.

"I need to answer to my God!" she'd cried when Uncle Harold had questioned her. "I can't keep these evil secrets any longer!"

Sonny had the misfortune of seeing the Adam's apple. The little weasel put it together that Miranda had been a man and instead of forgetting about it, his greed overcame him. He had asked Mildred about it and she would neither deny nor confirm, so he went straight to Ronald Goddard and tried to blackmail him. Bad idea. One afternoon, after Sonny had completed his gardening chores, Chevy met him in the shed. Without a word, Chevy plunged the pitchfork into him, a pitchfork specially purchased for the occasion. Sonny didn't stand a chance. Chevy was much younger and stronger, stood nearly a foot taller, and had killed him before Sonny's mind could assimilate what was happening. Chevy cleaned up the murder weapon then reported to Goddard, who made a grand pretense of finding poor, dead Sonny.

Uncle Harold sent an officer to City and County to check out Goddard's, the fake's, birth record. They found nothing. After checking in Kansas, they found the birth record of the real Ronald Goddard, but not a word on what this one's real name was. Uncle Harold was at an impasse, but he was not about to give up.

CHAPTER 36

The four sat in an interview room, the largest in University Station. Three sides of the room were glass. Sunlight streamed in from the east, slid through the room and flowed out of the window on the west, which afforded an afternoon view of the mountains. These were the two normal windows. The other window was one-way glass, providing a ringside seat to those who wanted to listen and watch. He had been brought in, accompanied by his two attorneys, amid flashing lights from the police cars and the blinding blinks from cameras clutched in the hands of probably every news service in the state. Grey suit, muted tie and that perfect hair gave the appearance that he was untouched by all of the hoopla. He had the attitude of an innocent man, contradicted by the handcuffs glinting beneath the cuffs of his pale, grey shirt. Once inside the station, he walked by all of us, the room more silent than it had been since it was built. He stoically stared straight ahead and went into the interview room.

Most of the cops that were not on duty that day, many of

whom had been comrades to me when I was a cop, sat or stood on the other side of that glass. I had been given a cushy chair, the captain's own, so that I could view in comfort. The guys and gals at the station had welcomed me as though I had captured a serial murderer that specialized in babies. They were all laughing and poking me, joking about me being a barnacle when I wanted to find something out. I kidded them back and shrugged off my heroism. When Goddard opened his mouth, we all shut up.

Goddard was talking, but he really wasn't saying anything. He would not admit to any knowledge of Chevy trying to hurt me and he looked perplexed when the subject of Frank's death was mentioned.

"Why, pray tell, would I have a man that I do not even know killed?" He began to bluster. "I'm a leading citizen in my community, and I don't associate with people like that man!"

Those were the only words that Goddard would say to Uncle Harold directly.

"Why didn't you tell the truth about where you were born and your real name?" Uncle Harold asked.

Whispered conference with one of his two lawyers.

"Goddard *is* his real name, and Mr. Goddard prefers not to answer at this time." One of them answered for him.

"Mr. *Whatever* his real name is," Uncle Harold emphasized, "is here because he is a murderer and a phony. He needs to answer the question!"

And that is how it went for nearly three hours. Uncle Harold would ask and Goddard would confer with one or both of his attorneys and they would relay to Uncle Harold that 'Mr. Goddard prefers not to answer at this time.' Goddard looked as unruffled as he had when he'd walked in. He occasionally sipped from the water glass in front of him, but other than that, he showed no signs of breaking.

I wanted to stay but I had to get back to my office. I needed to work on the Burkhardt file, so sighing, I wheeled the captain's chair back to him, told everyone bye, that I had to leave and drove back down to Shield.

Mrs. Goddard had disappeared. Rumor had it that she had gone to another reassignment clinic to improve on her womanliness, since the lack of the Chondroplasty surgery on her Adam's apple had been what had given her away. Though her medical record was sealed, Uncle Harold was able to get more information and he told me that she had not opted for the removal of the throat protuberance in her first reassignment operation. She hadn't had enough money at the time. Whatever steps she took, they were sufficient to remove her from the public eye.

But even those who wish to stay in the background have a way of showing up when revenge is in the air. I got back to my office and was sitting at my desk working on the Roland Burkhardt file when the phone rang.

"Nia Carter" I answered distractedly.

"Ms. Carter," a female voice whispered. "If you want information that will put Ronald Goddard away until the second coming, please meet me."

Roland Burkhardt was immediately forgotten.

"Who is this?" I had my suspicions.

"Just say you will meet me."

"Well, I can do that if you promise no one will try to bop me on the head and put me in a trunk," I said.

She chuckled. "I can assure you that my only intention is to help not hurt you."

"Ok. Where?"

"I'm in Ft. Collins and that's as close to Denver as I'll come. I hope you don't mind driving."

"Alright. Time?" I asked.

"What are you doing right now?"

"Nothing I can't do later. It'll take about two hours to get there."

"Good." she said. "You have a cell?"

"Yup."

"Call me when you get to Harmony Road." She gave me a phone number then hung up.

I called David.

"Hey, good lookin'," I said when the secretary put me through. "Want to go on a road trip?"

David groaned. "Are you working on a new case or the same old one with a G?"

"Same. G. But this is important. Really!"

I told him I had a feeling that I knew who had called, and that I needed to go to Ft. Collins. I knew he was frowning. He was silent for a while then sighed. "Come pick me up. I'll drive."

"Great! See you in about a half hour."

David drove and I stared out the window. He asked me why she needed to see me, and I told him I really didn't know, but if it would help put Goddard away, it would be worth it. When we got within sight of the huge Budweiser plant, I told him to look for the Harmony Road exit, which he did and when we were at the top of the turn off, I got my phone and tapped in the number she had given me. Two rings and I heard the smooth voice.

"Take a left and head toward the mountains. Stay on Harmony Road for about fifteen miles until you get to Westridge Drive. Turn left and continue until you get to the gate. I'll be waiting for you."

Ft. Collins is a laid-back town of clean air, hardworking citizens and Colorado State University. I vaguely knew the area she was describing. It was on the way to Horsetooth Reservoir, the site of countless parties, and I was sure the students still found their way to its shores on any given Friday night. We were there within twenty minutes and made the turn on Westridge. About two blocks of driving brought us to a massive gate, complete with guard, the entrance to a very upscale neighborhood along the lines of Beverly Hills,

California. The estates could vaguely be seen through stands of massive pine trees, each home proudly planted on at least an acre lot.

Miranda Goddard sat with her dainty elbow perched on the windowsill of a pale gold Cadillac XLR convertible. Her hair, which she had dyed, was a near match to the color of the car, and lightly wrapped in a white scarf. She looked as though she was ready for her close up, merely waiting for the film crew to arrive to make a television commercial of her drive on the twisting road to Horsetooth. My phone rang and as I answered it, I saw her lips moving.

"Follow me," she said in my ear then disconnected.

"Follow her," I told David.

She cruised by us, smiling at David.

"*That* used to be a man?" I nodded. "Whew! She looks better than most of the women I know!"

"Keep it in your jockeys, buddy."

Mrs. Goddard turned left and headed toward Horsetooth, and we followed. She drove up the dirt road south of the reservoir in a cloud of dust so thick, David nearly missed it when she abruptly turned left and headed up the hill. She arrived at her destination, a small clearing surrounded by trees so thick, only glimpses of the surrounding area were visible.

David and I got out and walked to her car where she still sat with her arm out the window. She looked a bit different from when I had seen her through the window of her house. Besides the new color of hair, she looked younger and her eyes, though the same pale turquoise, were turned up slightly on either side.

"Nice to finally meet you in person, you little pit bull you," she said to me, a smile curling her lips. "You are the most tenacious soul."

"Nice to meet you, too," I said. I introduced her to David, and she rewarded him with a brilliant smile, which caused him to grin back at her like the village idiot. I discreetly pinched his arm.

"Ok," she briskly changed her tone, and reaching into her handbag on the passenger seat, she withdrew a CD case and handed it to me. "This is what you need."

"I'm rather particular about my music, so if this is country, I don't think I want it." I turned the case over in my hands. It had no markings.

"Oh yeah, sweetie. You want to hear this, and it's not a CD. It's a DVD." Honey oozed in her voice.

"And how do I know if it is something I can use to get rid of your husband?"

"Ex-husband, emphasis on the ex. I'm divorcing that bastard and now; I'm preparing for my second marriage." She said with a small flip of her head. "And just because I'm a nice girl, I brought my laptop for you to check out the goods." Reaching to her right again, she picked up the laptop on the seat then turned and gave David a dazzling smile. David returned it with a goofy smile of his own. I punched him in the side with my elbow.

Handing him the laptop, she reached down to open the door, so we stepped back.

"It might be easier to view in your car since it's a bit darker." She put the convertible's top up.

She was a tall woman, about five eleven, and as she got out, I sneaked a look at her neck. I had to get a look at the Adam's apple, and she saw me.

"Is that what gave me away?" she said, looking down on me.

"Well, yeah, you gotta admit. Most women don't have one of those," I murmured.

"Well, most women don't have *cahones*, and neither do I, so just think of me as all woman." She was smiling and really didn't seem offended.

The three of us got into David's car, and taking the

computer from David, she opened and fired it up. I handed her the DVD and she put it into the tray. In a few moments, the screen flickered and there she was on the screen, sitting behind a desk smiling. Her television image began to speak.

"I always try to cover my ass. I married Ronald Goddard because he said he couldn't live without me. He's a kinky bastard but he fit my need – money. He paid for the remainder of my reassignment. Ron, or should I say Joseph, is a murderer in addition to being a pervert, and the only reason I married him was because of the fact that he had what I wanted. Like I said before – money."

"I met Joseph in Santa Fe some years ago, and he started pursuing me like a dog in heat; like no one I'd met before."

I held up my hand to interrupt her and she paused the video. "Joseph?" I asked.

"Hmm? Oh yes! His real name is Joseph Thompson. Born in Salinas, California."

I looked at David.

She started the DVD again. "I made inquiries and decided that since he was rich, I would stop running. He told me so much about his life, and it just didn't quite jive with the things I found out. I was suspicious of him from day one, so I made my preparations. When he asked me to marry him, I said yes right away. Small ceremony – his choice – in a little out of the way chapel there in New Mexico. He took me home to his ranch in Adobe Wells, that big old pile out on the plains away from everyone and everything. I hated that place."

"What he didn't know was that I had cameras mounted in our bedroom from day one, and all of our lovely high jinks were recorded for posterity. They were very well hidden, very inconspicuous, and they were positioned so that they recorded close ups and all shots in between. After we were married about six months, he made the confession which follows, and I knew I had *really* hit the mother lode."

Miranda leaned to the side and whispered to David and

me, "Microphones in the headboard are such an innovation."

The video changed and what followed made me blush. She and Goddard were lying in a huge satin covered bed talking; him with his arm curled up and his head resting on it, her with the sheets pulled down, her huge breasts fully exposed. I was embarrassed to look, mainly because they were so much bigger than my own. Knowing the camera was on, filming every move, she was smiling directly into the lens. Goddard's voice was quite audible.

"That was great!" he murmured, turning over to stroke her nipples.

Suddenly, he sat up on his elbow and turned to her. "Miranda, I need to tell you something. I'm not who you think I am."

She was looking at him with suspicious interest.

With a sigh, he started telling his story. "My real name is Joseph Thompson. Ron Goddard was my only friend, and I stole the dog tags off of his neck after he was dead in the jungle in Vietnam." He had lain back flat on the bed, staring up at the ceiling and the unflinching eye of a camera. Luckily, it was one of the ones that did a close up. So close up that tears could be seen twinkling in his eyes.

He continued in a voice that was nearly a monotone. "I'm getting old now and I feel as though I need to do something for my family. I left them in such bad shape." He gave a deep, mournful sigh. "I always wanted to be rich, but I was born in Salinas, California with a dead-beat father and a baby machine mother, poor as owl's shit, and I knew I could never have what was waiting for Ron. When I got to him, he was dead or almost dead, so I just thought it out and took the tags. We looked enough alike to be brothers, so I just became him. Ron's Aunt Judith was rich, and I envied him." He chuckled. "I still have his old beat-up bible, and my real name is on the wall of the Vietnam Memorial."

His narrative went on, chronicling the workings of a mind

so devious, so corrupt, that it bordered on insanity. Miranda didn't interrupt. He told about killing the prostitute, hiding out then coming to Colorado, claiming a fortune. He then described in detail the smothering of his 'aunt.' He smiled wistfully while describing her frozen expression and cloudy eyes. He told of how he had paid Tito to push the first Mrs. Goddard off a plateau while she was out riding her favorite horse, Shadow. Tito had startled the animal (and Edith had been drunk and not an accomplished rider), and the animal threw her off and down to a drop of nearly a hundred feet. Tito had then taken his time returning to be sure that if the fall didn't quite kill her, the searing sun, coupled with her injuries would do the deed and leave him in the clear. He and Goddard had gotten a big laugh out of that.

"Tito hated Edith. She always called him a wetback when she thought he couldn't hear her. He did that job well."

One twisted revelation was the birth of his illegitimate son, Isaac. He said that Mildred Reed was "too sweet to ignore," and he had raped her one afternoon when she was changing the bed linens in his wife's room. The baby had been sent to live with the housekeeper's sister and was raised as her own child. That secret and his fortune were safe.

"Edith was out that day at one of her bullshit charity luncheons, and I couldn't resist." He chuckled.

"Why are you telling me all of this?" Miranda asked.

"Ah, well, like I said. I'm getting old now and soft. I was thinking of trying to find my brother and sisters, and I might need help. I know you'd never betray me, so...will you help me?" He looked at her imploringly.

"Of course, darling. Anything." Miranda was smiling at him. She reminded me of a mongoose over a cobra.

The video changed and Miranda turned to us. "This one is from a few months ago. This is where he tells about killing your husband.

"He was threatening me. He'd hit me a few times. Wanted

to make sure I didn't talk about his first 'misdeeds.'" She was smiling at us, but not at him in the video. Her face was red and swollen, her left cheek sporting a bruise. Her hair was a mess and she looked rather plain without makeup.

"David, I didn't look my best in this one, so don't hold it against me," she murmured.

Goddard was standing over her yelling.

"You know what I can do to you!" He was breathing hard and then, as if he had just thought of something, he told her in a totally calm voice, "Let me tell you about when I came face to face with my only son. Mildred was away, Edith was out, and I was home alone; opened the front door and there stood Isaac. That little bastard had seen my face in a magazine. Dumb luck that. He brought some dumb kid with him from school. I made him believe I cared about him; sent him money, paid his way through college and kept tabs to make sure he kept quiet. I always had sent money to his parents. Kept them in a style few spooks could lay claim to, and in return, they never told him or anyone else a thing. The kid kept quiet, like I said, but one night he called to tell me that his friend, Frank Carter, had gotten drunk or high or something and was blabbing to anyone who would listen that I was Isaac's father. He called me to protect me." Goddard was shaking his head and laughing. "I sent Dorthmiller to Florida to shut him up. He found the little creep's wife, drowned her in the tub and went looking for Carter. Carter blew town as soon as he heard his wife was dead. Came here to get me. Came right here to this house! The nerve! I yelled for Dorthmiller, but he ran, jumped into his car, and took off. Dorthmiller followed and found him coming out of his parents' house, grabbed him, shot him, and dropped him in a lake."

He was smiling down on Miranda, stroking her hair and almost cooing. "That, my little balls-free darling, is what will happen to you if you ever decide to cross me."

She turned the video off, sat back and looked at us.

"Dorthmiller is my guy, Chevy?"

"The one you shot?" she asked. I nodded.

"Yup. That's the guy."

"So, Goddard – I mean Thompson – got to feeling guilty in his geriatric phase and wanted to purge his soul to make amends for his evil deeds?"

She nodded and I harrumphed.

David said, "Isn't that just the way?"

She nodded again and smiled.

I wiggled around a bit and Miranda noticed that I seemed uncomfortable. She said, somehow guessing the question I was hesitating to ask, "Yeah, he knew. About a month after I'd married him, I told him that I'd had the first stages of the surgery. He liked the idea. He figured I would never cross him because I didn't want anyone to find out that I'd...been a male."

She looked down then said, "My new lover knows too, and he has more money than old Ron. He's such a softie. Loved me even when Ron and I were married. We have been carrying on now for about a year. He's taking me out of the country tonight, which is why I wanted to get this to you. Now, I need to get going."

She ejected the disk and closed the laptop, handing the disk to me. We got out of her car and she scooted over to the passenger seat. She leaned into the backseat, picked up a big manila envelope and handed it to David.

"This is all the info I think you'll need: my attorney's name, affidavits to the authenticity of the recordings, everything. There are a lot of other recordings of stuff he told me in here, but I know these are the ones you need to convict his ass. I want to tell you, though, don't follow me and don't try to find me. You will not be able to, and I'm not about to set foot in this shitty state again. I'm out of here."

She reached up and kissed me on the cheek. "Pit bull, girl!

You are a pit bull!"

Sliding into the driver's seat, she started the engine, gave us a wave and took off.

CHAPTER 37

When the trial took place, Mildred Reed told her story with tearful accuracy, having a memory of the events that few could rival. Thompson had stepped up his attorney pool and hired what appeared to be an entire firm. But the real star witness was Miranda's video. Thompson's face drained of color. He looked around in panic, his face contorted in rage and what seemed like confusion when her face lit up the monitors in the courtroom. When the video ended, he turned and looked directly at me.

I smiled.

When confronted with the evidence, and unbeknownst to Thompson, Dorthmiller had told all that he knew in hopes of lessening his sentence. He had gone to Florida when Thompson ordered him to, looking for Frank, but instead found Darlene. He'd killed her when she wouldn't tell him where Frank was. He followed Frank to Denver, just as Thompson had said, and found Frank leaving Myrlie and John's. Dorthmiller then followed him. He'd shot him on the banks of Cherry Creek, weighted his body with rims from tires, and dropped him in. He was also in it for my attempted murder. His honesty was destined to not do him a bit of good. Uncle Harold was hopping mad that Chevy had tried to kill his favorite niece and he wanted blood. They were convicted for the murders of Frank and the Carters, Sonny, Darlene Moran, and Goddard's aunt. Tito was picked up and questioned about the death of Edith, denying everything. Didn't do him any good either, since the videos and Chevy's confessions were enough to convict him. None of the three will live to travel the highways and byways of Colorado or any other state, and they now spend their time in a Supermax prison in Florence, Colorado.

As for Thompson's beautiful 1948 Chevrolet convertible that had been used to kidnap me, I made a deal with the police department impound, and with David's help, it became my new vehicle. The car had been meticulously restored and updated with all the bells and whistles – navigation system, satellite radio, cruise control, electric windows, and heated seats. Uncle Harold told me that Thompson howled like a scorched cat when he heard that his precious car was now mine.

And David. He traded my Native American ring and bought me a one-carat, emerald cut diamond, with two half-carat trilliants on either side. I haven't given him an absolute yes yet, but he says he's patient and will wait.

"Who else would marry you?" he says, and those gorgeous eyes are calm again.

Days later, I polished the creamy yellow skin of my fabulous automobile to high sheen, cleaned the convertible top of dust, lowered it and motored out to Ft. Logan. It was a cool day, the leaves on the aspen signaling that soon snow would fly, and the snowbirds would descend for the best skiing in the country. It reminded me that, in spite of the constant visitors, I love this state and everything in it.

Walking across the carpeting of deep green in Ft. Logan National Cemetery, decorated here and there with the deposits from the ever-present Canada geese, I finally stood in front of Frank's crypt.

"Ok, so I did what I needed to. You knew I would, and now, you are avenged. Kick back and rest easy." I said. I turned to go and then I looked back and said, "One more thing, though. If at all possible, now that you are gone, could you please do something for me?"

I felt him ask, "Do what?"

"Watch over your son."

"Done."

ABOUT ATMOSPHERE PRESS

Atmosphere Press is an independent, full-service publisher for excellent books in all genres and for all audiences. Learn more about what we do at atmospherepress.com.

We encourage you to check out some of Atmosphere's latest releases, which are available at Amazon.com and via order from your local bookstore:

Twisted Silver Spoons, a novel by Karen M. Wicks

Queen of Crows, a novel by S.L. Wilton

The Summer Festival is Murder, a novel by Jill M. Lyon

The Past We Step Into, stories by Richard Scharine

The Museum of an Extinct Race, a novel by Jonathan Hale Rosen

Swimming with the Angels, a novel by Colin Kersey

Island of Dead Gods, a novel by Verena Mahlow

Cloakers, a novel by Alexandra Lapointe

Twins Daze, a novel by Jerry Petersen

Embargo on Hope, a novel by Justin Doyle

Abaddon Illusion, a novel by Lindsey Bakken

Blackland: A Utopian Novel, by Richard A. Jones

The Jesus Nut, a novel by John Prather

The Embers of Tradition, a novel by Chukwudum Okeke

Saints and Martyrs: A Novel, by Aaron Roe

When I Am Ashes, a novel by Amber Rose

Melancholy Vision: A Revolution Series Novel, by L.C. Hamilton

The Recoleta Stories, by Bryon Esmond Butler

ABOUT THE AUTHOR

Betti Louise Lee was born in Colorado and continues to live and work there. She attended Colorado State University in Ft. Collins, Colorado. Writing is a pastime that Betti has enjoyed since elementary school, having had her first short story published in the district newsletter when she was 11. Betti's blog is bettillee.com.

Made in the USA
Las Vegas, NV
25 February 2022

44603250R00163